W9-BZS-765

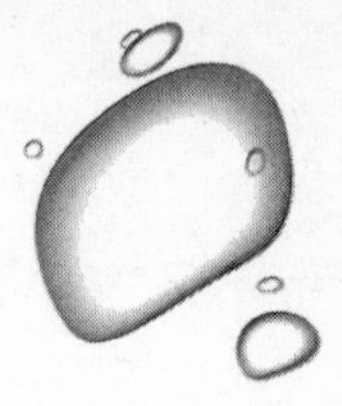

breathless

jessica warman

Walker & Company New York

For Colin

First published in the United States of America in 2009 by
Walker Publishing Company, Inc.
Visit Walker & Company's Web site at www.walkeryoungreaders.com

For information about permission to reproduce selections from this book, write to Permissions, Walker & Company, 175 Fifth Avenue, New York, New York 10010

Library of Congress Cataloging-in-Publication Data
Warman, Jessica.
Breathless / Jessica Warman.
p. cm.
Summary: At boarding school, Katie tries to focus on swimming and becoming popular instead of the painful memories of her institutionalized schizophrenic older brother.
ISBN-13: 978-0-8027-9849-7 • ISBN-10: 0-8027-9849-7
[1. Schizophrenia—Fiction. 2. Mental illness—Fiction. 3. Brothers and sisters—Fiction. 4. Boarding schools—Fiction. 5. Schools—Fiction. 6. Peer pressure—Fiction. 7. Swimming—Fiction.] I. Title.
PZ7.W2374Br 2009 [Fic]—dc22 2008042555

Book design by Danielle Delaney
Typeset by Westchester Book Composition
Printed in the U.S.A. by Quebecor World Fairfield
2 4 6 8 10 9 7 5 3

All papers used by Walker & Company are natural, recyclable products made from wood grown in well-managed forests. The manufacturing processes conform to the environmental regulations of the country of origin.

All I wanted was to say honestly to people:
"Have a look at yourselves and see how bad and dreary your lives are!" The important thing is that people should realize that, for when they do, they will most certainly create another and better life for themselves.
—Anton Chekhov

part one

chapter 1

There's a man feeding the koi in our fishpond because my parents don't want to do it themselves. Even though the pond has been there for years, the fish don't have names. The man comes twice a week to feed the fish, once a week to prune the rose bushes and mow the lawn, and once a month to wash the outsides of all the windows. This afternoon, from our place on the roof, my brother and I watch with detached interest as he tosses a handful of food pellets into the fishpond. He glances over his shoulder to look at us warily. My brother and I wave, and he quickly looks away. I don't know where my parents found him. I'm sure he has a name, but I don't know that, either.

Life hasn't always been like this. When I was a little girl, my family lived in a two-bedroom cottage in an area of rural Pennsylvania called the Bearlands. Even though I was so young, I remember almost everything about that life. I realize now that we were poor, but back then I never felt that way. My parents had paid their own way through college, and after we were born, my mom stayed home with me and my brother while my dad continued to work and go to medical school. They paid for everything themselves and we didn't have much of anything. We didn't have a TV or new clothes or lots of toys. We didn't even have a telephone. It was all very *Swiss Family Robinson*.

For the first few years of my life, I shared the same room as my brother. My mother painted dinosaur murals on our bedroom walls. Once I was old enough to speak, he and I stayed up past bedtime every night to make up stories about them. They scared the hell out of me, but I had my brother to keep me safe.

For years we lived that way, the four of us tucked back in the woods, alone in that cottage together. My dad went hunting, and we ate whatever he caught. I loved venison; I still do. My mom had a big garden in our yard, where she grew zucchini and tomatoes and lettuce. She took us for walks every day. We watched baby birds hatching from their eggs; we picked blueberries and raspberries and cultured wild yeast to make our own bread. We watched tadpoles grow into frogs, their eggs collected in a plastic bowl filled with water that sat on our kitchen windowsill. We sat very still as children—but never still enough—while our mom sketched our faces with quick precision. We played hide-and-seek in the yard while she stood at her easel a few feet away, never letting us out of her sight for too long.

But our dad was almost never home, and one night, while my mom read us a story at bedtime, we heard a car pulling onto the gravel outside our house.

"It's Daddy," I said, rushing to get out of bed. I hadn't seen him in days.

But my mother held out her arm in a panic. "It's not your daddy. Come with me. *Now.*"

The three of us hid on the floor of my closet and listened. My mother kept her hands over our mouths. My brother and I wrapped our arms around her. I remember the way her body shook with fear. There were two men; we never saw them, but we heard their boots and their voices. Later on—much later—I learned they broke into four other houses besides ours in the Bearlands that night. Because we were in the closet, we were the only family they left unharmed.

Less than a month later, we moved to Hillsburg. I was four. My parents chose the town because it was safer than the city, safer than the country, and had lots of kids. Our house was the biggest in town, but like most of the other houses on our street, it was also a mess: peeling paint, cracked sidewalks, ugly wallpaper, and leaky ceilings.

Our parents called the house a money pit. My brother and I didn't care. Our street was full of kids our ages. We had a nice big yard. My brother was so excited to go to a new, larger school, and I was thrilled by the possibility that, maybe someday, we could put a swimming pool in the backyard. Even then, at four years old, I could already swim like a sail slicing the wind on Narragansett Bay. My mom called me her water baby.

When I was five, a gallery in San Francisco started to sell her paintings, and after a while, she was making real money. Just after I turned six, my dad finished his MD and opened up a psychiatry practice. Pretty soon he had four offices in three counties, and we weren't poor anymore. But by then, our dad worked so much that he'd started to vanish. My brother and I even gave him a nickname, which he *hated*. We called him "the Ghost."

• • •

The less my dad was around, the more we seemed to *have.* My mom built a studio for herself at the bottom of our yard. My parents put in the swimming pool for me. We got a new minivan, new furniture, and a high stockade fence around our backyard that cut us off from our neighbors. Already, I know they had started to hate us. They were jealous. They watched us come and go, and the more we got, the less they smiled. It was right about that time when things started to go wrong with Will.

The summer before my sophomore year of high school feels hotter and muggier than those of any previous years. Lately I'm always sweaty and dirty. Instead of showering, I swim, which leaves me stinking of chlorine. When my brother is around, he doesn't shower much either. He and I both sleep into the afternoon on most days, and we spend the rest of our time in a haze of swimming and slow conversation and whatever trouble we can think to get into.

I've always had a swimmer's body, muscular but slim, and I keep my long blond hair—the same shade as the Ghost's used to be, before he turned gray—knotted into a messy ponytail, when it's not tucked underneath a swimming cap. This summer I'm usually barefoot, and always wearing the same ratty bikini covered in tiny, pink-lipped monkeys. The bathing suit hangs as though distracted from my body; it's a little too big for me and threatens to fall away with the pull of a thread. The look drives my parents crazy, especially my father, who thinks I should carry myself with more class.

"I'm fifteen," I remind him during one of his rare appearances in the afternoon.

He's unblinking. "That's right. You're fifteen." Then he likes to play the classic parent card. "I thought you were old enough to be treated like a *mature and responsible adult*."

If he were around enough to know better, he would understand I'm already quicker than that. "Mature and responsible is one thing. But this is Hillsburg, Dad. Look around." Our town's most recent claim to fame occurred when the police busted up a meth lab in the basement of a home daycare service. "I'm not sure where you think all this class is supposed to come from."

Before this summer started, I hadn't seen my brother in five months, which is how long it's been since his last stint in a psych unit. There have been so many episodes of his absence—three weeks here, six months there. All my childhood memories since we moved to Hillsburg fit together like a jigsaw puzzle, with pieces missing in the most conspicuous places: my birthday without my brother, age nine. Spring without him, age eleven. A whole childhood, not so whole.

For the longest time, the gaps in our relationship didn't seem to matter. I missed him so much that it only made me love him more once he came home again. After all, we'd been friends since the day I was born. He taught me my first swear words. We still have it on videotape. One time, when we still lived in the Bearlands, my grandpa Effie came to visit and brought his camcorder. He left the tape with us; I've watched it at least a hundred times on our ancient VCR. I'm hobbling across the living room in my diaper, moving toward my young mother's outstretched arms—I can't be more than two years old—when I stop and fall suddenly onto my ass and say, "Oh, shit!"

Back then, my mother still had a sense of humor about some things. She dissolves into giggles, her face so young and pretty and strange, before the tape fades to black. Her eyes are kind and hopeful, excited to see her children growing up.

Since I was twelve years old and he was seventeen, anytime the weather is remotely good enough, and anytime he's home, Will and I have snuck onto our roof to smoke and talk, wasting our afternoons taking delight in—as the Ghost would say—failing to meet our potential as Gifted Young People.

We are on the roof this afternoon, staring down at the koi man in the yard, at the glare of the sun reflecting off the surface of the pool. The heat on my back gives me goose bumps.

"There ain't a thing to do in this town but get baked," he says. He is always making wide statements like this, spreading his arms skyward in frustration as though the right plea might split open the town and free him.

"You got that right," I agree. Will hasn't been to a real school in years, so even though he's actually far more brilliant than me, I always try not to sound like I'm being too smart around him. He's sensitive about that kind of thing.

All afternoon we've been smoking this primo pot he got from someone he met at the hospital. Will tells me—and he should know—that crazy people always get the best drugs. Among the disgruntled teenage set, there seems to be an endless supply of whatever you want. All of Will's friends are from other psych hospitals all over the state. When he's home, he spends most of his time online in his bedroom.

Will asks, "Can you blame me for wanting to get high all the time?" And considering the circumstances—all that our parents and this town have put him through—I really can't.

Will grows serious, sliding his sunglasses down the bridge of his nose—our mother's nose—with his thumb and index finger, squinting against the backyard sunlight. "Hey. Katie."

"What?"

"You see that cat down there?"

I move my head next to his. "Where?"

"Down there—don't look!—down there next to the garage."

"Yeah. So?"

"It *knows.*" My big brother straightens his spine and puts a hand on my shoulder. "Stay here."

"Aw, Will, it doesn't know anything." A hint of a wheeze tickles my lungs. I ignore the feeling. "Gimme a cigarette."

"No, dude. Pay attention to me. *Look* at it. It knows we're high." He reaches absently into his shirt pocket and extends a soft pack of Marlboros in my direction. He giggles.

Right there, in his laugh, I can sense his emotional axis shifting a little, off-kilter. It's something I've come to call privately the kaleidoscope of crazy—shimmering and beautiful in certain lights, paisley and horrifying in others. Will is almost twenty-one and in certain lights looks more like twelve, in others closer to thirty. I know him as well as myself and not at all. All I can figure to do is hold on. He is my only brother.

Is he serious about the cat? I can't tell. "It's going to tell Mom and Dad," he murmurs, gazing at it. "Katie, Katie, Katie. It's going to tell on us."

"Come on, quit it. I need a lighter, too." Even now, after so many shaky recoveries that we hoped would last, it's important to always have my guard half prepared around Will. He can go like nothing, out of nowhere.

The kaleidoscope twists; the sun makes a slow tumble behind the clouds, into the hot shade. This is what always happens, every time my brother comes home: in the hospital, they get him on a steady dose of the right medications. They get his head on straight again, and once he's doing better, they send him home. After a while, he feels so good that he decides he can manage life himself, that he doesn't *need* to be medicated. So he stops taking his pills, and then everything starts all over again. The Ghost has told me this is typical of people like Will, that this very kind of thinking is why it's so hard to help them.

I know we shouldn't be getting high. But Will is right—what else is there to do? I don't have many friends in town, and Will doesn't have any. He almost never leaves our property when he's home. When I do spend time with my friends, leaving him alone here—especially to hang out with Hillsburg people—it always feels like I'm turning my back on him.

Will's face is badly sunburned, peeling by now from too many afternoons passed up here this season, gazing contemptuously at the town. Little Hillsburg—we call it Hellsburg. But on the roof of the biggest house in town, we are bigger than the whole place. I sometimes feel like, with only the flick of a finger, we could make the town disappear and we could stay here forever, undisturbed by the trash surrounding us. We are alone up here, masters of the afternoon, at least until our father gets home.

If it weren't for this town, and everything the people did to him, Will might not even be sick. He was smart as a kid—he still is—and it was too much for people here to handle. I think that seeing how smart he was, how successful our parents were becoming, made them realize how tiny and sad their own lives were.

Hillsburg is a network of cousins: everyone in the whole

town seems to be related to each other. They are poor. They go through people's garbage. They don't do things like go to college or look at art or read books or understand that not everyone is like them. Instead, they go to field parties and rebuild cars in their front yards and have their babies young and stay in Hillsburg for their whole lives. They hate us for being so different, for having so much more. I'll never understand why my parents stay here, especially after all that's happened to my brother.

Right now, we both watch in silence as the man who feeds the fish strolls away from the house. On his way out, he bends over to pet the cat we're talking about.

"How long has he been coming?" Will asks.

I shrug. "Maybe a year. Why?"

Will doesn't say anything.

"Why does it matter? He's hardly ever here."

My brother looks at me. His expression is so deadly serious that, when he speaks, I feel a tingle of electricity move through my spine. "Have you ever thought that maybe he's a spy for Mom and Dad?"

Things started to go really wrong for Will around junior high. He was on the basketball team—he loved basketball, and he was good at it. One night after practice he didn't come home. I was only in the third grade, but I remember how frantic my parents were, how once it got dark out, the local police went up to the school to look for him.

They found him in the locker room, alone, naked. For a few days he wouldn't tell us what had happened—he just refused to go to school. Finally, maybe a week later, our housekeeper showed up at our front door unannounced. Her son, Craig—who was on the basketball team too—was with her. The two of them sat down with my parents in our living room. Will stayed upstairs in his bedroom. I listened from the hallway as Craig explained how his teammates had locked Will in a bathroom stall after practice the night he disappeared. Then they'd stolen his clothes, done their best to make sure there was nothing else for him to wear—not even a towel—and had gone home. They'd thought it was hilarious.

My mother cried without making any sound, her shoulders trembling, the whole time Craig talked. Will didn't play basketball anymore after that. He didn't go back to school for the rest of that year—he stayed home, and my parents hired a private tutor. When he did go back, he started using whatever he could get his hands on—anything he could smoke or put up his nose, or whatever pills people would sell him—and that's when he started to fall apart. I know there's a chance he would have gotten sick anyway, but of course we'll never know for sure. What's wrong with Will, according to every doctor who's ever seen him, is *drug-induced* schizophrenia. Without all the bullying, he might never have gotten into all the drugs.

It took a few years before what was happening to him became clear; typically, schizophrenia doesn't begin to show itself until later in a person's adolescence or early twenties. But Will has never been typical, and people in this town were unusually cruel.

I puff on my cigarette now while he watches. "How am I doing?"

He takes a long, contemplative drag of his own smoke,

shaking his head. "You're inhaling okay, but you have to get used to keeping it in your mouth. Like this." He demonstrates, keeping a loose hold on the cigarette between his dry lips. "So you look tough and nobody messes with you."

"I don't want to look tough. I want to look sexy."

Will rolls his eyes, annoyed. "Why?" His gaze turns to the cat again. "So all the Hellsburg losers will want to take you out on the town?"

"No!"

He nods to himself, disgusted by the idea, determined to believe it. "Yeah, that's why."

"I'm a girl, Will. I want boys to like me."

"All right. Well, you've gotta quit calling them cigarettes, for one thing."

"Why?"

"'Cause they ain't." He removes the cigarette from his lips, holds it between stained fingers, stares at it. "They're fags."

"I've never heard anybody call them fags."

"That's what they call them in the city."

I snort. "Right."

"Shut up, Katie."

"Is that what they called them in the hospital?" Right away I know I shouldn't have said it. He bares his teeth at me, and even in the shade I can see the heat rising from the tarred roof, willowing around his slight figure. Behind his braces, his teeth are yellow and mossy, stubbornly crooked. Our orthodontist says Will is the worst patient he's had in thirty years of practice. Anytime his braces start bothering him, Will pries them from his teeth with a pair of pliers he keeps stashed in his room somewhere. My parents try to do sweeps of his bedroom every couple of weeks, looking for things that could get him in trouble, but somehow he manages to keep a lot hidden—random prescription pills; cigarettes by the carton; short stories that he writes about all kinds of awful, crazy things, scribbled on yellow legal paper; and his pliers. As a result of his stealth, he's had braces on and off for something like ten years. Which is funny when you think about it, because what's the point anymore? It isn't like they'll ever get him to wear his retainers.

He flicks his cigarette into the gutter and we both watch while its cherry eats at a dead leaf. Then Will leans forward on his knees and hocks a wad of spit onto the burning edge, turning the leaves over with his hand to hide our evidence. We've learned that we have to be careful, that in many ways our parents are better sneaks than we are. They pretend to be clueless to what's going on for a while, and then they seize on you.

The Ghost is the worst. He is a big fan of procedural television dramas and forensics. He takes sick pleasure at family meetings from producing Ziploc bags of evidence, sealed and labeled, displaying the paraphernalia he's discovered hidden around the house. Then he acts like he doesn't know what's going on until we get too bored or embarrassed and finally confess what we've been up to on the roof. He is good at almost everything. As far as I know, he's never failed once.

Well, maybe once. My mom says he'll never know how to take care of himself; he eats too much junk food. "Healthy eating and raising kids," he likes to say. "Those are two things I could never seem to get right."

At family meetings, he sits in an overstuffed recliner with a glass of wine at his side, obviously enjoying our misery. He clears his throat before speaking, holding up a bag so we can all get a good look at the evidence. "In the past week, I collected three handfuls of cigarette butts from the gutter, some of which had lipstick on them—Katie? There was also an empty bottle of crème de menthe. Anybody want to take credit for this?"

He'll look at my mom while she's furiously taking notes on a legal pad. We have a whole filing cabinet filled with minutes from family meetings, dating back, like, ten years, all of them in my mother's gorgeous cursive handwriting. While she writes, she keeps her head down, her ears trained to get all the highlights, her knuckles clenched white.

"Sweetheart?" he asks my mom. The Ghost is at his most intimidating when he's being sarcastic. "Were you drinking on the roof again? Because I can't imagine it could have been our children."

"Unthinkable," my mother says. She looks up for a moment, bats her eyelashes at him. "It must have been somebody else's children," she adds, as though she feels sorry for somebody else's long-suffering parents. "Those bad kids."

Even after two children and everything she's been through, everyone knows my mother is still a real beauty, soft and calm in contrast to the Ghost's harshness. Somehow she always seems *blurred,* as though to focus on anything that exists beyond a canvas might prove too difficult for her tiny frame to handle. When I was a very little girl, whenever she made me angry, I would imagine a strong wind simply blowing her away.

"Yes." The Ghost nods in agreement. "That must be it.

Somebody else's children wouldn't care if they created a fire hazard on our roof that could incinerate us all, would they?"

My mother and father have a secret language that I have never understood. They have been married since college and are still madly in love. I can't imagine why, since they have nothing in common besides me and Will, and all the two of us ever do is cause trouble.

As a result of these meetings, Will and I have learned that we have to be extra careful. We usually come up to the roof when our parents aren't home, which is often, or else late at night when they're asleep. This place has become the only place where I feel like I can know my own brother. I have never felt afraid as we lie beside each other, murmuring so as not to make too much noise. As Will says, "We wouldn't want to rouse the Ghost."

Sometimes, when we're sure that our parents aren't home and the neighbors aren't paying attention, we climb around in the pine tree that bows against the house on the farthest corner, over the living room, its branches thick enough to hold us as our bare feet sting from splinters and sap.

Even as I'm living it, something feels important about this day in particular. We're climbing around in the tree, hopping back and forth between its thick branches and the hot roof, when it occurs to me that I never feel too close to the edge, even with my brother right behind me.

"Willie," I say, turning around to face him. "It's too hot up here. Let's go swimming again."

"Don't call me that," he says. "I'm not a kid."

Will, Willie, William—our father's name. But the one thing

we all know about Will, the one thing we've known right from the beginning, is that he will never be like our father. Not even close.

Even for a Ghost, our father isn't around much; he works eighteen-hour days. When he is home, he spends most of his time locked in his office. I notice him mostly late at night, when I'm not sure if I'm asleep yet, and the murmur of his voice dictating psych reports filters up through my bedroom radiator. But always he is white, white, white: he has fine, grayish white hair that puffs along a tired ashen face and deep-set white eyeballs. He is wise and disappointed and so much older than he ought to be.

When I was a little girl, still in single digits, I'd sit on his lap in my pajamas and sip watery hot chocolate while he smoked a Marlboro; picked tobacco from his beard, which is full and also white—although he's no Santa; and held a flabby arm across my belly. We used to have an easygoing relationship that made me feel so loved, so precious to him, it seemed impossible that anything could ever change.

Despite all the golfing, which he does on the weekends, my father has always been out of shape, too much fat accumulated over muscles that have long since softened from his days as a college football hero. When I was a little girl, this didn't keep him from being godlike.

The Ghost is a psychiatrist. He calls himself a masseuse of the soul. His clients, stretched over a long career, number in the thousands. His ability to sympathize with strangers, to help them solve all their problems, has made him a wealthy man. So how is it fair that, within his own home, he became mostly quiet and unsympathetic? I know he is kind and loving and gentle. He spends his days chin-deep in other people's trauma, and you can tell it has hollowed him, made him brittle from endless days of drinking too much coffee while he sits in an overstuffed chair, listening.

For so many years I was his little girl. "What are you doing today?" I used to ask, peeling his grapefruit for him. All day after he'd gone, I used to sniff my hands and reconstruct the memory. I missed him constantly. Even when I was ten, I would still fit like a bundle on his lap, my toes barely touching the floor.

He leans his head back and squints at the ceiling. "Let's see, Kathryn." My father is the only person who doesn't call me Katie. "I'm at my office until noon, and then I'm having lunch with your mother."

"Can I come?"

"No. You'll be in school."

"Tuesday I go to the dentist. Can I come then?" And I burrow my head into the folds of his sweater to remind him that, wherever he goes, he belongs to me.

"Tuesday I'm in court all day."

"But *Dad* . . ."

"We'll see." He winks and touches a tar-stained fingertip to my nose. "Maybe I'll finish up early." He coughs, rearranging the contents of his chest, leaning away from the ashtray. I pat him on the back. "Cough it up, Dad. You have to stop smoking."

"Enough, Kathryn."

"You *do*."

"Okay." He snuffs out his cigarette, spreads his empty fingers like a magician. "See? I quit."

His eyes twinkle, pupils wide in the dimness, erasing his irises. I know how it feels to look at them, but I have no idea what color eyes the Ghost has.

I'm not sure what he would tell you about us. Probably he'd say that it was me who changed, that as little girls grow into young women, it is natural for them to pull away from their fathers. But I remember it differently. I remember a day when he looked at me and I felt, in his gaze, an impossible pressure to be something different. I was twelve years old; it was the first time he caught me smoking a cigarette. It was a look I would grow familiar with over the next few years, not just from the Ghost but from almost everyone around me.

What could I do? How was I supposed to be? I had no idea. The only thing I knew how to do, with any certainty, was swim.

chapter 2

I feel more drawn to the water than ever this summer. I blame the temperature and my boredom, but still I force myself to really move beneath the surface, to keep my pace so swift that I sometimes feel like my heart might explode. I've always done well in school—I get all As—but the only thing I really love is swimming. Sometimes I feel like I don't really exist outside the water.

Once in a while, my mother takes a break from painting to chase me around with a bottle of sunblock. She's lucky if she manages to do much more than swipe a few gobs onto my back. My suntan is uneven because of her, finger trails of her attempts to protect me left in stark white marks surrounded by bronze flesh. Each time she comes and goes, my brother and I follow her appearance with a slew of backhanded comments as she walks away. It isn't even noon yet, but her upper lip is already stained a deep crimson. Merlot, Pinot Noir, Cabernet—they're like grape juice in our house.

"She probably doesn't remember our names by now," Will says.

I jump in the water again before the sunblock has a chance to absorb. "After twelve," I say, putting a dramatic hand to my forehead, mimicking her breathy voice, "time for a little catnap."

Will dangles his feet from the diving board into the water, watching me with half interest and squinting into the sun, smoking cigarettes that he flicks onto the cement deck. He doesn't care that he's making a mess. The last thing I see before my head disappears underwater is his grin.

I am a swimmer by birth. I've been on some kind of team since age three, and I've always been the fastest. I swim every day, and every day I can feel myself getting a little better. After every twenty laps today, I get out of the pool. Will and I pretend to take a great interest in the ants mobbing the rhododendron bushes in the garden, keeping watch for each other while we take quick drags from a joint, giggling, feeling the sun bake the moisture from our skin, and it feels so good to be bad that I can hardly stand it.

"Hey," I say, "should you be doing this? Is it okay?"

"What do you mean?"

"You know—is it going to hurt you? Because of your medicine?"

His head comes forward, and he gives me a long, shaky look. His eyeballs look radioactive. I detect a small, almost imperceptible tremor from within the muscle fibers. "Don't worry about me, Katie. You're being dumb." He rubs his eyes with tight fists. The whites have turned the color of underripe watermelon. "You're just a kid."

After a few hours, the sun begins to creep down toward the horizon, and my vision starts to blur from keeping my eyes open underwater for so long. Will has fallen into a trance on the diving board, splayed on his back with a lit cigarette burning downward, its ashes breaking and falling into the water. I paddle over to him and swipe at his arm, his skin dry as a dead bat baking on the pavement.

"Hey."

When he doesn't answer, for a minute I think he might be asleep. But then he murmurs, "Hmmmm?"

"Let's go up to the roof again."

He sits up, squinting at me. "Are you sure? Mom's home."

I lick my lips in contemplation. I can be tough; I'll show him. "I don't care. What's she gonna do about it?"

"Huh."

"Huh."

He shrugs. His squint breaks into a grin. "Okay. Let's go."

We're dancing around on the roof—me in my bathing suit, him in an old pair of sweatpants cut off at the knees, shirtless, doing the robot to a Beastie Boys CD and shifting our feet on the hot roof to keep our soles from burning, when, from out of nowhere, the cat we saw earlier falls from the pine tree and lands right between us—*smack*—and the music skips, slows down, as though it's keeping up with the mood.

"Oh my God," I say, trying not to laugh in spite of the cat. "We're in the Bible. It's raining *creatures*."

We kneel down to get a better look. It's a sorry sight. Since we last saw it, just a few hours ago, the cat looks like it has been in a fight—its tail is bent at a painful angle, its breathing is too quick, and its tabby fur is matted and sad. Will picks it up and cradles it in his arms. He walks to the edge of the roof, looking around kind of panicked like somebody might see him and think he's done something wrong. I have never known him to be anything but gentle with animals.

"I'm going to drop it. Onto the ground," he says, licking his dry lips, nervous. His gaze flickers to our neighbors' windows, to the surrounding houses. Even though it hasn't happened yet, I feel the kaleidoscope turning, the whole summer and then some ready to spill and sour.

"Will, don't. You'll kill it."

He sounds certain. "No, I won't. Cats can fall long distances. They always land on their feet."

I lean over the edge and take a good look at the drop. Even I don't think the fall will be too far—it can't be more than ten, maybe fifteen feet. I almost give up trying to stop him then—he's older, after all, and I usually do what he says. But I can't help myself from trying, just this time.

"Why not get some help?" I ask. "Why not take it downstairs and give it some milk and food? We could call a veterinarian."

"No," Will says, "we shouldn't get involved. We should just drop the thing. Trust me, Katie, it'll be fine."

I watch him drop the kitty. He does it carefully, releasing his hands from around the torso, and I expect it to fall softly onto the mulch below.

For a moment, I believe everything is going to be all right. It seems to fall in slow motion, its legs limp beneath it, a wide bed of soft mulch ready to break its fall, and then it will jump to its feet again and be on its way.

We underestimated. Maybe we couldn't really tell how far it was—we were so large up there. Everything else looked so small and close and meaningless.

The cat hits a big, flat rock in the mulch with a dull thud and goes instantly still, its big empty eyes looking up at us with nothing behind them, and there's no movement anywhere, not even from us. It feels like the stillness begins from the cat on the ground and moves outward, holding on to us tightly, keeping us from breathing. It feels awful.

Somebody might have loved it. Somebody might be looking for it, and my brother has just killed it.

After what feels like a long stretch of time, Will puts a shaky arm around me. I feel his fingernails on my sunburn, a tingle that goes down my arm and spreads to my whole body, like I'm going to shiver until I throw up.

"Katie." His voice is scratchy. "I didn't mean to do that."

"I know you didn't."

"What should we do?"

I don't know why, but I giggle. "There's nothing we can do now. Bury it?"

And he's giggling, too. "Maybe Mom will want to paint it first."

Flick. Swoosh. Out of nowhere, the Ghost appears behind the window. He has obviously been looking for us, has appeared with perfect, omnipotent parental timing. For a second I think maybe that's why I am cold—you can sense him sometimes like that. We turn around, hands behind our backs, shoulder to shoulder while the Ghost opens the window and clumsily climbs out. He wears tinted bifocals with lenses that turn black in the sun. A cigarette is held between his teeth, smoke billowing around his features, sunlight obstructing our view of his face.

Will snorts at him, nudging me. "You look like the devil, Dad."

The Ghost is not amused. "What are you two doing out here?"

I stare at my feet, biting the inside of my mouth. I can still feel the silent pull of what's on the ground beneath us, and I can feel tears forming at the corners of my dry eyes.

"We aren't doing anything, man. We're just hanging out." Will takes a defiant drag from his cigarette.

"Kathryn? What's going on? I thought I told you kids not to come out here anymore." Our father is more concerned about the neighbors seeing us than he is about our personal safety. Even though everybody in the whole town knows otherwise, my father likes people to believe that our family is doing just fine.

I shake my head. "I just wanted to get some sun."

"Go to your room." He's rough, grabbing my arm and shoving me toward the window, but he's really interested in Will, you can tell—Will thinks our dad is out to get him. Sometimes I think he's right.

The Ghost snaps his fingers at Will, who is trying to follow me inside. "Not you, William. Stay there."

"Aw, man, it's hot out here."

"Shut up."

"Ha."

"What's that?"

"Nothing."

The Ghost starts pacing back and forth on the roof in full business dress, looking around for some evidence that we've been up to no good. God, he must be burning up in those clothes, but I don't remember ever seeing him in anything different, not since we moved to Hillsburg. He looks ridiculous in the light: weathered, faded, in need of a haircut and a good night's sleep. I can't see him from the window when he makes it over to the edge where Will dropped the cat, but I can tell he's seen it by the way Will's shoulders droop and the sweat that has gathered on his brow seems to heat up and seep down his face.

I hear the Ghost say, "Did you do this?"

Will doesn't answer him. He'll let him think what he wants before begging him to believe the truth.

"He didn't do anythi—"

"Katie, shut up!" Will shouts to me. "Listen to Dad. Go to your room."

I sit in the hallway instead, just to the left of the window, on the same landing above the stairs where Will and I used to wait in our pj's on Christmas morning for our parents to make coffee and set up the video camera. Through the open window I can still hear their conversation.

"What the hell are you doing up here? Almost twenty-one years old and you're on the roof of our home with your little sister doing God knows what. People are going to think you're—"

"That I'm what? Crazy?"

"Your sister is busy. She should be with friends her own age."

The truth is, I'm not allowed to do much of anything outside swim team and school activities, because the Ghost is convinced I'll be corrupted by Bad Influences. For someone with so many degrees hanging on his office walls, he's dumb as can be about how it feels to be a teenager.

"I haven't seen her in how many months? I just want to spend some *time* with her . . ." I imagine Will looking anywhere but at the Ghost.

"And this is your idea of fun? Animal torture? I suppose next you'll be teaching her how to forge prescriptions."

"God, Dad." Will's voice is shaking. He's trying to be strong, but I know he's terrified of the Ghost. "You don't know anything. Whatever you think of me, you can't believe *Katie* would ever—"

"Do whatever you tell her to do? I don't know? How am I supposed to know? The two of you shut me out of your lives—Kathryn, *I said go to your room.*"

I don't know how he even saw me. He pokes his head through the window, leaving Will on the roof alone. "Now."

"It was an accident. Dad—Daddy—we thought it would land on its feet."

For a minute, I almost think he believes me. "Okay. All right, Katie. Now go."

I have no choice except to listen to him—otherwise, I'll be grounded for like a month. But something like this, I know, is no good. Will would have been upset enough by the cat alone, without the Ghost getting involved and making assumptions. It seems like our dad wants to think only the worst of him. Sometimes I wonder what would happen if our parents could just understand that none of this is my brother's fault.

Five o'clock p.m., ninety-two degrees outside: my mother tells me the temperature accusingly, as though I've turned up a universal thermostat just to make her uncomfortable. She blows hair out of her eyes while she bends forward on her knees to cover the dead cat in a shallow grave of dirt and mulch underneath a rhododendron bush. I sit cross-legged on the ground, coaxing an earthworm around my ring finger, imagining a wedding in the backyard someday.

I hold up my hand. "What do you think, Mom?"

She laughs, says "Nice, brat," and musses my hair with a dirty hand. We kind of look at each other for a second, and then she says, "I love you, Katie. You know that, don't you?" She's drunk.

Six o'clock p.m., living room, freezing cold in the air-conditioning: my mother leans her head on my father's shoulder, wrinkling her nose at his cigarette smoke while he thumbs through pages of statistical analysis, the doctoral thesis of one of his interns. I stand across from them in a sweatshirt and my bikini bottoms, a Japanese pear held between my teeth, which are perfectly, naturally straight.

The Ghost looks me up and down for a minute. "Why don't you put some clothes on? You're not a baby anymore. You look like you're in your underwear." He averts his gaze. "It's embarrassing."

"Why aren't you nicer to him?"

He looks back down, pretends not to have heard.

"Why, Dad? He didn't do anything wrong. I told you it was an accident, and you've got him stuck up in his room like he's on house arrest, and he didn't even *do* anything." And I repeat what I've heard Will say countless times: "You want him to be just like you, and you can't accept that he'll never be that way. You want him to be—"

"Kathryn, there is a time for foolish loyalty. Now is not the time." As though there's any need to remind me again, he adds, "You're a kid."

"I'm *fifteen.*" After everything we've been through with Will, I sure don't feel like a kid.

"I know. That's how you're acting." He goes back to his reading.

I take a bite of my pear, give it a few good chews, and gather the pulp in my cheek. After Will and the Ghost came in from the roof, my brother spent the rest of the afternoon in his room, headphones on his ears. The only sounds from his room were the tapping of his fingers on his keyboard—probably firing e-mails to his latest group of friends from the latest hospital—and his breath, which I listened to from outside his closed door until I got hungry. I'm amazed my parents let him have a computer in his room at all.

"Believe me," I say to the Ghost, "the second I turn eighteen, I'm packing everything I own and getting out of here. There's no way you'll keep me *imprisoned* until I'm twenty years old."

The Ghost seems to suppress a smirk. "Imprisoned? Kathryn, you can't even begin to—" And he stops. "Never mind."

"What? I can't even begin to what? To understand?"

He murmurs to my mother, "This is a sick family." His head is down now, palm over my mother's hand. "Sick," he repeats.

I stand there for another few moments, waiting for him to say something else to me. When he doesn't, I gather my hair in a pile on top of my head and rise toward him on one strong leg, pointing my toe outward, and spit my mouthful of pear onto the pages spread on his lap.

He looks up, stunned, confused by what has just occurred. I am immediately sorry but not really—not sorry enough to stop. His eyes are mine. I am his. I am satisfied, knowing he will feel my anger in his blood.

"I hate you," I say, keeping his gaze. "You hear me?" I look at my mother, who stares at me, trembling. "You too. I hate both of you."

The Ghost uses his handkerchief to wipe away the pear and turns the page in the thesis he's reading.

My mother looks around, notices the pulp in the handkerchief, startled. She does that a lot when she's drunk—just kind of spaces out for a while. "I just put away laundry in Will's room. He wasn't there. His door was open, and I was in his room for a few minutes, putting things in drawers. . . ." A flutter of panic, frantic as a pair of damaged wings, takes hold of her voice. "Katie? Where's Willie?"

The doorbell rings.

Beth George, our neighbor a few houses down, stands alone on our front porch. She's in her midforties and has something like six kids already and is visibly pregnant again. Every member of the George family has bright red hair. Beth's husband has been in and out of jail for DUI so many times that even our teachers at school make open jokes about it, and none of the George kids seem to care.

Beth looks at each of us. When she speaks, her tone is nervous but not panicked. "I think you ought to know," she says, "your son's been knockin' on people's doors, tellin' them to come watch him. He's on the swing set in my backyard. He's got a knife, and he says he's gonna kill himself."

My parents and I start to run. When we get to Beth's house, we have to climb over a pile of broken cinderblocks at the edge of her yard. Other neighbors are already there. I can hear them trying to talk to him, saying things like, "Come on, Will, your parents are coming any minute, everything's going to be okay."

Someone—it sounds like one of the older George girls—yelps. "Mom!" she screams. "He won't stop, he's doing it . . . MOM!"

In my rush to reach my brother, I slip on the edge of a

cinderblock and fall forward. My hands and knees break my fall, but I can feel pain tearing through my shin as it makes contact with the edge of the block. Nobody moves to help me; they're all crowded around my brother. Some people have turned to look away. I see Henry Reuben, one of the local firefighters, pushing through everyone to reach my brother.

I hear my mom screaming before I see Will. She screams, "Ambulance! Someone call an ambulance, now!"

"They're coming," Donny George—Beth's husband—tells my mother. "Don't worry. We already called. They're on their way." He looks at me for a moment as I try to make my way past him, and says, "You know you're bleedin', don't you, Katie?"

But I don't anymore. My mother is on top of my brother like a blanket, my father is kneeling at his side. On the ground beside them is the serrated knife that my mom uses to carve turkeys and ham on the holidays, blood all over the blade and the white handle. Even before I reach him, I can tell that the wounds are very deep, that Will was not messing around. He usually isn't.

He seems unconscious. There is blood everywhere, coming from his arm, following the beating of his heart, and my mother holds his arm in the air while my father takes off his necktie and knots it so tightly around Will's bicep that my brother opens his eyes and screams. But when that only slows the blood, my father takes off his shirt and then my mother takes off her shirt, and the two of them are there beside him, my mom wearing only a worn-out white bra, my neighbors standing there murmuring to themselves, but none of them—not one—moving to help. I am amazed the Georges thought to call an ambulance at all.

When the ambulance comes, they get him inside and I try

to follow and come along with my parents, and for a minute I think I'll get away with it, but then the Ghost sees me trying to climb into the back and says, "Kathryn, *no*."

Will is conscious, barely, upright on the gurney, his arm held in the air by one of the EMTs.

It's like a nightmare—the kind where you want to scream, but you can't make any noise. "Will," I try to shout, and my voice comes out barely above a hoarse whisper. He doesn't hear me.

I try it again. "Will." Nothing. Again, I scream, "*Will*," and his eyelids flutter, his gaze takes its time focusing on me, and before I say anything, he says, to me and my parents, "I had to do it. You wanted me to. Everyone wanted me to."

My mom chokes on a sob. One of the EMTs hands her a gown to put over her bra, just as his partner is cutting off my brother's shirt. The doors are pulled shut, the lights go on, loud and red and spinning down the otherwise empty street, and I stand there with the rest of the crowd watching my family drive away, me and the whole town left to gaze at my brother's blood all over the George family swing set.

When I was a little girl, until I was eight or nine, I used to crawl into bed with my parents when I got scared at night. After it gets dark tonight, when I still haven't heard from my parents, I lie on Will's unmade bed and stare up at his ceiling. The paint is old, cracking in places, and the ceiling is still covered in stick-on, glow-in-the-dark stars that our mom put up in both of our bedrooms when we were kids. It was a careful task for her, with great attention given to detail. There is nothing random in the stars' arrangements. I stare at the Big Dipper and the Little Dipper, at the Hunting Dogs and the Great Bear and the Dragon. In the corner closest to the window, my mom created a detailed profile of my brother's young face. Even though he's so much older now, it is still unmistakably Will.

My parents get home a little after eleven. The Ghost stands in my brother's doorway, watching as my mom comes toward me to give me a hug. As soon as her arms are around me, she begins to sob.

"Is he okay?" I try to ask, but it's such a dumb question that I start shaking and crying instead.

My mom takes a deep, shaky breath. The Ghost is still in the doorway, a lit cigarette between his fingers, watching us like we're strangers.

"He's okay, sweetie," my mom says. "He'll be okay."

"We should all go to sleep," the Ghost says. "We can talk about things in the morning."

But I know they won't talk to me about anything. I know from experience that Will is likely at Forbes Regional Hospital right now, probably sedated and asleep, because that's what they used to do when this started. It is hard to believe he has been this sick for only a few years; it feels like this has been going on forever. When it started, they used to explain things to me more carefully. I've had it explained by guidance counselors, family therapists, and neighbors who don't have any idea what they're talking about. It got to the point where the same kind of things kept happening, over and over again, and there wasn't any point in explaining anymore.

• • •

Once I'm sure my parents are asleep, I creep out of my own bed and go downstairs to find a cigarette. I go back to Will's room, ease the window open, and slip outside, onto the roof.

The night is still too warm, the air sticky and unpleasant, so thick that each exhale of smoke seems to hover like a cloud for a few seconds, right in front of my face, before I blow it aside with the next breath.

When I'm finished, I turn to go back inside, and there he is: the Ghost is leaning with his head out the window, staring at me.

I expect him to do *something*—to start yelling, or to slam the window in disgust, or to order me inside—but he just looks at me. It's the same look of concentration I've seen him get when he's on the golf course, trying to figure out the right angle for a putt. It's the same look I bet I get when I'm on a starting block, gazing at the water beneath me, waiting for the whistle.

For the next few days, everything is quiet. The Ghost goes to work as usual. My mom spends long hours painting in her studio, and I stay outside by the pool, all by myself, swimming so much each day that my muscles ache into the night and keep me awake, staring at the plastic stars, bright and motionless above my bed. Things are too calm. Even my mother and the Ghost don't seem to be talking much. I can tell something's coming. The longer the quiet stretches, the more worried I get.

And then it happens. Three weeks before I'm supposed to start my sophomore year of high school, I wake up on a Saturday morning to find my parents sitting on either side of me in bed. They're both already dressed in nice clothes. My mom is sipping coffee from a plastic mug the size of her head. She's wearing a pantsuit and a full face of makeup and a delicate string of pearls around her neck, none of which I have *ever* seen her wear before. A glance at the Ghost's watch tells me it's not even seven in the morning.

"Katie," my mom pronounces, brushing my hair from my forehead.

"Go away," I murmur. I close my eyes again, trying to pretend they're not there.

"Kathryn," the Ghost says. "Get up." When I don't move, he claps his hands. "Get up!"

I sit up, throw the covers off of me, and glare at both of them. "What. Is. It?"

"We're going on a little trip," my mother says.

It doesn't even occur to me that I might be going to see Will; they haven't let me visit him in a hospital in over a year.

"We've found a place where we think you might do a little better." Before I can ask her what kind of place it is, she hurries to explain. "It's not to punish you or anything like that, sweetie, it's to help you because we want to see you reach your full potential. You and your brother are so gifted, and we want you to have every opportunity to maximize those gifts—"

"It's okay," the Ghost interrupts. I'm still half-asleep. He hands me a thick booklet. "She can read."

The front of the booklet says, "Woodsdale Academy: Preparing Students for Excellence since 1814." Beneath the heading, in smaller letters, it reads, "A Coeducational College Preparatory School for Boarding Students in Grades 9–12." And beneath that, right there on the cover, is a picture of three girls and two boys, each of them wearing swimsuits and caps, beaming at me with perfect white teeth. They're seated on the edge of a glistening, Olympic-sized indoor pool. Their arms are around each other, matching maroon towels slung over their shoulders, and they all look so happy to see me. Behind them there's a banner:

OHIO VALLEY
ATHLETIC CONFERENCE
CHAMPIONS

I flip through the booklet, looking at all the pictures. There are students strolling arm-in-arm through a lush autumn landscape, each of them wearing neat uniforms and carrying full backpacks. A more candid shot shows two girls in what appears to be a dorm room. They're both wearing Woodsdale Academy T-shirts, their hair set in pink curlers, heads tilted together as they grin at the camera like they've never had more fun in their lives. In another shot, a teacher leans helpfully over a student's shoulder as he peers into a microscope.

"Where is it?" I ask.

"Close," my mother says. "Really close. We can visit you all the time."

"Four hours away," the Ghost clarifies. "It's in West Virginia."

I close the brochure and stare at the cover again, at the glistening swimmers who have never met me and won't know a thing about me except that I can swim faster than any of them.

"The last set of admissions tests for the year is this afternoon," the Ghost says. "You need to get dressed."

I glance at both of them, back and forth. My mother's eyes are dewy. Her eyelids flutter nervously as she takes long, loud sips of coffee.

Finally, I look at the Ghost. I feel like, if I stare at him long enough, maybe he'll break down and show some warmth, hug me or cry or *something,* but the longer I stare at him, the steadier his gaze seems to get.

"Do I have a choice?" I ask.

He doesn't even blink. "No."

I want to fight with him for the sake of fighting. Because, I mean, who wants to get sent to *boarding school*? And then I think about the last few weeks, about what school will be like when I go back and everybody wants to know about Will and I won't have anything to tell them, and depending on what they've heard I might have to fake a headache and spend the afternoon on a cot in the nurse's office, waiting for the day to be over. And then I'll come home to what? My mom. The pool in our yard. In a month or so, it will be too cold and they'll have to cover it for the fall and winter, and all I'll have is Rec swimming four days a week, two hours a day.

Who wants to get sent away to boarding school? I do.

I shrug. "Okay. I'll get dressed."

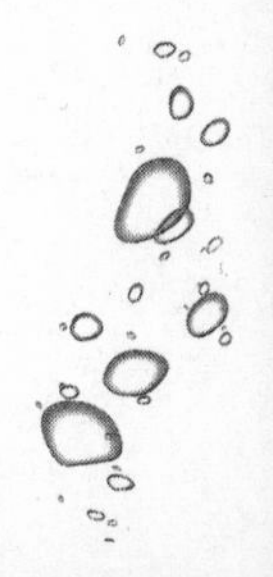

part two

chapter 3

Woodsdale's campus is nicer than any school I've ever seen in my life. Most of the buildings, including the main school building, are restored old mansions. The administrative building is all wide hallways and winding stairwells and shiny hardwood floors covered with Oriental rugs. After the admissions test, which takes only an hour or so and isn't hard, I sit beside my parents in the admissions director's office and watch the Ghost write a check. I figure the real "admissions test" is whether or not the check clears.

The admissions director, Dr. Waugh, is a lean, blond woman with a South African accent. She leans against the front of her desk and beams down at me. "Katie," she pronounces. "We're so thrilled to welcome you to Woodsdale."

Before I can say anything—like reminding her they couldn't possibly have had time to score my admissions test—she continues. "There are only two new sophomore girls this year. You and your roommate. Her name is Madeline Moon. She comes to us from a boarding school in Connecticut, and I'm sure you two will really hit it off."

Dr. Waugh doesn't seem like the kind of person to use the expression "hit it off" in everyday conversation, unless she's talking to someone like me, who comes from someplace like Hillsburg. Dr. Waugh wears tailored black pants that look *expensive,* a white shirt with a narrow black tie, and high-heeled white sandals. Her office isn't air-conditioned and it's at least ninety degrees outside but she isn't sweating at all. On her ring finger, there's a band with a single diamond so big I can't stop staring at it. The wall behind her desk is covered with half a dozen framed degrees and certifications of merit, most of which are from Harvard; the others are from Brown.

"So . . . are there other new kids? In other grades?" I ask.

She shakes her head. "Most of our students begin their Woodsdale career in ninth grade, but we certainly make exceptions for . . . special circumstances."

"So there's nobody else? Just me and, uh, Madeline?"

She nods. "That's right." And then she leans over, her face only a few inches from mine, and smiles so big that I can see all the fillings in her bottom teeth and feel her warm spearmint breath on my face. "Don't be nervous, Kathryn. We're a family here. Everything will be fine."

They call the two weeks before school begins "preseason," which is an intensive, all-day, every-day practice session for school athletes to prepare for the upcoming year. Even though swimming is a winter sport, there is practice year-round for the varsity team. So, three days after my first visit, my parents drive me back to Woodsdale—this time with our car packed full of my things—and drop me off at my dorm, Wallace Hall.

We hug each other. None of it feels real. My mother has tears in her eyes, and the Ghost cups my chin in his hands and says, "I'm proud of you." He smiles. Even though the room is piled with boxes of my stuff, there is a tactile void surrounding us, so heavy that it's like standing in the eye of a hurricane and trying to pretend the weather is perfect. The room is big, bigger than my room at home. Its walls are bare, the bunk beds unmade—there's no sign yet of Madeline Moon. I can't stop thinking about what Will would say about all of this.

"Shipping my little sister off to boarding school? Oh, that's low." He'd shake his head in disappointment over the whole sorry situation; probably light a cigarette in the middle of the room, indifferent to the smoke alarm going off. "You know what you should do, Katie? You should get yourself kicked out right away for something so bad it gives the Ghost a heart attack."

Over the next day or so, the dorm fills up with other girls. Wallace Hall is a long, narrow building with a single hallway and rooms on either side. On one end of the building, there's a huge common room with tables and sofas and a piano and TV. On the other end there's a huge apartment where our house mother, Mrs. Martin, lives with her husband.

All of the girls seem to know each other. Most of them are freshmen or sophomores, except for a couple of dorm assistants, who are seniors. Even the freshmen all know each other from somewhere—either they went to the same private schools or the same summer camps or *something.*

Everyone seems friendly at first; girls introduce themselves, look me over, and then continue talking to their roommates or other friends. In my first twelve hours, I meet an Alison, a

Gretchen, an Estella (who is gorgeous, probably the most beautiful girl I've ever seen), a Lindsey, and one of our dorm assistants, a senior named Jill. Jill is the only person who doesn't smile when she meets me.

The night before my first practice, I stay in my room, listening to all of their loud voices lilting down the hallway from the common room, too afraid to leave even to use the bathroom. Their laughter gets so loud that it makes me flinch in reflex a few times. They are all such good friends already, obviously so comfortable, their lives so easy, I can't imagine what they would think of me if they knew how I'd come to be here with them.

Since Madeline isn't here yet, I've claimed the top bunk for myself. I lie in bed, listening, staring at the blank ceiling above me until it gets so dark in the room that I can't see anything at all. Finally, a little after eleven, I hear Jill's heavy footsteps coming down the hallway, the sound of her voice booming into the common room, ordering everyone to bed. As they trickle down the hallway into their bedrooms, one of them complains loudly that school hasn't even started yet and she isn't their mommy and they aren't freaking *preschoolers,* loudly enough that Jill comes out of her room and screeches, "If I hear one more word you'll all be pulling weeds outside the field house tomorrow until your fingers are bleeding!"

I wait, staring at the ceiling, until the whole dorm is quiet, until the last giggle drifts into silence. Then I get my toothbrush and towel and sneak down the hallway to the bathroom to brush my teeth and wash my face.

On my way back from the bathroom, I notice a crack of light coming from the doorway that leads to the common room. Before I can hurry back to my own room, the door opens a little, and I see that it's Estella, her back pressed against the door. She's practically being smothered by a tall blond guy as the two of them hold on to each other like they'll die if they let go, faces mashed together, and I stand there frozen until the boy opens his eyes a little bit and sees me in my pj's, staring at them. He pulls away from Estella, whispers something into her ear. Estella turns and gives me a long, appraising stare. She's wearing nothing but day-of-the-week (Sunday) underpants and a pink tank top. Her long red hair spills wet and clingy over her shoulders and down her back. She stands on her tiptoes, whispers something to the boy—who is every bit as beautiful as she is—and then gives him a quick kiss on the nose before heading back into the dorm.

She doesn't say anything as she passes me. She just holds a finger to her lips, which are curled into a slight smile, goes, "Shhhh," and walks away, closing the door to her room without a sound.

My first swimming practice starts the following morning at eight sharp. There's breakfast beforehand in the cafeteria, everyone except me in T-shirts and Woodsdale Academy–issue maroon sweatpants cut off at the thigh to make shorts. I show up five minutes before breakfast ends so I won't have to talk to anyone.

Everyone looks tired and annoyed while they eat scrambled eggs and buttered toast and bacon. Nobody says much of anything above a sleepy murmur here and there. Estella is the only person whose name I know for sure. She's sitting with the boy from the previous night. She feeds him bites of her toast and murmurs into his ear while he smiles and keeps his free hand on her bare thigh. Neither of them even looks at me.

I've been swimming almost my whole life, but I've never been at a practice like this before. The pool seems so clean and flat and cool that I don't dare even dip my toe in before someone tells me. Everybody but me is wearing a matching maroon swimsuit—to *practice*—and each of the girls has her last name printed over her right breast in delicate white lettering. They all have matching maroon swim caps with big white *W*'s printed on the side. Even the lining of their goggles is maroon.

There are sixteen members of the coed varsity swim team this year. Everybody looks at me—my black one-piece is worn thin and doesn't say my name anywhere, and my swim cap is pink, with tiny white elephants all over it—but nobody says anything. Our coach, Mr. Solinger, waits with his hands clasped behind his back while we all line up along the wall facing the shallow end of the pool.

His face is dead serious, even stern, for a good long minute, before he breaks into a grin. "Hey, team," he says. "Everyone have a nice summer?"

We all nod.

"Ready to work hard?"

We nod again. Does he even *notice* me? He doesn't make eye contact, just strolls up and down the maroon-and-white tile in his bare feet, hands clasped behind his back.

"Ready to win the OVACs again?" He's talking about the Ohio Valley Athletic Conference. From what I understand, it's a big deal.

This time, nobody nods. "Yes!" they all shout, their enthusiasm overwhelming, and when I look at their faces, there's an obvious ferocity in all of their eyes. The girl beside me catches my gaze. Her eyes flicker up and down my body, taking it all in. She whispers, "What's your name?"

"Katie," I whisper back.

"I'm Grace. I'm captain this year for the girls' team."

"Oh." I try to smile. The last name on her swimsuit reads "Waugh," and I wonder if she's related to the admissions director.

"Solinger told me you're good. What do you swim?" she whispers.

I hesitate. "Everything."

She pauses. "Yeah, but what's your best stroke?"

I hesitate again. From the side of her swim cap, I notice a few blond hairs peeking out. She has the same long legs as Dr. Waugh, the same sleek confidence.

"Everything," I say.

Her grin disappears. She stares forward, and I watch as she bites her lower lip and gazes at the water, shoulders creeping up just a bit toward her ears.

"I'm sure you've all noticed we have a new face this year," Coach Solinger continues, and all of a sudden all eyes are on me. "This is Kathryn Kitrell."

"Katie," I say. Like I said, nobody calls me Kathryn except the Ghost. I'm determined to keep it that way.

Solinger nods. "Okay then, Katie. So, kids, Katie here comes to us from Pennsylvania. She's a sophomore, and last year she broke more than a few records in her state finals. I think you'll all be very glad that she's decided to join us."

He looks at me, gives me a lopsided grin. "Katie. We have

only one rule for our practices. Somebody want to tell her what it is?"

Almost before the words are out of his mouth, Grace's hand goes up. She gives me a deliberate, icy look, and says, "Practice isn't over until someone pukes into the gutter."

Solinger nods. "Right-o. Okay kids—drills are on the board." He nods at a chalkboard behind him, four columns of writing divided into four strokes, each stroke divided into a series of different drills. It's going to take all day.

Before I know what's happening, everyone around me is in the water, goggles on, shaking their arms and bouncing up and down and shuffling into place. Within seconds, I'm the only one left standing on the ceramic tile deck beside the pool, and everyone is staring at me, half smiling. I know what they're all thinking: *she'll be the one who pukes.*

Solinger gives me a gentle push toward the water. "Go on, Kitrell. Lane one."

I get in. Even though the water is much colder than I'm used to, it's the first time since I've gotten to Woodsdale that I can feel myself relax, from my face to my stomach, right down to my toes.

Sure enough, around 11:45, after almost four hours in the water, a girl in lane 6 whose swimsuit reads "Dodd" hoists herself over the edge of the deep end and loses what's left of her breakfast.

For the past half hour, the boys' varsity water polo team has been standing on deck in their swimsuits, tossing medicine balls around, waiting for their turn in the water.

"Oh, thank *God,*" one of them says, loud enough for everyone to hear. When I turn to look, out of breath and treading water halfway down the deep end, I see that it's the same boy from last night—Estella's boyfriend.

Swimmers are hopping out of the pool in a hurry. Most of the puke has missed the gutter and is spreading across the surface of the water. Solinger is already heading toward the deep end with a net.

One of the boys on the varsity swim team sidles up beside Estella's boyfriend, nudges him, and says, "It's always Dodd."

The two of them grin. They're both gorgeous. They look like they could be brothers, but Estella's boyfriend is a little taller, his grin a little more rotten. "Hey, Jamie," he calls across the room. "Jamie Dodd! You ought to see a doctor about that weak tummy!"

Glancing to make sure Solinger's back is turned, Jamie holds up both middle fingers and mouths a string of obscenities. She's still a little pale.

In the locker room, while everyone is pulling on their clothes, Jamie says to nobody in particular, "I hate Stetson McClure."

"You should stop throwing up all the time, then," Grace snaps. "Besides, he's just kidding."

"I get cramps if I don't eat for more than a few hours. Then I swallow some pool water and I can't help it, I just—"

"Then quit," Grace says, "or stop whining." She glances at me. I'm trying to pull on my clothes as quickly as possible over my swimsuit. "I was sure you'd be the one to puke. What's your name again?"

When Grace tugs off her swim cap, I see she has the same wavy blond hair as her mother. Her legs look like they haven't been shaved all summer, which tells me she's serious about swimming. The more body hair you have, the more drag it creates in the water. When you finally do shave, right before a race, you can go a few seconds faster.

"Katie," I say. "Katie Kitrell."

Grace only nods. "Well, Katie, you need to get down to the school store and order your suits, like, now."

"I didn't think I'd have to wear my meet suit for practice—"

"These *are* our practice suits," Jamie says, frowning at Grace behind her back. She mouths a few more choice words in Grace's direction and gives me a little smile. Jamie has braces on her teeth, and since she's just barfed all over the pool, she needs to *brush.*

"Oh. I didn't realize. Well, what do you wear for meets?"

Grace doesn't blink. "We wear our meet suits."

"Okay. Well, what's the difference between our practice suits and our meet suits?" Swimsuits are expensive. I can't imagine having a custom suit printed just for practice.

"We wear our practice suits for practice. We wear our meet suits for meets." Grace pulls on a maroon sweatshirt that says "CAPTAIN" in big white block letters across her chest. "Got it?"

I'm standing naked in the middle of my dorm room, toweling off from my shower after practice, when an unseen hand slips a heavy ivory envelope beneath my door. Inside the envelope is an invitation to the annual—no kidding—*tea party* for Woodsdale girls. It says the dress code is "white glove."

I don't know what "white glove" means. I'm still shook up

by how intense practice was, how mean Grace was, and I don't want to risk showing up in the wrong pair of freaking *gloves* for a tea party.

When I first met our house mother, Mrs. Martin, she'd made me promise I'd come straight to her with any questions or problems. The tea party is definitely both.

"I was thinking I'd skip it," I tell her, standing in the doorway to the hall that connects her apartment to the rest of the dorm.

"Oh no, sweetie. It's compulsory."

"Compulsory?" I raise my eyebrows, put my hands on my hips, hoping she'll admit she's only kidding.

"Mandatory," she repeats, like I don't know what "compulsory" means. "If you don't go, you'll get a demerit." She shakes her head at me. "You don't want to start your Woodsdale career that way. Besides, tea parties are fun. You'll see."

Before I know it, I'm blinking back tears. "I don't have any white gloves."

"Oh, honey. Come on." And she leads me down the hallway, into her home, past the kitchen and the living room, where her husband is asleep in his bathrobe on the sofa. Once we're in her bedroom, she goes to a bottom dresser drawer and produces a stack of impossibly white gloves in all different sizes, each of them ironed crisp and cleaner than anything I've ever seen. "Don't be afraid," she tells me, winking. "You aren't the first new girl, you know. You just have to understand what people expect from you."

I pull a glove over my palm, my fingers still wrinkled from swimming all morning. "What do they expect?"

She seems surprised by the question. "Well, they expect you to succeed. They expect greatness. And"—her powdered nose wrinkles—"oh, I don't know, a sense of gratitude. Have you ever read *King Lear*?"

I shake my head. It's already far more of an explanation than I was expecting.

"I'll show you—right here." We go to the bookshelf in the living room. She plucks a leather-bound copy of Shakespeare's *Collected Works* off the shelf, goes directly to a bookmarked passage, and reads aloud: " 'Her voice was ever soft, gentle and low. An excellent thing in a woman.' You'll read this . . . in senior-year English, I think." She replaces the book on the shelf and reaches outward to squeeze my gloved hand. "But remember it now."

From the sofa, her husband—who I'd thought was asleep—sits upright and gives us both a big grin. "Best advice you'll ever hear, sweetie," he says, winking at me before lying back down and turning up the volume on the TV.

Everything here is monogrammed: the awnings on the front porch of the headmaster's house; the stone walkway leading to the front door; the napkins, the teacups, the plates—they all bear the Woodsdale Academy insignia, which is a large capital *W* with a smaller capital *A* formed in the *W*'s center, all contained within a circle. I can hear Will hissing over my shoulder; I can almost feel his breath and smell nicotine and rotten teeth and teaberry gum. He says, "Kind of looks like a pentagram, doesn't it?"

Everybody sits around sipping from teacups that barely hold anything, balancing their elbows on crossed legs while the female faculty wander about, mostly talking to each other.

"There you are," somebody says from behind me. It's Estella. Her friend Lindsey is beside her. They're both smiling.

"Hi," I say.

"Hi," Lindsey says.

Estella narrows her eyes. "I think you forgot something."

Oh, God. I'm probably wearing the wrong shade of pastel, or my skirt is an inch too high.

"Your name tag," she supplies. "Over there, on the table in the foyer. If Dr. Waugh sees you without it, she'll come over and bother us."

I stare at their name tags. *Lindsey Maxwell-Hutton. Estella Delilah Brinkley-Wallace.* I suddenly feel incredibly inadequate with only two names. I can sense these girls, with their lineage on such display, staring at me with what must be pity, sizing me up based on my borrowed gloves and my simple name: Kathryn Kitrell. It looks ridiculous in calligraphy, even on the paper name tag.

I follow them—I don't know what else to do—to the corner of the living room, where we can lean against one of the wall-to-wall bookshelves.

Lindsey puts me at ease almost right away. "I wish we could take these stupid gloves off," she says, talking around a mouthful of egg-salad sandwich. "I have to borrow them from my mom every year. She keeps them in her nightstand drawer." Lindsay shudders. "I'm afraid she and my dad use them for some kind of weird sex game." She holds out her hands, asks the question to nobody in particular: "Who still wears white gloves? Freakin' Queen Elizabeth?"

Let your breath out, I think. I never have to remind myself when I'm swimming; only on dry ground. "I know, right? I've never owned a pair either. I had to borrow them from Mrs. Martin."

Estella—who is drinking coffee, not tea—perks up. "That cow," she declares. Her voice is so sweet that everything she says, no matter how nasty, sounds pretty. "You'd be smart to avoid her. I mean"—her gaze rakes me up and down—"once you return those gloves."

Estella's name tag takes up two full lines of script: "Estella Delilah Brinkley-Wallace." I've never met anybody—not anybody—with any one of those names, let alone all four of them. Her face looks like it could have been sketched by Michelangelo. She would look more appropriate in a toga, a crown of olive leaves adorning her crimson hair.

Then it dawns on me. "Your last name is Wallace? As in—"

"Wallace Hall," she finishes, grinning. "That's right. My father donated the building to the school two years ago."

"Your *step*father," Lindsey murmurs.

"Either way. So, Katie. Tell us all about you."

I'd assumed Estella wasn't the least bit interested in me. But her gaze is steady and almost fascinated. Nobody like her has ever shown an interest in me before.

"Ummm . . ."

"Where are you from? Why didn't you start last year?" Her tone is verging on accusatory.

"Well, I'm from Pennsylvania, and I didn't start last year because . . ." I shrug. "I don't know. My parents just decided to send me this year instead."

"Really?" She raises one perfectly groomed eyebrow, the mildest grin on her face. "Are you sure you didn't get kicked out of your last school? Why would your parents just decide out of *nowhere* to send you here?"

I can feel my eyes widen. The whole room seems to get smaller. When I open my mouth, my voice is shaky. "They just did."

"Do you have any brothers or sisters?" Lindsey asks. She

seems genuinely interested, kind, excited to meet someone new. She's pretty, soft and curvy, and is wearing a shade too much makeup. Even though it's the first time I'm talking to her, there's something kind of desperate about her. But she seems genuinely nice, and I like her already.

When she asks about brothers and sisters, I stare down at our hands—at all of our hands, white gloves pulled taught and flawless over our fingers—and all I can think about is Will and the blood everywhere the last time I saw him. I remember watching from my window as Donny George stood with a hose in his backyard, rinsing the blood from his kids' swing set, spraying down the concrete walkway in his yard. It took him forever. As I'm thinking about it, I can feel my shin aching where I fell on the cinderblocks in the Georges' yard and took a chunk out of my flesh.

The words leave my mouth before I can stop them. "I had a brother," I say.

"Oh." It takes them a moment to fully understand. Then Estella says, *"Oh,"* and leans forward just a little; I can hear her breath quicken. She nods her head, satisfied. "So *that's* why you're here?"

I nod. Part of me wants to punch her in her beautiful face. She's so *entertained* by me. "Kind of."

"Oh, my God." Lindsey puts a hand on my arm. "That's awful, Katie."

Estella puts her hand on my other arm. Her grip is tighter than Lindsey's. "Do you mind if I ask . . . what happened?"

I don't know what to say. I don't want to lie, but I can't imagine anything more awful than the truth. "There was an accident," I say.

They both nod, looking at me differently now. For a few

awkward seconds we stand there, nobody speaking, all three of us sweating in our gloves. Estella seems to glisten, even though she continues to drink coffee so hot that I can still see steam rising from its surface.

"So. Well. Where are you going to volunteer?" Lindsey wants to know.

I'm grateful for the change of subject. "Oh, I haven't decided yet."

"But you know it's mandatory?" Estella asks. She closes her eyes for a moment, like she's so irritated that she can hardly contain herself. "Everything at this stupid place is mandatory." Even though I don't know if I even like her, I know I want to be her friend. She's so annoyed by everything, so intimidating, that just standing there talking to her—knowing she can bear being around me—makes me feel good.

All of the Woodsdale Academy students are required to volunteer for five hours a week. According to the school literature, volunteering is designed to "foster a bond with the greater community and a sense of responsibility to mankind." I'm guessing it's really because it looks so good on college applications.

"I read to blind people," Estella says, "Tuesday and Wednesday afternoons." Then she whooshes the idea away with the flick of her wrist. "But you can't do that, because all the blind people in Woodsdale are already taken."

"Why don't you come to the soup kitchen with me? My mom organizes the group for Saturday mornings. We start next month," Lindsey offers.

"Ooh, that might be good," Estella reasons. "Since you're on the swim team, you'll have all kinds of Saturday-morning meets. That means you'll almost never have to actually go volunteer."

I don't have any reason to say no. "Okay, sure. But wait—your mom is in charge of the volunteers?"

Lindsey nods.

"But where do you live? I mean, where do your parents live?"

They look at each other, and then back at me, confused. "We live in Woodsdale."

"So . . . why do you live on campus if your parents live in town?"

Estella opens her mouth like she's about to say something, closes it, opens it again. "Because it's . . . you know . . . *boarding school.*"

"Oh. Right." The idea of living so close to your family while still living on campus seems silly. I mean, why pay all that extra money for room and board when you could just drive your kid to school every day?

"So you two knew each other before you came here?"

"All our lives," they say, almost in unison.

There's a brief pause. I can't think of anything to say. Finally, I shift my focus to Lindsey. Her smile is constant. "I think it will be fun to volunteer," I say.

Estella narrows her eyes at me. "Katie, are you a Democrat or a Republican? Because if you're a Democrat . . ."

"We aren't old enough to vote," Lindsey says, putting another triangle of sandwich in her mouth. "It doesn't matter."

"Yes it does." Estella licks her lips. "My mother's first husband was a Democrat."

Lindsey stares at the ceiling. When I follow her gaze, I notice that even the exposed wooden beams are painted in a maroon-and-white checkerboard pattern. "You mean your father?"

"Yes." Estella presses her lips together. "My biological

father." And she sighs, saying, "You should meet my sister. She's also a Democrat. She's at Princeton now, but let me tell you, she's headed nowhere in life."

There is a smear of egg salad at the edge of Lindsey's mouth as she grins at me and says, "My mother says that Estella is a living example of the trauma divorce inflicts on families."

Estella whips her head to the side, glaring. "Really, Linds? *My* mother says you need to stop eating carbs."

Lindsey blinks at me, still smiling. "See what I mean?"

The next few days are filled with swimming practices so intense that, by the end of the week, my muscles ache so badly I can barely get up from a sitting position by myself. Each day, I come back from practice expecting to find that Madeline Moon has arrived, but every night I go to bed by myself, in my otherwise empty room. I usually fall asleep early, exhausted from practice, and as I drift off I can hear the sounds of the other girls talking and giggling in their rooms, keeping their voices low so that Jill doesn't come banging on their door.

After about a week of tentative talk with Lindsey and Estella, Lindsey comes knocking at my door one night, just as I'm about to fall asleep.

"It's nine thirty, Katie," she says when she sees me in my pj's. "You weren't going to bed, were you?"

I shrug. "I have to be up early for practice." It's actually the latest I've stayed up all week.

Lindsey moves past me, into the room. And then, before the door has a chance to close behind her, Estella pushes herself in.

She watches as I yawn. I stretch my arms over my head, wincing. She snorts. "What are you, eighty years old?" She laughs out loud.

"We're going to wax our legs," Lindsey tells me, leaning against Madeline Moon's bare desk. I notice that Estella is carrying a basket of supplies: a container of hot wax in what looks like a tiny Crock-Pot, wide wooden sticks for spreading the wax onto our legs, and long strips of cloth to yank the hair out from the roots.

"We've been growing our hair out for, like, six weeks in order to wax right before school starts," Lindsey explains.

"And we noticed your legs are hairy as hell," Estella says. "But I don't know—are your bones too fragile for wax strips? We wouldn't want Granny to break a hip."

I shake my head at Lindsey, trying to ignore Estella. "I can't do it." And I explain to them how drag works in the water, and that it would look bad if I showed up to practice with smooth legs.

Estella frowns. "What about your armpits and bikini line?" She wrinkles her nose at me. "You've got to do *something,* Katie." Her gaze drifts to my legs. "You look like Sasquatch."

I take a moment to consider. It isn't that much hair. Besides, here I am with two girls who are obviously interested in being my friends—although I'm still not sure why—and if I tell them to leave so I can go to sleep, they might not come back. "I guess that's okay."

"Put on your swimsuit, then," Estella says, slipping out of her boxer shorts, anxious to get started on her fuzzy legs. She stands in the middle of my room, wearing nothing but a white thong and matching white tank top. "I'll do your bikini line, okay?" She gives me an exaggerated wink, followed by that huge, irresistible grin of hers. "Don't worry, Katie baby. It won't hurt a bit."

But it *does* hurt—so bad, in fact, that after just half of her right leg (which is bleeding already), Estella hops out my window and strolls, half-naked, into the woods behind the dorm to take a break and smoke a cigarette.

Lindsey and I both watch her from a distance, the white of her top and underpants glowing beneath the moonlight. She seems unafraid of being caught and takes her time, running her free hand through her long hair, absently searching for split ends in the almost-dark.

"Is she always like this?" I ask, trying to keep my voice down.

Lindsey nods. "She's something, huh?"

I know I'm taking a risk, since I barely know Lindsey. But I ask, "Why do you think she's . . . I don't know . . ."

"Such a bitch?" Lindsey supplies. She doesn't even look up from her waxing.

"Well, yeah."

Lindsey shrugs. "Duh, Katie. Just *look* at her. She's like that because she can be. She's my best friend, you know, and she's not even nice to me. Like, the summer between seventh and eighth grades, my parents hired me a trainer and I lost, like, fifteen pounds. When we went back to school, Estella told everyone I'd been to fat camp. It's just her way of getting attention. Or whatever."

She yanks away a section of hair, closing her eyes momentarily to let the pain subside. Pinpricks of blood appear in bursts where her hairs have been ripped from their roots. "Don't take her personally. She wouldn't be here if she didn't like you. And, Katie," she continues, "she's the most popular girl in the whole *school,* and she wants to be your friend. So, I mean—who cares what she's like?"

I glance out the window. Estella has finished her first cigarette and lit another. Anyone looking out their window could spot her. It's almost like she's daring Jill to come out and catch her.

"Why does she want to be my friend, though? She doesn't even know me."

"Because . . . you're mysterious. Here you are, arrived out of nowhere with this tragic past . . . *ouch!*" She has yanked away another sheet of wax. "Where's your roommate, huh? What's her name?"

"Madeline Moon."

"Right. Fifty bucks says she never shows up. Anyway, people like you, Katie. You shouldn't be so surprised."

"Why do you like me, then?"

Lindsey shrugs, stirring the wax. "You're nice. You're pretty. Like I said, you're mysterious. We need to expand our group a little bit. Lately Estella's always busy with Stetson or something, and everyone else we hang out with . . . they only want to be friends so they can get invited to parties and, you know, be *seen* with us."

"But you said she's the most popular girl in school," I say, confused.

"Yeah. So?"

"Well . . . doesn't she have a ton of close friends?"

Lindsey looks me in the eye. "She has a bunch of people who think they're her friends. But I'm the only person who really knows her."

"Oh." I nod, pretending to understand.

"This isn't public school, Katie. Things are more complicated here. Just trust me." Glancing at the window, Lindsey lowers her voice. "Here she comes. Shut up."

The day before school starts, I'm walking back from dinner with Lindsey. Estella is still in the cafeteria, sharing a sundae with Stetson McClure, who, Estella has informed me, Belongs To Her. Stetson is captain of the boys' water polo team and has yet to say a word to me even though I've sat at the same meal table with him and Lindsey and Estella and a few other people more than once.

Lindsey is telling me about the parties she has, almost every weekend, at her parents' house. I'm only half listening, tired and full and homesick in an achy way I've been feeling all week—homesick for an impossible place. My parents have called every night to check in and see how I'm doing. When I ask about Will, they say he's fine, and then they clam up. Our conversations are never more than three or four minutes.

". . . plus," Lindsey continues, oblivious to my distraction, "we have an indoor pool. It's huge. My mom has a family history of arthritis, so she can only do low-impact aerobics."

I perk up at the mention of the pool. "So you have pool parties, like, every weekend?"

She shrugs. "Pretty much."

"What do you do there?" I ask.

She shrugs again. "Whatever we want. Get drunk, mostly. Smoke up. You know—normal teenager stuff, I guess." She squints at me. "Why? What did you do at parties back home?"

I shake my head. "Oh, the same thing. You know—normal stuff." *Got high with my clinically insane brother. Smoked cigarettes stolen from my supernatural father. The usual.*

Lindsey lowers her voice. "What's your family like? You haven't mentioned them. I mean, besides your brother."

When I look away, she rushes on, "I'm sorry—I shouldn't have said anything. It's just—there was an accident, you said?"

Once again, I hear the words coming out of my mouth automatically. I keep telling myself that as long as I don't say "dead," it isn't really a lie.

"Yes." I nod. "It happened very close to our house." *Not untrue.*

"Katie, I'm so sorry." Her look is full of pity. "And . . . I mean, what kind of accident? What happened?"

"It was . . . It was a mess." I stare at her, pronouncing the next few words without having to force any false emotion into my voice. I just want her to stop asking questions. "Then he was just gone." *Technically not untrue.*

I can tell she wants to ask more, but my look shuts her up. And then, when we turn the corner that brings us into the bottom of our dorm's driveway, I put my hand on her elbow, point with my other hand, and say, "Hey! Look at that!"

A Woodsdale Academy shuttle van (shiny maroon, the Woodsdale insignia painted in white on its side) is parked in the driveway. The school groundskeeper, Papa Rosedaddy (obviously not his real name, although nobody—not even Mrs. Martin—seems to know what his real name *is*), is hoisting a suitcase from the back. Mr. and Mrs. Martin are carrying smaller suitcases, one in each hand, toward the dorm. Behind all of them, her head down, a curtain of long black hair hiding her face as she follows them inside, is a girl who can only be my new roommate, Madeline Moon.

chapter 4

When I walk into my room, Mr. and Mrs. Martin are gone. It's just me and Madeline and all of our stuff. I don't know how she's managed to do it so quickly, but Madeline has switched my sheets to the bottom bunk, claiming the top bunk for herself. Neither of us mentions it, but right away it sets an unsettling tone to the whole roommate relationship.

At first, she doesn't say anything to me—not even hello. She stands in the center of the room, lips pressed together, her small Asian features delicate and soft, and says, "This is crap."

Before I can respond at all, she continues. "Do we get laptops? I mean, do they issue them on the first day, or what?"

I shake my head. Woodsdale is what they call a cyber-secure campus. There are computer labs in school, and most kids have laptops of their own in their rooms, but there's no Internet access anywhere except the main academic building. We also aren't allowed to have cell phones—each room has its own landline—or PDAs or iPods or anything like that. Breaking any of these rules is supposedly punishable by expulsion, although Lindsey has assured me you'd just get a ton of work details.

When I explain this to Madeline, she looks on the verge of furious tears. I realize she doesn't even know my name yet. "So," I say, trying to ignore her obvious anger, "I'm Katie Kitrell, and I'm a sophomore too. And you're Madeline Moon?"

"Mazzie."

"Huh?"

"Ma-zz-ie," she pronounces. "Don't call me Madeline. And my last name isn't Moon. It's Moon-Park."

Another hyphenated last name. Great.

"Okay. Mazzie."

She nods. "Look—Katie? Let me just tell you now that I don't want to be here. This school is a joke. I mean, as far as boarding schools go, it's at the bottom of the totem pole. What is it, like, seventy percent of graduating students matriculate to top-tier colleges?"

"I think it's . . . eighty-five? Maybe ninety?"

She snorts. "That's what they *tell* you."

I don't know what to say. But I don't have time to come up with any kind of response before she continues with, "The last school I was at, in Connecticut, had a ninety-five percent matriculation rate to top-tier colleges. It cost about twice as much as this place." She shakes her head at me, like she can't believe I'm not as disgusted as she is to be someplace so clearly inferior.

"Well if you don't mind my asking, why did you leave your last school?"

She pauses, glares at me, and says, "I don't know. It's not important."

"Uh . . ."

"Why did you leave *your* last school?" She puts her tiny fists on her hips and smirks. When she narrows her eyes at me, they almost disappear. "If you don't mind my asking."

I don't hesitate. She deserves to feel bad. "My brother died."

And then—right there, in that moment, which I know I'll always remember, right down to the red-and-white-striped tank top Mazzie is wearing, the small beads of sweat on her high forehead, the bronze of her summer tan and her almost-labored breath—I feel a door closing, my brother's face behind it.

I feel awful. In this moment, I miss him more than ever. But I also feel relief, a kind of deep satisfaction now that I've managed to complete the lie I've been trying to tell for weeks. I feel, for the first time since I watched Will being driven away in the ambulance, like I can breathe on dry land again.

Just like every other year, there's a kind of death in the air as the summer is squelched by autumn. It is a lonely feeling. At night, I lie in bed and listen to Mazzie breathing above me, thankful for her warm sound in the dark. Even though she's still barely willing to speak to me, it feels better than being all by myself. Sometimes I pretend she is Will, and that I know exactly where he is and what's happening to him, right there above me. Sometimes I try not to think about it, and I don't pretend anything. Mostly, though, I pretend that everything I've told everyone is true: my big brother is dead. In that scenario, at least, we all get some rest.

For the entire first week of classes, aside from our brief exchanges when we come and go from the room, Mazzie and I hardly speak to each other. At breakfast and dinner, it's mandatory that you eat family-style, seated with your roommate and a few other girls from your dorm, along with a handful of boys and at least one faculty member to head the table. When we're forced to eat together, Mazzie and I sit across from each other, wordlessly passing food.

In spite of this, we quickly settle into a rhythm as roommates; we learn from each other's slowing actions when it's time to turn out the light at night; we shake each other awake in the morning if one of us—usually Mazzie—sleeps through the alarm. The telephone in our room doesn't ring once all week. It's typical of the Ghost and my mom; now that they know I'm tucked away, they don't feel any need to get in touch. It doesn't bother me so much. It's not like I want to talk to them, anyway.

The person I do want to talk to is Mazzie. I feel like, if she'd just give me the chance, we'd have a lot to say to each other. It seems like we are both alone in the world, families out there somewhere, for whatever reasons disinterested in making contact, and we both seem determined that it's okay with us—isn't it? I can't help but feel so sorry for her, even though she took my bed without asking, even though she can't seem to stand being around anyone. As far as I can tell, she hasn't made any friends so far. Whenever Lindsey and Estella come into our room, she makes herself scarce; it's almost like she can slip away before they even know she's around.

There's something else, too: from the first night she arrived at Woodsdale, and every night afterward, Mazzie has talked in her sleep. It starts with the grinding of her teeth; that's how I know she's out. Then, after ten or twenty minutes, she starts murmuring to herself. Her voice is angry and sad at the same time. More than once, I've gotten out of bed to watch her. I've thought about shaking her awake, or even putting my arms around her and holding on tight so she can't struggle away. I want her to know that, whatever she's dreaming, I've probably known worse.

But I get the feeling she wouldn't appreciate it if I woke her, or tried to comfort her in any way. When she talks during her dreams, she speaks Korean, her guard up even in sleep.

The more I get to know Lindsey and Estella, the more I like both of them. Well, not Estella as much. But I at least understand where Lindsey is coming from when she defends her. Right away, it's obvious there are advantages to being her friend. On the first day of school, I'm standing at the back of the lunch line when Estella, Stetson, and Lindsey walk past me. Without a word—she doesn't even *look* at me—Estella takes my arm and yanks me out of line, leading me toward the front with them. None of the people we cut ahead of say anything.

Later that day, in study hall, I'm sitting a few rows away from Estella, looking over the pile of Latin homework that's already been assigned. She and Stetson are in the back row, deep in hushed conversation. There's no way I'd have the nerve to join them. As I'm staring at a page of conjugations, I feel something hit the back of my head. It's a balled-up piece of paper. When I open it, it reads,

Hey Sasquatch—
I'm going to pluck your eyebrows for you tonight. C U in my room after dinner.
XOXO
—E

I don't know whether to feel embarrassed—I mean, she *did* just throw paper at my head—or happy. When I look back at her, she gives me a wave, fluttering each of her long, manicured fingers individually. And when I glance around at everyone else in study hall, nobody is laughing at me. If anything, the other girls seem curious to know what the note says.

Estella, I think, *knows* how obnoxious she is. She's more clever than people give her credit for. It seems like everyone assumes she's a spoiled bimbo, when she's neither. I can see it in the way she looks around sometimes, quietly, her face tight with concentration, just taking everything in. If people weren't so quick to judge, just based on what she looked like, she might not be able to get away with so much. Then again—her stepdad *is* on the board of directors.

A few weeks into the year, I'm sitting at lunch with Estella and Lindsey. I've started eating with them every day. "You have an accent, you know," Estella informs me. So far she's plucked my eyebrows, showed me how to roll the waistband of my skirt up so that it's at least a few inches shorter than regulation (although none of the teachers say anything), and openly expressed her hopelessness that I'll ever be able to properly apply eyeliner. I keep waiting for the day when I can relax around her. So far, it isn't looking good.

"Do I?"

"Yes. Very Pittsburgh. My mother's first husband is originally from Pittsburgh." She shakes her head, oblivious to the hint of a West Virginia drawl in her thick, accusing tone. As her hair spills over her broad shoulders, her movement sends a swirl of perfume across the table. It smells so good—so clean and lovely—I can almost see it. "He trained himself to get rid of it. You should do the same thing." She digs into her cake—Estella eats three huge pieces of cake for lunch every day, and her body is perfect—and chews silently, staring at me.

"You're so mean," Lindsey says, staring at her own untouched piece of cake. The minute she takes a bite, Estella will narrow her eyes and kind of cock her head to one side, looking at me, expecting us to share a smirk.

"I am not *mean*. I'm *honest*. You know, nobody is ever straightforward. But sometimes people need to hear the truth."

"Hey, look"—I put my hand on Lindsey's arm—"there she is." We've been trying to spot Mazzie every day at lunch, without any luck. Now the three of us stare as she takes small steps, balancing her tray in one hand, looking around the room for a place to sit. I catch her gaze and try to wave her over to us.

"You know, she's super smart," Lindsey says. "She's in my advanced abstract mathematics class."

"She's in my advanced abstract mathematics class," Estella mocks. Even though she's pretty smart, there's no question Estella isn't good at math. She's taking geometry for the second year in a row. "Big deal. Eat your cake already. You know you want to." Underneath the table, she kicks Lindsey.

"Ow!" Lindsey's eyes well up with tears. "That really hurt!" Estella is cocaptain of the girls' field-hockey team, and you can tell who the other team members are by the way their shins are covered in bruises so purple as to be almost black. Each day after school, they cringe as they peel off their knee socks. Only Estella and the other cocaptain—Amanda Hopwood—are almost bruise-free.

"Go get her," Lindsey urges me.

"Yeah," Estella echoes, giving me a much lighter kick under the table, "go get her." She rubs her hands together. "She can't avoid us forever."

"I don't know," I say, watching as Mazzie—who pretended not to notice my wave—sits by herself and begins to eat at a deliberate, fast pace. "Maybe we should leave her alone for now."

I feel protective of Mazzie already. I'm not sure why. Maybe because, at first, it also occurred to me to hide out during lunch, as she's likely been doing up until today, but I managed to force myself to do otherwise. Or maybe because I keep hearing her talking in her sleep, her voice as angry as ever. I'm not sure why I don't tell Estella and Lindsey about Mazzie's restless nights—it's definitely a juicy piece of info. I just don't. Somehow it feels cruel even for me to *know,* because I think Mazzie would be mortified if she found out.

Things loosen up after the first couple of months at school. On paper, Woodsdale Academy is a model of academic excellence. Its students' days are planned down to the minute. We wake up in time to get dressed and hurry to breakfast by 7:15. Homeroom starts at 7:50. Classes begin at 8:00 and last until 3:00. Every student is required to participate in at least one extracurricular event, preferably a sport, and practice is held at a minimum from 3:30 to 5:30 every day. A sit-down, family-style dinner follows from 6:00 to 7:00. Study hall in the dorms—bedroom doors open, no talking or music allowed—lasts from 7:30 to 9:30. Lights out is at 11:00 for underclassmen, midnight for upperclassmen.

But most of their "model of excellence" is a load of crap. It's just so people like the Ghost can feel great about packing up their kids and sending them away. Once you know what you're doing, it's easy to break the rules. Take our uniforms, for example. In the student handbook, there are five whole pages devoted to their care and cleaning. During our first dorm meeting of the new school year, we even have a visit from a member of the housekeeping staff, who explains how we should hang and fold each article of clothing in order to keep our shirts and skirts in pristine condition. As we lounge on the sofas and on the floor, we pretend to pay attention as she demonstrates how to properly fold—never roll—a pair of nylon-and-cotton-blend knee socks to be stored in our drawers.

This is how it really works: after school every day, most of us have loosened our ties and untucked our shirts before we even get back to the dorm. At the end of the hallway, there are two piles: one for neckties, and one for navy blue knee socks. We add our own clothes to the pile, toss our shirts over the back of our desk chairs, and leave our skirts wherever they happen to fall on the floor of our bedroom. Anytime we put on our uniform, we pluck a tie and a pair of socks from the collective pile. At the end of the week, when they come to collect our laundry, the housekeepers know where to find everything. In the student handbook, "improper uniform maintenance" is supposed to be punishable by half a dozen demerits. But nobody ever mentions what a departure we've made from Woodsdale procedure—not even Jill, who is usually so rule conscious that, as Estella loves to say, "She would have made a great Nazi."

It's the same kind of thing with sports and academics. Officially, academics come first No Matter What. But Woodsdale has a widespread reputation for its fine swimmers. The varsity team practices year-round, and we compete in scrimmages all fall.

In my first scrimmage, I come in first in every one of my

heats. Most of the other girls tell me how excited they are to have me on the team this year, but I'd bet anything they glare at me the second I turn my back, especially Grace.

The following Monday, Coach Solinger tracks me down during a boring lesson on sentence diagramming in English class, tapping me gently on the elbow and nodding at the door.

No matter what time of year it is, Solinger looks like he just wandered off a beach in Malibu. His blond hair is sun streaked, and he's always in swimming trunks, flip-flops, and some kind of T-shirt. I guess he gets away with it because he's the swimming coach. Today he's wearing a threadbare Tom Petty T-shirt that you just know he's had since college.

Solinger is flirty and has a reputation for picking favorites among his varsity swimmers.

"Katie, I have to tell you, you're my favorite swimmer," he declares, leaning against the wall in the empty hallway, gazing at me with a combination of hope and adoration. He rubs an open palm against his whiskery chin, shaking his head. "I simply don't know where they found you."

He's probably in his late thirties now, but I heard he spent the early part of his twenties swimming professionally, and even had a mediocre turn in the Olympics, where he walked away without a medal. He has his doctorate in sports medicine, and I can already tell he's a great coach. He's so cute, it's embarrassing to make eye contact, especially when we're alone in the hallway like this.

My breath catches. "Hillsburg, Pennsylvania," I supply.

"What?"

"They found me in Hillsburg. It's about an hour east of Pittsburgh."

"Oh. Right." He grins for a split second before growing serious. "Listen," he continues, "your schoolwork is important. I mean, nothing is more important than your education, right?"

I'm not sure I'm completely sold on the idea. So far, it seems to me that good looks and money are more important than anything. But whatever—Woodsdale's slogan for the year (they have a new one every fall) is, "Education is the most valuable tool a person can have." "Right," I agree. "I mean, it's the most valuable tool a person can have."

Solinger continues to rub his chin. "You're going to be our key swimmer this year on girls' varsity. I hope that isn't too much pressure for you."

I shake my head. Pressure can feel good, especially if you can push through it. Swimming is all about forcing your way through endless resistance.

"What you need to do," he continues, "is practice, practice, practice." He pauses, waiting for a reaction from me. When I don't say anything, he adds, "Practice." Then he puts his hands on my shoulders and squeezes. "Practice. Practice. Practice."

I nod. "Three thirty. I'll be there."

"That's not what I mean." He takes me by the elbow. "Come with me."

I glance toward the classroom door. "What about—"

"Don't worry. You're clear." And he tugs me down the hallway, in the direction of the pool.

In a few minutes, I'm standing on deck beside Solinger, feeling ridiculous in my full school uniform. At the opposite end of the pool, in a three-lane area sequestered by buoyed ropes, the ninth-grade girls' phys ed class is running through a synchronized swimming routine to some kind of classical music. They wear identical maroon swimsuits and bathing caps made of thick, fancy latex that covers their ears. They are operating—all of them—on an insane level of concentration. The effect is both eerie and beautiful, all of them wet and cloaked in stinging fluorescent light.

At first I think Solinger and I are the only people in the natatorium besides the girls. But then I notice somebody swimming in the lane closest to me. His body is parallel with the water, almost beneath it, moving quickly and without too much visible effort, exactly the way it should be.

Solinger kneels at the head of the lane, waiting for the swimmer to reach us. Before the body can curl into a flip turn, Solinger grabs hold of an ear, tugging the swimmer to his feet.

I'd recognized him just by the way he moves in the water. But to see his face as he stares upward at us, his faint scowl at being interrupted, his annoyance with the ninth graders at the other end of the pool—all of it combined with the way he looks dripping wet, his hair stuffed beneath a swimming cap so that only a few lone, blond curls escape from a corner behind his ear—only one thought goes through my mind: *I love boarding school.*

Drew Bailey spits into the water, his breath heavy. "What is it? I'm in the middle of a five hundred."

Solinger, annoyed, says, "Keep your panties on, Bailey. Get out for a minute."

Drew pulls his goggles away from his face, perching them on his forehead to reveal big blue eyes. "But I'm in the middle of—"

"Uh-huh." Solinger snaps his fingers. "Up."

Drew stands between us, still panting, oblivious to a white thread of booger at the edge of his nostril. "What's up? I've got"—he glances at the clock—"thirty minutes before I have to be in chem lab. I've got a B minus, and I can't be late or I'll lose points, five points for every minute you're late. Education is the most valuable . . ." He realizes Solinger is smirking at him. "Oh, forget it."

Solinger strokes his shadow of a beard. His other hand is on the small of my back. He gives it a reassuring pat, as if to say, *I know. What. A. Jerk.* "You won't lose any points. I'll take care of it."

Drew shakes his head. "You said that about trig, and I—"

"Later." He nudges us together. "Katie Kitrell, Drew Bailey. Drew is our number one on the boys' varsity. Drew, this is the girl I was telling you about."

Drew nods, looking at Solinger, not me. I'm not sure why Solinger is even explaining any of this to us—I guess he wants to make a formal introduction. Drew and I have been in practice together every day after school, but the girls' and boys' scrimmage meets are separate, so we haven't exactly had a chance to see each other in action. "I know who she is. She hangs around with Estella." Drew finally looks in my general direction, narrows his eyes, and mouths, *"Trouble."* I notice that he's wearing a thin silver chain with a tiny crucifix around his neck.

Right away I'm curious about what his problem is with Estella, because Drew's best friend is none other than Stetson McClure. The two of them are always eating lunch together and talking around the pool, when water polo and swim team practices overlap.

Solinger couldn't be less interested. "Shake hands," he directs.

When neither of us moves, Solinger reaches out to physically lift our hands and bring them together, pumping our arms in a forced shake. Drew avoids making eye contact for as long as possible. Finally, after we shake hands, he wipes his nose clean and meets my gaze. But he doesn't smile.

Drew is a junior, like Stetson. He's fast, I know, and oh my God is he cute. He's at least six foot four, strong, and kind of effortlessly graceful, which is why he's such a good swimmer.

Solinger takes a step back. "I want you two to practice together, every day. Before breakfast and now, third period."

I blink at him. "But I have English."

"Not anymore, you don't. You'll have study hall, which means you come here. English is seventh period for you now."

Drew scratches the back of his head, working a finger beneath his bathing cap. "I thought I could come and go whenever I felt like it. Good God, you'd think they could turn down the Rachmaninoff just a *little,* wouldn't you?"

Finally, I find my voice. "The what?"

He looks at me like I'm stupid. "The music? This is Rachmaninoff's Ninth Symphony." His mouth hangs open. "You've never *heard* this before?"

Before I can say anything else, Solinger interrupts with, "Ladies, ladies, ladies. I want you to work together. Run drills, time each other, keep each other in check. I have intramurals with the freshmen. I can't be here, and I don't want you two working completely uncoached."

I'm too embarrassed to look at Drew again. I'm just standing there in my uniform, actually sweating because the air in the natatorium is so warm and muggy, but I feel almost naked. "It's fine with me."

Drew is confused and on the verge of furious. "But, Coach." He lowers his voice. "She's a *girl*."

"Oh, she is? I hadn't noticed. Forget everything I said then. As you were." He gives Drew a light slap against the back of his head. "She's a girl. So what?"

Drew opens his mouth, looks at me, looks at Solinger—and says nothing. He only scowls.

Solinger gives me a wide, satisfied grin, like everything's just peachy. "Your suit is in your locker, right, Kitrell?"

I nod.

"Well? Whatcha waiting for? Go get changed."

When I get back from the locker room, Solinger is gone. Drew watches as I slide into my own lane and position my goggles on my face. He nods at the chalkboard to the right of the pool, where a series of drills is written in chicken scratch: *2X100 free, 2X100 back, 2X100 breast. 500 free.*

"That's today," he says. "He'll change it for the afternoon and morning."

"Are you going to—" I'm about to ask him if he wants to time me, if he has a stopwatch I can use, but he holds up a palm, stopping me midquestion. "Listen . . . Katie. You should know, those friends of yours have a bad reputation. Especially Estella." He shakes his head, looks at me with exaggerated pity. "You should be careful. That chick is nuts."

And before I can say anything in response, he's gone, his face below water. When I finish my first drill, I stand up in the shallow end of the pool to find myself almost alone, watching a crooked line of tired freshmen as they move single file toward the girls' locker room, the music playing to the end on low, echoing against every corner of the room, as though addressing me and my ignorance alone.

The next few weeks are a blur of swimming and schoolwork and scrimmages and more schoolwork—I'm so tired and overwhelmed that I don't even make it off campus on the weekends. Lindsey and Estella are busy too—everyone is—but Estella manages to go out with Stetson every weekend, and Lindsey often goes home to see her parents. The fact that my only friends in the dorm are gone most weekends makes the time I spend with Mazzie all the more excruciating. She still talks in her sleep, and she still ignores me almost all the time. I get frequent updates from Lindsey about Mazzie's stellar performance in advanced abstract mathematics, but beyond that, I don't know the first thing about her aside from the fact that she seemed to appear from out of nowhere and wants to disappear more badly than anything.

For our entire first week of practice, Drew doesn't say much to me. Then, on a Monday, after he's finished swimming and stretching, he takes a seat on the bench beside the pool and watches as I glide to the end of a 500-meter free.

I stand at the shallow end, catching my breath, tugging off my goggles and swim cap. My whole body feels warm and energized.

"Nice job," Drew says.

I'm still trying to catch my breath. "Thanks." I hop out of the water and glance at the clock on the wall. "Wow. We've got twenty minutes until next period."

When I look at him, as I stand there dripping wet, I notice that his gaze is taking in my whole body, like he's seeing me for the first time. That's something about swimming that I've always found kind of odd—it's like you're standing around in your underwear, soaking wet, but nobody acknowledges that everyone around them is half-naked. I mean, Drew's in a *Speedo.* I can see every ripple in his body, right down to the V-shape of his hips, which I do my absolute best not to stare at.

Right now, it's obvious he's noticing me too. There's nobody here but the two of us, our breath audible and deep, our cheeks flushed. For a few seconds we stay that way, silent, staring at each other's bodies.

"So . . . what should we do with the rest of the time?" I ask. "Should we do more drills?"

The moment between us dissolves. Drew tugs off his swim cap. There are those curls again. I *love* them. "I'm too tired," he says. But then he stands up, strolls over to the edge of the pool, and sits down, letting his legs dangle into the water. He lies on his back and stares at the ceiling. "Katie."

"What?"

"Come here."

I have no idea where his interest is coming from; a week ago he didn't even want to look at me. But I'm not going to argue. Trying my best to be casual, I take a seat beside him.

He's still looking at the ceiling. "You're really good. You know that, right?"

"Yes." I dip my legs into the water beside his. "Swimming is the only thing I'm good at."

He sits up. "That's probably not true. You get good grades, don't you?"

"Well, yeah. I guess I meant that swimming is the only thing I really love to do."

His gaze drifts to my shoulders, my chest, my legs, and finally back to my face. "I can tell you love it." He hesitates. "You look really good—really graceful, I mean—in the water."

Oh. My. God. I have to struggle to find my voice. "Thanks."

He nods. "Do you think you'll keep swimming? I mean, I'm sure you'll get a scholarship somewhere, but after college?"

"I hope so. Maybe I can coach."

"You don't think you'll try to go pro?"

He and I both know this isn't a realistic option—if it were, I'd have been at a swimming academy somewhere since like age ten—so I wonder why he's even mentioning it. Maybe he's trying to make me feel good. The possibility makes my face grow hot. "Well," I say, "I can swim in college, and swim in a league after that, but I'm not good enough to go to the Olympics. I mean, maybe a few years ago, if I'd had a good coach and had been really focused . . ." *If my parents hadn't been preoccupied with my brother as he was losing his mind.* I shake my head firmly. "I don't think I'd want that, anyway."

"Oh, no?" His voice seems genuinely interested. "Why not?"

"Because I love it so much. The fact that I'm fast is just, like, icing. I told you, it's the only thing I really love to do. And if I had pressure that intense on me—well, what if I stopped loving it? Then what would I have?" I shake my head. "Nothing."

Drew narrows his eyes. "That's really interesting," he murmurs.

"You think?"

He nods. "Did you watch the Olympics this summer?"

"Of course."

"How about that Margo Duvall?" He's talking about the girl who took home nine gold medals in swimming.

"I know," I say, getting excited. "When she finished the two hundred IM, she stood up and looked around, and she knew she'd won, but she—"

"She wasn't even breathing heavily!" Drew finishes.

"I *know,* right?" I shake my head. "Just thinking about being that fast gives me goose bumps."

"But you'd never want to be like her?"

I shrug. "In theory, sure. But . . . no, not really. Swimming is . . ." I struggle for the right words, amazed that Drew and I are talking so intimately. "It's *mine.* I love competing in meets and everything, but once you get to that level, it's not really about swimming anymore, is it?"

Drew shakes his head, looking over at me again. "No, it isn't. You know, I believe that people need to find what they love to do most in the world, what they're *best* at, and then they need to use that ability to make the world better."

His eyes are so sincere, so hopeful and kind. "That's amazing," I say. "I've never heard anyone put it that way."

Drew nods. "Like, the thing I love to do the most is to be outdoors and to be physical. So I spend a lot of time volunteering, especially for Habitat for Humanity. That way, I get to be outside and do a lot of work with my hands, but when the work is over, I get to watch someone who's had a way rougher life than me get a nice place to live."

I could cry if I let myself. If I squinted, maybe tilted my head a little bit, I could probably see a halo above Drew's curls.

"You make it sound so simple," I say. Our gazes are locked together.

"It is simple."

I force myself to swallow before I start drooling. "But I'm no Margo Duvall."

Drew grins. "That's right. You're Katie Kitrell." He hesitates. "I think that's even better."

We sit there in silence for a few seconds. I feel so dizzy that I'm almost nauseous. Drew looks like he's about to say something else, when his eyes flicker to the clock. "Katie."

"Hmmm?"

"We're late." And just as quickly as our conversation started, it ends. He hops out of the pool. "I've gotta go." As he's heading toward the locker room, he turns around, walking backward, looking at me while I start to towel off. "This was fun," he says. He stops at the door to the boys' locker room.

I nod. "Yeah, it was."

He gives me another smile. "We'll talk more tomorrow, okay?"

On a Friday afternoon, I'm sitting in art class, putting the finishing touches on my handmade mosaic of what's supposed to be the Woodsdale Academy Insignia. Our teacher, Mrs. Averly, who is at least in her seventies, pauses over my shoulder. I don't say anything as I squint at my project, trying to force an already glued maroon square into a better position.

She clears her throat. "Kathryn?"

"Katie." I push the mosaic away, sighing. "Yes?"

One of the things that's interesting about Woodsdale is that you can take your electives whenever you want throughout all of high school. So what ends up happening is classes get filled with students from all different grades. There's some kind of educational philosophy behind it, I'm sure, but I know I'd much rather be with people my own age who aren't so intimidating. I'm at the same table with Grace Waugh, whose mosaic is flawless, and her best friend, Leslie Carter. Leslie's father is on Woodsdale's board of directors.

The two of them nudge each other, their grins spreading as Mrs. Averly says, "That is really very poor work. It looks like you haven't put the slightest bit of effort into—"

"I think she's been distracted, Mrs. Averly," Grace says.

"Oh? By what?"

Grace gives me a demure smile. "By Drew."

Drew is on the opposite end of the room, working on his own, perfect mosaic of a big white cross surrounded by small ceramic depictions of what I assume are robed Christians. Drew is the president of the Fellowship of Christian Athletes and seems genuine about his faith. Before every swim meet, he leads a circle of swimmers in a prayer. Even though I've started to do almost anything for a chance to be near him, I never join in; Will and I decided a long time ago that religion just wasn't for us.

The thing that gets me is, Grace is right; I *have* been distracted by Drew. He and I have been finishing our drills early most days and talking more and more. We both seem to know, without openly acknowledging it, that there's something happening between us. And for the past few weeks in art class, we've been glancing in each other's direction, smiling. If we didn't have assigned seats, I might have the nerve to sit with him.

Mrs. Averly looks at me, then at Drew. Everybody loves Drew, especially the teachers. She beams at his mosaic. "Well . . . you'll have to redo that, Katie, if you want to pass the assignment." She pauses, then adds, "It looks like a pentagram."

Once Mrs. Averly is out of earshot, Grace and Leslie engage in deliberately loud conversation.

"I think she likes him," Grace says, "because he's the captain of the boys' team, and she thinks she's going to be the next captain of the girls' team."

"Really?" Leslie asks, her tone mockingly innocent. "And then I guess she thinks they'll be boyfriend and girlfriend, like Estella and Stetson?"

"Yes, I'm pretty sure that's what she thinks."

I'm humiliated. I've never had anything like this happen to me before, and what's even worse is that Drew can hear every word they're saying.

"Do you think that might happen?" Leslie asks.

"Oh, no. I mean, first of all, she won't be captain because nobody else on the team likes her enough to vote for her."

What she's saying doesn't make *sense*—Solinger is the one who chooses the captains—but I don't even have the nerve to look up, let alone say anything.

"And if she isn't captain, then it seems dumb to think that Drew would go out with her, doesn't it?"

"Well," Grace says, "even if by some miracle she did make captain, he still wouldn't go out with her."

"Oh yeah? Why not?"

"Because," Grace says, and now she raises her voice a little higher, just to be sure everyone around her can hear. "Where do I even start? First of all, she comes from trash. Her brother was killed in some kind of crazy car accident. I heard he was drunk. And Drew would never date someone like that. Besides, she's not even pretty enough for him."

My hand is closed around my sloppy mosaic, ready to hurl it at Grace's face. But then what would happen? I'd get in trouble—I could even get expelled, maybe. In the meantime, though, I'm sitting there with my head down, and there's no way I can stop them, the tears are coming, hitting the table and rolling off the edge and landing in droplets that hover unabsorbed on the surface of my wool skirt. I don't know what else to do. I get up and leave the room. It takes all my willpower not to break into a run before I reach the door.

The bathroom has three stalls, and there's no lock on the door; all I can do is hope that Grace and Leslie don't try to follow me in. All of the stalls are empty for now. I lean against the wall beside the sink, catching my breath, before I let myself start crying hard. I slide down the wall and sit on the cold tile floor, my legs folded, trying to breathe. Just breathe.

And while I'm sitting there, all my sniffling and deep breaths echoing off of the walls, I hear something else—the sound of something shifting in the cabinet beneath the sink.

For a second, I forget all about Grace and Leslie and Drew and Will. I become completely silent. I stop breathing, listening.

I hear it again: a slight crunching sound, quick breathing, and as freaked out as I am to look in the cupboard, there's something familiar in the sounds.

When I try to open the door, there's a split second where I think it's locked, until I realize there's somebody on the other side, holding it shut. I pull harder—the person inside lets go, which sends me falling backward onto my butt, out of breath, a sharp pain going through my lower back.

Right there—under the sink in the first-floor girls' bathroom, her tiny body curled into an impossibly small ball, legs gathered behind the pipes, hands in their usual tight fists—is Mazzie.

"What are you doing here?" she says.

I almost laugh. "What am I doing here? What are *you* doing—you're under the freaking sink!"

She doesn't smile. "Yeah. I know where I am, Katie."

We sit there, staring at each other, for a good long minute. Finally, for the first time since I've met her, Mazzie's voice breaks into something besides hostility. "Don't tell," she says. "Please?"

"Is this where you are all the time? We look for you at lunch. I always thought you were—"

"Shh!" She looks panicked, and I realize that somebody's heading toward the bathroom. Without thinking, I push the door to the sink closed, stand up, and pretend to be washing my hands.

It's another girl from my art class, Mary Ann Bowers. She's a freshman.

"Katie," Mary Ann says, "I'm supposed to give you a message."

Oh, God. I can only imagine what Grace or Leslie—or even Mrs. Averly—has sent her to tell me. Even though Mazzie's the one hiding under the sink, I'm so embarrassed by what she's going to overhear.

"Drew is in the hall waiting for you," she says. "He wants you to come out and talk to him."

"Uh, okay." I'm still pretending to wash my hands. "Just give me a minute alone in here. Tell him I'll be right out."

As soon as the door closes behind Mary Ann, I crouch down again and open the door. I give Mazzie my hand, offering to help her out from under the sink.

She shakes her head. "That's okay. I'm going to stay here." She hesitates. Then she says, "Thanks."

"Are you okay?"

She nods. "You should go meet Drew, shouldn't you?"

I shrug. "I don't have to, not right away. Are you sure you're all right?"

Mazzie doesn't say anything for a moment or two. Finally, she gives me the slightest smile. "Sure. I'm okay." She glances at her watch. "I've got five more minutes before Spanish. Please close the door."

Just as I'm about to, though, she reaches out and grabs me by the wrist—it's the first time we've ever really touched each other, and I feel a spark of surprise at the strength of her grip, those tiny fingers holding on to me so tightly that I couldn't get free if I tried.

She says, "I have a message for you too, Katie." Her smile gets a little bigger. "Your brother called."

Drew is still there in the otherwise deserted hallway, waiting for me. I'm so shook up that I almost walk right past him—he's right outside the door to the girls' bathroom—but he catches me by the sleeve of my blazer.

It's obvious I've been crying. "Katie, come here," he says, and he gives me a hug.

I let myself lean against him, my head against his chest. If any of the faculty see us like this, we'll both get demerits. He's so much bigger than me, his arms so strong and warm, that I can't help but cry into them. I feel so sick with guilt that I can't hold it in for another second. When did my brother call? Was it this morning, after I'd left early to go eat breakfast with Lindsey? Or last night, when we were in the common room until lights-out, pretending to do English homework when we were really keeping watch for each other while we took turns sneaking outside to smoke cigarettes?

"It's okay," Drew says. Then he cups my chin in his hand, tilting my face upward and looking into my eyes, and says, "You don't have to be embarrassed, okay? I know you like me."

"What?" The bell rings, and the halls start to fill up with students. At least I won't have to go back to art class. "You think I'm crying because I'm embarrassed because—because you think I know you know I like you?"

His hands are on my shoulders. His grip feels so good, a part of me wants nothing else but to sink back into his arms.

He looks confused for a minute, thinking about what I've just said, distracted by the people around us. I step back from him. Finally, he says, "Yes. That's why you're crying—isn't it? And," he adds, lowering his voice, leaning in slightly, "because of everything else Grace said. About, you know, all those other things."

"Uh . . ." What else am I supposed to tell him? "Yes." I nod my head. "I guess so." And really, when I think about it, it's all kind of the truth—in a way.

The two-minute warning bell rings. The halls start to empty again as everyone makes their way back into class. Drew glances at the clock on the wall behind me. "Katie, I have to go to trig, okay? But listen . . . we'll talk more. Soon." He puts his hands back on my shoulders, then lets them slide down my arms, his fingertips lingering against mine for just an instant before he backs away. "Okay?"

The door to the girls' bathroom opens, and Mazzie strolls out. I turn to watch her, but she doesn't even give us a glance as she passes. By the time I turn back, Drew is also gone.

Not long after he's left my sight, it occurs to me that I'm so sick about Will, I don't even remember what Drew and I just talked about. I'm left standing there all by myself, confused and horrified by what Mazzie knows and who she might tell, and there's a part of me aware of the fact that I've got a vocab quiz in Latin class in about thirty seconds, and I'm going to be late, and there's nothing I can do about any of it.

chapter 5

Things aren't the same after I find Mazzie under the sink. A few days later, when I'm almost asleep, she says, "Tell me why you lied about your brother."

Most people would ask, instead of giving an order, but as I'm learning, Mazzie isn't most people.

So even though I know she could tell everyone, and probably ruin everything I have going for me at Woodsdale, I tell her. I tell her everything. When I'm finished, she says, "Oh. So you're a freak."

If it came from anybody else, I'd be offended by the label. But hearing Mazzie say it, along with the fact that she's finally willing to *talk* to me, gives me a strange sense of relief and satisfaction. "Yeah."

"And a liar."

"Yeah, I guess I am. Mazzie, why were you under the sink?"

"You know," she continues, and I can *hear* her smiling above me, "I could tell there was something different about you, Katie. I've tried so hard to hate you. . . . You're really annoying, you know?"

"Thank you."

"You and Lindsey and Estella hanging around together all the time, talking about swimming and boys and swimming and boys, and everyone following the three of you around like your farts smell like hot fudge . . . it just makes me want to barf."

"What were you doing under the sink?"

"But I've been thinking that I should probably come out with you sometimes . . . I think I'm going to be stuck here, so I should probably make some friends. Okay?"

Can she hear me smiling now? "Mazzie, you'll have to come to parties. You'll have to talk about swimming and boys and you'll have to . . . you know, *talk* to people."

"I know that. I'm not stupid." She pauses. "Now, Katie, when I talk to people, should I tell them your secret? Or is that just between us?"

"That's funny. I don't know, should I mention where you like to spend your study halls?"

"Hmmm." She pretends to think about it. "You know what? I changed my mind. I do hate you, Katie."

"I hate you too, Mazzie."

She sighs. "Good night, freak."

"Good night, loser."

About a week later, I'm awake in bed, listening to Mazzie as she mutters in her sleep. I feel the mattress shifting above me as she kicks the covers away. When she's not talking to herself—still in Korean—she keeps grinding her teeth.

The muttering grows louder than I've ever heard it. I sit up in bed, unsure of what to do. It's painful to listen to her, obviously so unhappy. I have to do *something*, don't I?

So I get up, switch on the reading lamp on my desk, climb halfway up the ladder to the top bunk, and give her a tentative shake. "Mazzie," I whisper.

She's so sweaty that, even in our air-conditioned room, her hair sticks to her face in wet strands.

"Mazzie!" I almost shout.

She sits up, opens her eyes, and looks at me with wild panic. She reaches out and grabs me by the arm; her palm is clammy. Without a word, she reaches into her mouth with her free hand and removes a thick piece of red plastic. It's a mouth guard, meant to keep people from grinding away the enamel on their teeth. Will has one that he never wears. It might keep her teeth safe, but the noise is still awful. When I get a closer look at the mouth guard, I see that the plastic is worn so thin from the grinding of her teeth that it's almost translucent.

"What's the matter?" She looks at the clock. "Katie, it's practically the middle of the night. What the hell are you doing waking—"

"You were having a nightmare. You were talking in your sleep." I keep my voice low. "You were loud."

For a few seconds, it seems like she doesn't believe me. "I was talking in my sleep."

"Yes."

"What was I saying?"

I shrug. Without asking, I climb all the way up the ladder and sit across from her in bed. Her sheets are damp with sweat. "You were speaking Korean."

She's relieved to hear it, I can tell. "Oh. It was nothing, Katie. I have nightmares sometimes."

"You have to tell me what's wrong," I say.

"I do, do I?" She picks up the mouth guard, studying it. "Why would I tell you anything?"

"Because I told you everything about my family." I hesitate. "And because you've been doing this every night since you got here."

She blinks a few times. I peer at her—are those tears I see? Is Mazzie going to cry?

"Mazzie, you should tell someone what's wrong. I mean, you have to *want* to tell someone, don't you?"

She stares at her sheets. "I don't know."

"I felt better when I told you about Will."

She shakes her head. "That's different."

"Why did you come here? Why do you hide under the sink?"

She studies my face. "If you tell anyone, I swear to God I'll tell everyone about your brother."

I nod. "Okay. I won't say anything." I pretend to zip my lips shut and lock them with my fingers, tossing the invisible key over the side of the bed.

She shuts her eyes again. "I'm a freak, just like you."

"What do you mean?"

"My mom died."

Oh God. What am I supposed to say? "Oh, Mazzie . . ."

"She always called me Madeline." She shakes her head. "So don't *ever* call me Madeline again."

I nod. "Okay, I won't. When did—"

"Seven weeks ago."

I feel like I've been punched in the stomach. I can't breathe. Her mother died seven weeks ago, and she's *here*? *Alone?*

"Why are you here? Why aren't you with your family?"

She shakes her head. "It was just me and my parents." Her

eyes are closed, tiny tears falling one right after the other down her porcelain cheeks. "My dad isn't . . . he's not an emotional kind of guy."

I sit there, stunned, waiting for her to continue. I want to reach out to her and touch her hand or put my arms around her, but I'm afraid she'd clam up and push me away. So I just listen.

"I'm a first-generation American. So my parents wanted to send me to the best schools. My mom wanted me to be a doctor." She hesitates. "That's what she was."

"What happened to her?"

Mazzie ignores the question. "After she died, all I wanted was to go back to school and see my old friends. My dad didn't talk to me for almost a month. He just worked all the time." She shrugs. "It's not his fault, I guess. He doesn't know what to say to me."

"But how did you end up here?"

She wipes her eyes hard with closed fists, as though she's willing the tears to stop. "Without my mom's income, there wasn't enough money to send me back to my old school. So here I am." Her tone is bitter. "West Virginia is a lot cheaper than Connecticut."

The air around me feels suffocating. "Oh, Mazzie."

"I didn't even know I was coming here, Katie. Not until we were in the car, on the way to the airport. I haven't talked to my father since then."

And here I am, mopey and broken-hearted over Will, who's alive and as well as he'll ever be. No wonder Mazzie acts like she can't stand me.

"I miss my friends," she says.

"I'll be your friend."

She smirks. "Gee, thanks."

"I mean it. I won't tell anyone anything, and I'll wake you up when you have nightmares." Finally, I reach out to close my hand over her wrist. She doesn't pull away. "It'll be okay."

She leans toward me and starts to cry again. Before I have time to understand what's happening, she burrows her head against my shoulder and sobs. It goes on and on, until finally the sobs turn to deep, heavy breaths. I keep my arms around her as we sit there, imagining that I can absorb some of the pain she's feeling, that I can somehow give her some relief.

After what feels like forever, Mazzie abruptly stops crying. She sits up straight, wipes the hair from her eyes, and says, "I don't want to talk about this anymore."

I nod. "Okay."

She finds her mouth guard among the covers, reaches toward me, and uses the corner of my T-shirt to wipe it off.

"Let's go to bed, Katie."

"Okay." I climb down the ladder and get into my own bed. But I can't sleep. I lie awake for the next few hours, until the first signs of light appear beneath our blinds, listening to Mazzie. She still grinds her teeth, but otherwise, for the first time all school year, she's quiet.

After that night, Mazzie makes herself scarce for a while. I don't even see her at breakfast or lunch. I'm tempted to try and find her, to check under the sink every time I'm in the bathroom during school, but I don't. I figure she'll come to me when she's ready.

A few weeks later, I'm eating lunch with Lindsey and Estella. The three of us seem more comfortable together now. Sometimes

I feel like Lindsey and Estella are both relieved to have someone to talk to besides each other.

Lindsey is chewing on a piece of her hair, looking over her bio notes for the test she has after lunch. Estella is just about to dig into her second piece of chocolate cake. I'm glancing across the room, stealing looks at Drew, when out of nowhere, Mazzie plops her tray down beside me and takes a seat.

We all look at her, startled.

"Well, well, well," Estella says, chewing with her mouth open. "If it isn't Katie's missing roommate."

Mazzie's nervous; I can tell by the way she brushes the hair from her eyes. There's a slight tremble to her fingers as she picks up her fork. But nobody else seems to notice.

"You're Stetson's girlfriend, right?" Mazzie asks.

Estella nods, grinning.

"What is he, like, your trophy boyfriend?"

Estella's grin widens. "That's right."

Mazzie nods, satisfied. She appears to relax a little bit. I've noticed that she's always at her most comfortable when she's on the offensive. "So you form personal relationships based almost totally on physical appearance."

For the first time that I've ever seen, Estella appears at a loss for words—but only for a second. She licks icing from her fork. "It's like my father always says," she tells Mazzie, "it's not how you feel on the inside that counts; it's how you look on the outside."

Mazzie looks Estella up and down. "Sounds like a great way to live."

Estella grins again. "I think so." To me, she says, "I *like* her, Katie."

"I'm so glad you're here," I tell Mazzie, almost breathless.

"We're always hoping you'll eat with us, so it's great you finally—"

"Katie. Keep your panties on. I'm just hungry, that's all." She gives an exaggerated sigh. "I guess if I have to eat with someone, it might as well be you."

"You don't have to eat with anyone," Lindsey says. "You could always eat alone if you wanted to."

"Shut *up*," Estella says, and I feel the table shift as she kicks Lindsey under it. "She's eating with us from now on." She looks at Mazzie expectantly. "Aren't you?"

Mazzie hesitates for only a second. "Sure."

"You're kind of a mystery—just like Katie!" Lindsey continues, oblivious to the delicacy of the situation. "Where did you come from? I mean, it's weird for students to transfer here after their freshman year, so we've just been wondering why—"

"Her old school closed," I supply.

Lindsey blinks at me. "Really?" She switches her gaze to Mazzie. "It did?"

Beside me, I can sense Mazzie relaxing a bit more. "They didn't have enough funding," she says. "Low enrollment. That kind of thing."

"That happens sometimes with private schools," Estella says. "My father says—"

"Your *step*father," Lindsey murmurs.

"Whatever." She points her fork at Mazzie. "If your last school closed, I'm sure there was a good reason. You're very lucky to be here."

Mazzie nods. I can only imagine what she'll say about this conversation later. "I know I am."

"Look at us!" Lindsey says, pleased. "We're a foursome

now." When she reaches across the table to close her hand over Mazzie's, I see Mazzie flinch, almost imperceptibly. "I can tell we're all going to be good friends," she says. She claps her hands together. "Oh, this is great! Isn't it great, Katie?"

For the first time, I find myself wishing I could be alone with Mazzie. Things might still be raw with her, but at least we can be honest with each other.

Lindsey might have a point, though. Everybody needs friends, and now I've got them. And if Mazzie is with us, then at least I've got one person who knows the truth about me and is willing to put up with me anyway.

The first party I go to is at Lindsey's house, just before winter break. Even though Mazzie has been eating lunch with us for weeks now, it's the first time I can convince her to come off campus.

The four of us—me, Lindsey, Estella, and Mazzie—are supposed to meet up early in the evening to help Lindsey decorate. When Mazzie and I get to her yard—the house is close enough to campus that we can walk in just a few minutes—Mazzie stops me, closing her hand over mine. "Katie. What is she doing?"

We both peer through the branches of the maple tree in Lindsey's front yard. Behind the tree, there's an expanse of well-maintained lawn, the grass littered with only a few stray leaves since the gardener's last visit. The house stands beyond the lawn, huge and dark except for several strands of Christmas lights strung across a trio of sliding glass doors that lead to the indoor pool. Estella stands on the patio outside the doors, dressed in a tiny yellow bikini and a threadbare gray cardigan, white flip-flops on her feet. She's smoking what I think at first is just a cigarette, but then I smell it: that familiar, heavy sweetness that colors so many of my memories from summers with Will.

"Oh my God. Is that . . . marijuana?" Mazzie asks as we keep walking. By now we're close enough for Estella to hear.

"Shh." I nod.

Mazzie grips my arm more tightly, her fingernails digging into me. Her voice is a whisper. She's scared. "I don't want to go. Let's go home. Okay?"

Home. She means back to the dorm. Part of me wants to go with her, but it's too late. We've been spotted. Besides, tonight is supposed to be a big night for me.

Estella peers at us. "Mazzie, I can *hear* you. Would you relax? Her parents aren't home, you know."

"Why are you in your bathing suit?" Despite her ability to bring Estella down a peg or two, Mazzie still doesn't like her much. "It's forty degrees out here. You look stupid."

"*You* look stupid." Estella takes one last hit of the joint before kneeling over to put it out on the cement patio. She drops the remaining half into the pocket of her cardigan. She looks past us, shading her gaze against the sunset. "Where are Drew and Stetson?"

It's been weeks since our art class encounter, and Drew and I are only starting to spend more time together outside of swimming practice—although we have been sitting together in art, to Grace and Leslie's horror. Since Drew is so beloved by the faculty, he actually convinced Mrs. Averly to change the seating chart for him.

Tonight, though, I'm told things are supposed to change. As we sit beside the indoor pool, our feet dangling in the water, Estella says to me, "Drew is only coming tonight because he wants to see you."

I smile, trying to be coy. "That's not true."

"It is," Lindsey says from behind the bar. The pool at Lindsey's house is unlike anything I've ever seen before: aside from the pool, there's an entire wall lined with shelves of liquor and a full-length oak bar. On the opposite wall, a spiral staircase leads to a balcony with a pool table and exercise equipment. "You know otherwise Drew doesn't want to be in the same room as Estella," she yells.

I nod. "So I've heard. Why is that?"

Estella shakes her head. "No good reason. He thinks I'm going to"—she leans in closer, lowers her voice in a mock whisper—"*hell*."

"You *are* going to hell." It's Mazzie.

Estella shrugs. "What can I say? He doesn't like me. I don't know why."

"Oh, you don't?" Lindsey is mixing vodka and cherry pop together in a glass. "Last year," she tells us, making a face as she takes a sip of her drink, "Estella and Drew went out on a date. *One* date. It was right after his sixteenth birthday and he'd just gotten a Land Rover. Estella asked him to go to Michelle DellaCorte-McCarthy's birthday party with her. And once they got there—"

"Drew was completely boring and I knew I wasn't going to have any fun with him, and we never went out again, and that's the whole—"

"No, it isn't!" Lindsey takes another sip of her drink—it's like she's getting braver with every swig. "Estella got really, really drunk. Like, so drunk that Drew had to leave early and take her home because she was acting stupid. And on the way home—"

"She threw up all over my car."

We all look toward the sliding glass doors. Drew and

Stetson are standing side by side. Drew has a smile for everyone, including Estella, but I can tell it's forced. When he looks at me, though, he seems to relax.

Estella stands up, peeling off her cardigan to expose her bikini as she approaches Stetson. "It's okay, Drew," she says. "Stetson is more my type."

Stetson grins at all of us. "Lucky me."

Outside it's cool and growing colder. By the time everyone arrives, it's probably in the thirties. But inside there's steam rising off the pool, the heat turned on in the rest of the house and spilling into the room even though we don't need it. Everybody is sweating.

After midnight sometime, I'm surprised to see Drew leaning over the bar, talking animatedly with Stetson, both of them drinking beer, passing a joint back and forth. Drew has told me before that he doesn't drink or smoke. In fact, his exact words were that he tries to live by "God's Law." At the time, it seemed obvious he was serious. Watching him now, I feel a twinge of confusion. Doesn't what he's doing now make him kind of a hypocrite?

I'm pretty sure the only person at the whole party who isn't drinking or smoking or doing *something* like that is Mazzie. She's in the pool with a bunch of other people, playing volleyball, and she looks like she's having a perfectly good time. She's even smiling.

I make my way to the bar, stepping over half a dozen warm bodies on beach towels.

Just be coy. Be aggressive—like a tiger! Boys like that. But not too aggressive. "I thought you didn't do things like this," I say, putting my arm around Drew like it's the most normal thing in the world.

I have a cigarette in one hand, and a vodka and Cherry Coke in the other. With every mouthful of my drink, I have to stifle a gag.

"It's a party, honey," Stetson says. "Right, Drew?" Stetson has never—not once—called me by my first name. I think this is the first time all year he's spoken to me directly.

Drew looks around at the rest of the party. He suddenly seems annoyed. "Can we go outside?"

I look around the room. The air is getting so thick with smoke that I can barely make out faces anymore. What are Lindsey's parents going to say about this? Are they even going to care? They're at a conference this weekend for—get this—research scientists who have written science fiction novels dealing directly with the theory of relativity and its questionability.

It's freezing outside, and I'm in my wet bathing suit. I start shivering the moment we step out the door. Drew, who is clumsy and drunk and sweet all at once, gives me his puffy Gore-Tex coat to wear. It covers only my upper half, but I pretend not to mind the cold as we stand outside, huddled close together on the patio. The noise from inside is just a background din of voices now.

Drew takes a step closer to me and says, "Be warm," putting his hands on my cheeks. My teeth are chattering a little; I can feel my wet hair going quickly brittle in the cold, goose bumps rising up and down my bare legs.

"Katie," Drew says. I can tell he isn't used to drinking. "Katie, Katie, Katie."

Chatter, chatter, chatter. "Hmmm?" I smile. "There are, like, thirty rooms inside with heat. Do you want to go in and talk—"

"No." He takes a deep breath. "This will be quick." His hands are still on my face, and I can feel them shaking a little. "I really like you," he says.

As quickly as the cold came over me, it disappears. There is warmth everywhere. I knew it might be coming tonight, sure, but now that it's actually happening and I'm standing here with him—so cute and tall and liked by everyone, including me more than ever, whether he's a hypocrite or not—before I can stop myself, I ask him, "Why?"

He steps closer, so that our bodies would be touching if it weren't for the very thick layer of Gore-Tex between us. "Why not?"

I imagine how Mazzie might respond: *How much time do you have?*

As excited as I am, I'm confused. Why me? I'm not as pretty as half of the other girls in school, I'm not rich the way everyone else is. The only things that are special about me are that I'm a fast swimmer and a big liar.

"You're talented and innocent and sweet and . . . you seem kind of lost, Katie." He brings his face closer, so that our cold noses are touching. "Do you ever feel lost?"

I nod. "Sometimes."

"I want to help you. Can I help you?"

"Yes."

He kisses the tip of my nose. I close my eyes. I hope people can see us from inside, especially Grace. He kisses my eyelids, my cheeks, my chin, my forehead—everywhere but my mouth. "Do you want to come to church with me sometime soon?" he murmurs.

It's not what I was expecting. "Uhhh . . . okay."

More kisses. My earlobes. My neck. I start kissing back, but every time I try to kiss him on the lips, he tilts his head away. After a few minutes of this, he says, "Oh, God. I need to go inside." For someone so religious, I'm kind of shocked by how lax Drew is with his language. Wouldn't some people consider him blasphemous for invoking the name of God—whether he's drunk or not?

He leads me inside by the hand—*every* other girl is watching us, even if they're pretending not to—and leaves me by the bar with Stetson before disappearing into the bathroom.

"You know what he's doing in there, right?" Stetson asks. He is behind the bar, casually prying open the lock on a glass case of what appears to be very old and expensive scotch. "He's throwing up. He'll be sick for, like, three days." The lock opens. Stetson looks at the bottles for a few minutes, picking them up to examine their labels more closely, and then puts them all back, replacing the lock without taking so much as a sip.

"You have to loosen him up for us," he says to me, lighting a cigarette between his teeth, which are just a tad crooked. "Okay? Drew is my boy, but he's uptight as hell."

"He wants me to go to church with him," I say. I can't believe I'm actually *talking* to Stetson McClure. I'm amazed I'm able to form a complete sentence.

Stetson shakes his head. "He's just nervous. He likes you." He blows smoke in my face. "Sorry. He does, though. A lot. He talks about you all the time. And Drew could have any chick he wants, you know? But he's picky, so you should be flattered." Picking up his drink, he starts to walk away. "You're a lucky girl."

It's a little past three in the morning, and pretty much everyone is asleep in different rooms all over the house. As far as I know, Drew is still in the bathroom downstairs, sick as a dog.

I'm by myself in one of the spare bedrooms on the third floor. I haven't been able to fall asleep, even though I'm so tired and thirsty that my muscles are starting to cramp up.

The door creaks open. It's Mazzie.

She perches herself on the edge of the bed and pokes at my head. "Hey. Are you awake?"

I nod.

"Do you want to go home?"

I nod again.

She pauses, thinking about it. "We don't have a car. It's the middle of the night."

"It's okay. We can walk."

It has started snowing, a thick wet layer of slush that won't stick. There are no cars on the road, nothing but big white flakes falling onto our faces, erasing the buildings around us, and the low swish of our feet on the road as we try to keep our footing, a soft wheeze humming from the bottom of my lungs from too much smoking.

In the middle of National Road, Mazzie turns to me without any warning. She grabs my arm and we both fall down, and then we're sitting there in the middle of the bare road, and for a few seconds we just sit there, quiet, listening to the eerie silent noise of snow falling against land.

Snow covers Mazzie's eyelashes, making her look like a tiny ice princess—the closest she will ever come to wearing makeup.

"You look pretty," I say.

"Shut up."

"I'm serious."

But she doesn't want to hear it. Instead she says, "So—you and Drew?"

I nod. "I think so."

She starts to get up, pulling me along with her. "I don't like him."

"You don't like anyone," I say. I grin at her. "Except me."

We're both standing now, but neither of us seems in a hurry to get back to the dorms. There is such constant pressure at Woodsdale, with academics and swimming and this whole new social life, sometimes I don't realize how tense I am until I'm with Mazzie, and I notice its absence. The only other time I feel this way is when I'm underwater. I've started to realize that, when it is only the two of us, I feel a kind of separateness from everyone else. Sometimes she tells me things about myself that even I don't know.

"No," she says, "I don't like you."

But even though Mazzie isn't a snob like Estella or a pushover like Lindsey, she still knows a different world than me. She's never set foot inside a public school. Her opinion of Woodsdale as subpar, as far as boarding schools go, hasn't changed. I've told her everything about me and I still know so little about her. But I can't imagine anything she could possibly tell me that would make me like her less.

Back in our room we strip down to our underwear, red faced and breathing heavily from the trek. I know she will grind her teeth all night, giving a beat to my wheeze. It will sound like this: *crunch-phee-crunch-phee-crunch-phee*—it's almost like our song. After so many nights of the same thing here, I cannot fall asleep without its melody.

chapter 6

Will is home. My parents don't even tell me. But I know, as soon as I walk in the front door for winter break, that he's here somewhere. On the family photo that hangs over the mantel in the living room, my brother has drawn big red horns and a tail on the Ghost with permanent marker.

I've been dreading Christmas break up to this point. I even considered staying at Woodsdale—there are a few kids who do that, mostly from other countries and different religions that don't celebrate Christmas—but the Ghost wasn't about to let that happen.

I run up the steps to Will's room, knock on the door, and open it before he can even respond.

I want to close my eyes and turn away. I cover my mouth with my hand. He looks like a different person: twenty, maybe thirty pounds lighter, paler than the Ghost himself. He's shirtless, on his back in bed, headphones over his ears, tapping a bare foot as he gazes at the ceiling. He doesn't notice me. His music is so loud that I can clearly hear it outside the headphones. He's so thin that each of his ribs is visible. I can see his hip bones beneath his jeans.

More than anything, though, it is his arm that makes me want to look away. His wounds have healed into a network of scars that cross and weave over each other like a map leading to nowhere. They are deep and thick and will never fade. The injuries are so bad that they go beyond simple scarring; they're a deformity.

I remember everything again, like a flood that I've been blocking since I left for school: all the blood, my mother covered in it, the Ghost pale and horrified as he knotted his tie around Will's arm, all the neighbors standing there watching.

If I were still at Woodsdale right now, I wouldn't have to deal with any of this. I could be swimming, or else driving around with Lindsey and Estella, music blasting from the car speakers, without a care in the world.

"Katie," Will says, sitting up as soon as he notices me. He slips his headphones off. The music becomes louder, heavy and grating. I'm amazed he can hear anything.

I try to smile. When he crosses the room to hug me, I can feel the veins in the soft tissue connecting his ribs.

He closes the door and we sit on his bed. We both light cigarettes.

"I'm surprised you still smoke," he says. There's a new hoarseness to his voice. "They let you smoke at that fancy school?"

I shake my head. "Just when I go out on weekends."

"Yeah, I figured." His eyes look huge. His cheekbones, which I've never noticed before, are high and pronounced. This is not my brother.

"I tried to call you," he says.

I nod. "I know. I'm sorry. I'm so busy there, I leave really early for school and you didn't leave a number or anything, so"—I pause—"well, you didn't call back. If I'd been there when you called, I would have talked to you."

He shrugs. "It wasn't important or nothing. Just wanted to, you know, shoot the shit. See if you were homesick." He tries to smile. His teeth are yellow and more crooked than ever, the braces gone. "A big brother has to look out for his little sister, you know?"

I nod. "Sure. It's okay." We stare at each other in the smoke-filled room, the music coming from his headphones like a fly in the room that's driving me nuts. It doesn't seem to bother him.

"Hey"—he's excited all of a sudden—"didja see what I did to the picture down there?"

I nod, forcing a smile. "Great work."

"Mom just had it reframed and everything." He claps his hands, downright giddy. "She's gonna cry. Oh God, I can't wait."

"She just had it reframed?"

"Yes." He elbows me, fist to his mouth, snickering. "The Ghost is gonna soil his tightie-whities, Katie."

Watching him, I feel the annoyance spread into a mixture of anger and pity. It's an odd feeling to have. I feel the same way about my parents as Will does, for sure. But he's twenty-one. He's a *grown-up.* And our mom cries all the time already. Why would he want to make things worse?

"Katie, you know what we should do? We should give him cloven hooves, too. Damn, I should have thought of that before. Hey—what the hell's the matter with you?"

"I missed you," I say. My eyes are filling with tears. He looks away. "I was homesick for you." I reach for his bad arm but he pulls away quick, like a reflex. I wonder if it still hurts.

"Shut up, Katie."

"I was worried about you."

"You shoulda been there when I called. What were you doing—out riding ponies? At a polo match? Out playing tennis with someone named Bunny?"

"I couldn't help it, Will."

"Okay." He nods. "Okay, then, I'll call you more. Okay?"

But that's not what I want, either.

His voice is weaker than I've ever heard it. He says, "Don't be homesick, all right? No good home to be sick for, that's what I say."

Even though I sleep late, Will always sleeps later. It's not unusual for him to sleep eighteen hours a day. He's been up at least once already, and is now asleep in the basement, the TV blaring so loud that I can't imagine how it's not keeping him awake. His whole body is covered, right up to his chin, in a thick white comforter. I stand close to him for a moment, listening to the sound of his breath, before I go back upstairs.

On the kitchen counter, there's a note from my mom.

Katie,

Good morning, sleepyhead! Gone to a watercolor workshop for the day. Empty the dishwasher if you get the chance. Call me when you wake up. No car today—we want to actually see you for once!

—Mom

I pick up the phone. There's only one person I can think to call. Candy Huzak was my friend before I went to Woodsdale, and I know she'll want to see me. Besides, I'm dying to get out of the house; I don't know what I'll say to Will when he wakes up.

"Katie freakin' Kitrell!" Candy's voice has its familiar, impoverished twang. "Hell yeah, come on up! Just give me a while, okay? I've gotta do a few things." She giggles. "Gotta give my girl a proper homecoming, you know?"

My mom is sloppy, too trusting for her own good. The Ghost would have thought to pocket the car keys on his way out, but my keys are right where I left them the night before, on top of the microwave, next to a carton of the Ghost's cigarettes. Not that it matters; I can walk to almost anywhere I'd want to go from here. Hillsburg doesn't even have a traffic light. Yet they've got a historical society that keeps its members busy trying to get government grants for improvement; I know because my parents are devoted members. All that's happened so far is that the vendors for the annual historical festival have switched to deep-frying in vegetable oil instead of peanut oil.

Regardless, it's *cold* outside—too cold to walk anywhere without my nose going numb. And I know that my mother won't be back for hours, that the Ghost is working God knows where—it isn't like they'll even know if I take the car. I don't bother with the dishwasher. When we were younger and our mom would ask us for help around the house, Will and I both used to get a kick out of saying, "That's okay, Mom. You go ahead and do it." Eventually we got a housekeeper, but I guess she's not here today.

I wander around the empty house for a while in my pj's, tinkle a few notes on the piano in the living room, go nose-to-nose in a staring contest with my parents' cat, Priscilla, and smoke a few cigarettes while catching the end of the midday news. I go up to my room and get back into bed for an hour or so and spend the whole time debating whether or not to fall back asleep. I reread my favorite scenes from *Wuthering Heights,* especially the part where Heathcliff bribes the gravedigger to let him sleep on Catherine's grave. I go into Will's empty room and poke around for anything interesting, listening to a Phish bootleg with headphones, paging through a copy of *Playboy* from his closet.

I've been taking a gender studies class at Woodsdale; students are encouraged to take it every year. Our professor is a man, a great-looking guy in his early thirties, on loan from the local university. They do that sometimes—recruit local college professors to teach advanced courses.

During our last class before winter break, we had a long discussion about what he called the "normalization" of pornography in our society. This professor—his name is Dr. George, but he tells everyone to call him Evan—is really cute, married, and is deeply concerned with our self-esteem. All the girls have crushes on him.

"Pornography," he told us, "is a way of anesthetizing ourselves to our own humanity. I'm sure all you girls have been told by many of the boys you know—maybe even by many of the adults you know—that it's something men look at out of necessity. That it isn't a big deal. Am I right?"

Sitting in class that day, he took a moment to look each of us in the eye as he spoke. "I'm here to tell you, as a heterosexual man, that it isn't something you have to tolerate. It isn't something a man can't live without. You girls all deserve to be treated in a way that makes you feel valued and comfortable. Please, girls"—he seemed almost ready to cry for us—"please don't let anybody tell you differently."

I bury the magazine under the newspaper in the kitchen compactor and replace its spot in the closet with my dog-eared copy of *The Yellow Wallpaper,* then head off to the shower. It's two thirty in the afternoon, and I'm not even dressed yet.

When I knock on Candy Huzak's door, she's holding her two-year-old daughter in one arm and smoking a Kool cigarette with her free hand. Her apartment, which she shares with her older sister, is low-income housing. It's the kind of place where you don't even want to sit down on the furniture because you start thinking about what kind of fluids might be dried onto the upholstery. I've known Candy since elementary school. We were in the *gifted* class together. It's funny, you never stop along the way to think about who will end up pregnant at fifteen or dropping out of college or dying in the river, like Greg Phillips did last summer.

Candy is a single mom now, and she thinks she's got it made with her own place. The rooms in the apartment are sectioned off with piles of dirty clothes, baby toys, and clusters of empty beer bottles whose labels she's peeled away as she's watched her afternoon soaps.

We plant Holly, her daughter, on the carpet in front of *The Little Mermaid* while we talk and go through a stack of old *Cosmopolitan* magazines, ripping out the perfume samples so we can tape them up around her bathroom mirror later on. I feel embarrassed just thinking about what my friends from Woodsdale would say if they could see me. I don't think there's an actual book in this whole apartment.

I sink back into the sofa, imagining what kinds of microorganisms are leaping onto my body while Candy gives me the update on Hillsburg's happenings.

"You know Kelly Lang—she's pregnant with her second kid. And Keith Mitchell is supposed to be the dad, even though she married my cousin Tim right after high school. You know Tim? He graduated from the Triangle Tech in Grotto Falls last year?" She digs through her purse for a pack of cigarettes, which she opens and holds toward my face. The smell of marijuana wafts between us. "See that? I got this dope from Tim a few months ago, right?" She lights up a Kool. Her fingernails are all different lengths, ridged and jagged and covered in dull, chipped polish. I look at her and can't understand for a *second* what she's thinking—I can't believe she's smoking around her child. I would *never* tell any of my friends at Woodsdale that the Ghost still smokes in our house. It's just so . . . second-class.

Even the air in her apartment feels dirty. I don't want to get high around her daughter; the idea makes me feel sick to my stomach. So I'm relieved when Candy says, "We can smoke up after Holly goes down for her nap."

Even so, there's just no way. "I can't smoke anymore," I lie. "They give us random drug tests at school."

"No kidding? God, that sucks. Katie, we all told you you shoulda failed that admissions test. Even my *mom* told you so."

The silence in the room would be more than awkward if Candy and I hadn't known each other for so long. But it stretches on, all the way to the end of *The Little Mermaid*. I can't stop noticing all the patches of filth in her apartment: the kitchen sink overflowing with dirty dishes; the toilet in dire need of a good scrubbing; even the television screen is covered in sticky fingerprints so noticeable that they almost make it hard to see what's happening on the TV.

Remembering my mom's note from this morning, I ask, "Hey, can I use your phone?"

My mother's voice sounds far away, distracted, like she always is when she's painting. "Candy and I are going to do some Christmas shopping today. What do you want for Christmas, Mom?"

"Do you want to make cookies with me when I get home tonight?" she asks. She doesn't remember that I wasn't supposed to take the car.

"What time?"

"Around eight."

Christmas cookies with my mom? What's next, mother-daughter basket weaving classes?

But her voice is so hopeful, so genuine and distant, that I feel terrible disappointing her. "Whatever. Sure, that sounds great."

When I get back to the living room, I notice it's already dark outside. I wish I hadn't even come here—the whole day is wasted. I never realized what trash Candy was until I got to Woodsdale. I can't imagine Lindsey or Estella, or even Mazzie, ever meeting her, and what they might think of me if they did.

Smoking a cigarette, she says, "Someday I'll be sitting in my high-rise office, drinking champagne with my feet up while my assistant does all my work for me."

All I want to do is leave. But I don't want to go home, either. I just want to go back to school.

"What do you want to do?" I ask her.

She shrugs. "I'm thinking about becoming one of them, uh, radiologers?"

"You mean a radiologist?"

"Uh-huh." She doesn't even have a high school education. "One of them people who takes X-rays at hospitals."

"Oh. You mean an X-ray technician?"

She shakes her head. "No, I mean a radiologer—radiologist—whatever you called it. You know how much money they make?"

I shake my head. "How much?"

"They make, like, thirty grand! Can you imagine making that much money? I'm telling you, once I get back to school, it's all gonna happen for me, Katie."

Sure it is, I think. *You're really on your way.*

At ten o'clock that night, I let the car idle in the driveway. Before I go anywhere, I sit with my eyes closed for a few moments, taking deep breaths, trying to brace myself for whatever's waiting for me inside. It's always a crapshoot with my mom. There's a chance she doesn't even remember the plans we made. And then, of course, there's Will. Who knows what kind of mood he's in? He might be furious that I went to see Candy instead of spending time with him, or he might have slept all day.

Our house is always too dark at night because my parents refuse to use overhead lights. The Ghost tells me it reminds him of how poor he was as a kid, growing up in railroad housing with bare lightbulbs glaring overhead. In the evenings, my parents rely on candles and table lamps. It makes the whole place feel kind of haunted.

My mother stands before the blender in the kitchen, holding a margarita glass in one hand, a half-empty bottle of tequila in the other. I think it's the good stuff—at least, it's the same kind that Lindsey's parents buy. She's probably drunk. The rest of the house is dark, almost silent except for light, faraway sounds of the cat pattering around the foyer.

"Hey, Mom. I'm so sorry I'm late."

I'm used to seeing her drunk, but I can't help but picture her waiting for me in the kitchen, measuring and sorting the ingredients for cookies, then getting all sad as the evening dragged on and I didn't show, eventually tapping the bar for company and getting started on the cookies by herself.

I feel dizzy. It occurs to me that I haven't eaten all day.

I look around the kitchen. "Oh—did you start baking cookies already?" I pretend to be surprised, as though our plans were for, like, 9:55 p.m.

My mother sniffles a little bit, shaking her head, staring at me. "Fuck you," she mouths, without making any sound.

Under normal circumstances, my parents do not swear. The rare times when I've heard them say "fuck" have been burned into my brain forever. And my own mother—my *mommy,* for godsakes—does not say "fuck you" to her daughter. The words feel like a punch in the stomach. Worse than that, even, because I know I deserve it.

I take a step backward. "What did you say, Mom?"

But she only stares at the floor. And then she says out loud, without looking up, "Go to bed, Katie." She turns her back to me and resumes folding flour into the dough, sipping her margarita.

I look around, awestruck. The kitchen is all marble countertops and track lighting and sleek appliances. When I was younger, before my parents had any money, it was dark and dingy. Half the time, the stove didn't even work. Still, my mom and Will and I would spend entire afternoons in here, pureeing fruit to make homemade sugar-free fruit leather in the dehydrator. Or else we'd bake loaves of wheat bread, turning it into a little science experiment as we watched the yeast bubble to life in water.

But that was when we first moved to Hillsburg, before people had a chance to get to know us, to decide they hated us. Will and I had to go to school and listen to everyone call us rich kids all the time. For a while, it was okay—but then the teachers started doing it, too.

Will was smart—he *is* smart. He used to get good grades, so good that he skipped the fourth grade, and they were thinking about letting him skip fifth, too. One day, in eighth grade, he got caught playing with a Game Boy during class. Back then nobody else had them yet, at least not in Hillsburg. The teacher took it away and let everyone else in the class play with it. "Since you're so rich, your parents can just buy you a new one," he said.

But that wasn't all. For a few months after that, from the beginning of the year until Christmas break, the teacher put Will's desk in the corner of the room, facing a wall, away from everyone else. When my parents found out—at their parent-teacher conference, just before the holidays—the Ghost went apeshit. I can still remember him on the phone with the superintendent. That was one time I heard him swear a lot.

I don't fit in my bed anymore. When I sprawl out on my back my arms and legs hang off the sides. It's hot in here. I get up and strip down to my underpants, hear voices downstairs, winding through the rooms and up the stairwell. The Ghost must be home. He and my mother speak in low voices to each other. I picture them in the kitchen, him hunched over and her on tiptoes to kiss. He probably won't even come upstairs to say hello to me. They'll stay down there all night and drink wine together. I don't know why they even bothered having kids, if they're so obsessed with each other.

The shelves in my bedroom are filled with all the books I've ever read and rows of swimming trophies and ribbons and medals. Nothing has been touched since I left for school. Above my little bed is an oil painting my mother did of me as an infant, sleeping on my back. I know she loves the way it hangs above me while *I* sleep in real life: Katie sleeping above Katie sleeping. Sometimes when I'm home, I wake up to find her standing in my doorway, looking at us. I wonder if she does the same thing when I'm not here. Probably not—there used to be a similar painting of Will above his bed, but it disappeared the first time he left.

As I'm lying in bed, the phone rings. It's past eleven; most likely it's some kind of psychiatric emergency for the Ghost.

A few seconds after it stops ringing, my dad taps lightly at my door, holding out the phone. "It's for you," he says.

"Am I calling too late?" Drew's voice is almost a whisper. My stomach does a somersault.

"How did you get my number?"

"I stopped by your dorm earlier today, since you mentioned you might be staying for Christmas. Mrs. Martin gave it to me."

I don't want to risk anyone in the house overhearing my conversation, so I throw on my terry-cloth robe and go outside to the backyard. I stand in ankle-deep snow, wearing only my sneakers, while we talk.

"I was going to see if you wanted to come to Christmas Eve mass with me if you were still on campus," he says.

The whole God situation with Drew makes me more than a little uncomfortable. He's just so *genuine* about the whole thing. I've been to church with him a couple of times, and it's starting to irritate me that Drew—who seems to have had an easy life with lots of friends and love and *nothing* to make him question whether or not there's a God—is so devout. Will always says that agnosticism is the only true religion, and most of the time I think he's right. After everything I've seen from this town and the people in it, after how they treated Will and our family, and what happened to Will because of them, I can't imagine feeling anything *but* doubt about something as big as God. It's a great idea, and I hope it's all true . . . but that's the best I can do for now.

"Mazzie told me she'd come with me," he says.

"Mazzie?" I feel a rush of warmth that goes all the way to the tips of my toes. "You're taking *her*?"

Drew pauses. I can tell he's really contemplating what to say next. "We're just going as acquaintances, you know. She offered to come, and I couldn't say no. It wouldn't be—you know—Christian of me."

Mazzie is a Buddhist, and she thinks Drew is about the most annoying person on earth. She's going with him as a joke; I'm certain I'll be subjected to the highlights of her experience as soon as I get back to campus.

But that's not really why I'm surprised. Mazzie hadn't told me she was staying on campus for winter break. Now that I think about it, she might have gone out of her way not to mention it. I feel like crying for her. I want to call her, but she'd only hang up on me for waking her.

"Katie? You still there?"

"Yes." I pull my robe more tightly around my body. The air in the yard is damp and so cold that I can feel my core going numb.

"I wanted to call you because . . . I've been thinking about you a lot," Drew says. "I miss seeing you every day. I miss you a lot."

My cheeks burn as I beam. "I miss you, too."

"When are you coming back?"

"Soon," I say, and I know it's true as the word leaves my mouth. "As soon as I can."

Will is waiting for me in his doorway. "Come in," he whispers, his tone urgent. He shuts the door behind him. "We need to talk."

It's the first time I've seen him awake all day, and I'm horrified all over again by the way he looks.

I sit on his bed as Will paces in a tight circle in front of me, smoking, his breath quick. "What were you doing on the phone?" he asks. He reminds me of a caged animal. His steps get faster and closer together. "Were you talking about me?"

"Will, no. I was talking to a friend from school—"

"Telling them what a loser I am? Telling them you can't wait to get back to school so you never have to come home again and see your crazy loser of a brother?"

"No!" Downstairs, our parents are still awake, I can hear their voices lilting up the stairs. With every circle, my brother inches a little closer to me.

His voice gets louder. "I am your *elder.*" He points a bony finger in my face, the nail chewed down past the skin so that I'm staring at a bloody stub. "You respect me!" He's almost shouting now. "What gives you the right to talk about me with your spoiled rich friends? You do not speak about me without my *permission,* do you understand? You think you're better than me because you go to some fancy prep school for rich kids now? You probably tell them all about me, don't you? You tell them you wish I'd died. You stood there and didn't do anything, just like everyone else. Everyone was laughing, saying that loser Will would have been better off if he'd died, right? And you laughed too, didn't you?"

Where are our parents? "Will—no, I would never laugh at you. Will, I love you, please calm down, okay? Come here, just sit down and talk to me—look! Look at my leg." I pull my robe apart and show him the deep gouge in my shin. "I was in such a hurry to reach you that I fell on the cinderblocks and cut myself, and I didn't even care. I wanted to go with you, but they wouldn't let me."

The Ghost appears in the doorway. I hadn't even heard his footsteps on the stairs. It's the first time in a long time that I can remember being grateful to see him. It's the first time I've *ever* been scared to be alone with my brother.

"Will," the Ghost says, his voice soft but firm. "Kathryn."

Will stops, shifts his glare to the Ghost. "We're just having a friendly conversation, man."

The Ghost puts a hand to his lips and carefully removes an almost invisible piece of tobacco from the corner of his mouth. "It's too late for this," he pronounces calmly. The corners of his mouth twitch into the slightest sarcastic smile, but his eyes don't move. "Time for all the good boys and girls to go to bed."

But I can't sleep. Once my parents go to bed, even though it's almost the middle of the night, I creep downstairs and pick up the phone and dial my dorm room.

Our answering machine picks up on the third ring. "Mazzie Moon . . . ," I murmur. "Mazzie Moon, are you awake?"

Beep. "Good God, Katie, what the hell do you want? You know it's, like, two in the morning?"

But I can tell from the sound of her voice that she wasn't sleeping.

"If I could see you, I'd smack you across your dumb face," she says.

"Why didn't you tell me you were staying for break?"

She pauses. "Oh. You talked to Drew." She adds, as an afterthought, "*That* loser."

"You're the one who's going to mass with him."

"Yeah, well, you know I'm always looking for a good laugh."

I close my eyes and smile, clutching the phone, wanting more than anything to be there with her, alone in our room, safe.

"I'm going to come back early," I tell her.

She gives an exaggerated yawn. "Please don't."

"Mazzie, what are you doing there? Why didn't you go home?"

"How's your dead brother doing?"

"Don't change the subject."

She yawns again. "I'm very tired, Katie."

"You are wide-awake. You're probably sitting at your desk studying calculus, aren't you?"

". . ."

"Are you?"

"No, I'm not."

"Okay. Chemistry, then."

". . ."

"I'm right."

"I hate you, Katie. When are you coming back?"

"As soon as I can."

There's a long pause, her end of the line silent except for the grinding of her teeth, which she doesn't realize she's doing. "I can't say I'm completely disappointed," she says. And then, without so much as a good night, she hangs up on me.

chapter 7

The night before school starts after winter break, Mazzie and I are sitting beside each other in my bottom bunk, reading our shared copy of *Crime and Punishment* for English class, when Jill, our dorm assistant, pounds a fist against the door.

"Kitrell," she says, her lips pressed together in contempt. Jill is thickly built, a little too masculine to be pretty, and takes herself very seriously as an authority figure. Estella has recently started a rumor that Jill is a hermaphrodite. "You've got a visitor."

"But it's—"

"I know, it's after lights-out. This is complete insubordination, and if it were up to me, you'd be on work details every weekend until you graduate." She glares at me. "But Mrs. Martin says it's okay. Just this once." She takes a deep breath of resignation. "Supposedly it's official swimming business, but you and I both know better than that. Don't we?"

Before I manage to throw my slippers on and grab a robe and take a quick look in the mirror, Jill has pushed her way into our room. When she sees that our reading light is on and that Mazzie is sitting atop the covers on my bed—that Mazzie isn't even in her pajamas yet—Jill appears on the verge of rage. "Mazzie Moon!" she barks, her voice dipping so deep that I can see how she really, really *could* have a penis. "Get your butt in bed, *now*." And as we're leaving the room, Jill snaps off the reading lamp, leaving Mazzie fully dressed in the darkness.

Drew is in the vestibule between the hallway and the common room. When he sees me, he lets out a deep breath. "Hi," he says.

"Hi." Behind us, in the common room, I can hear the low murmur of giggly voices, the sound of a chair falling over.

"Estella and Stetson," he explains.

"Oh. Sure."

The vestibule is almost dark. Outside it's snowing; there are almost-melted snowflakes on Drew's hair, on his face, and as he steps closer to me and takes my hands in his, I can feel that he's chilled through. He isn't wearing a coat or anything; I'm certain he and Stetson (who are roommates) snuck out their window to get here.

"I hear you have some official swimming business to discuss with me," I say, grinning.

"Very official," he says. His teeth are chattering a little bit, even though it's warm in the vestibule.

"Are you cold?" I put my hands on his shoulders, rubbing his arms.

He shakes his head. "Maybe a little nervous."

There's a sudden, conspicuous silence in the common room, which probably means Estella and Stetson are under a blanket on the sofa. She is the only person at Woodsdale who could ever get away with that kind of thing without facing expulsion.

But facing any kind of punishment isn't really an issue for her, since she'll never get caught. There's a part of me that would give anything to have what she has.

"I was going to throw stones at your window," Drew says, still shaking a little bit. "I thought it would be romantic."

Just knowing he had the idea makes me fall in love with him a little bit. "Why didn't you?"

"Because it's so cold. And I didn't want Mazzie to yell at me." He licks his lips. Our arms are around each other now, our noses almost touching. "Besides, there's something I want to ask you, and I wanted to do it in private."

My heart starts to flutter. *Please, please, please don't ask me to go to church with you again.*

"I know we've been spending a lot of time together lately. I wanted to tell you that I've been having a great time."

"Me too." I'm afraid I'll start crying, staring at his clear blue eyes, so big and sincere and nervous.

"So, I wanted to ask you if you wanted to be . . . ah . . . exclusive."

I am melting into a puddle of Katie-water. I don't deserve him. How can he possibly want me?

But he does. "I'm crazy about you, Katie," he says. "Every time I'm away from you, you're the only thing I can think about."

All I can do is gaze up at him and try to stay upright, clinging to his waist with my arms.

"Katie? You didn't answer my question."

"Oh, right. Well, *duh,* Drew. Yes!"

He lets out a deep breath, which I didn't realize he'd been holding. "Oh, wow. You have no idea how happy I am."

Then, for the first time, he kisses me on the mouth. It feels like I've been waiting for this moment my whole life. I don't have much to compare him to, but I can tell he's a *good* kisser. We back against the wall, still kissing, and oh my *God* I can't believe this is happening to me. On the other side of the door to the common room, I can hear Estella and Stetson again. I open my eyes and see the double doors cracked open slightly; they are staring at us, snickering, Estella biting her fist to suppress her giggles. But I don't even care.

After word spreads that Drew and I are an official couple, life seems almost perfect. Aside from shooting wicked glances in my direction whenever they see me, Grace Waugh and Leslie Carter pretty much leave me alone. Even Estella's attitude toward me seems to soften, at least temporarily. Sometimes I don't even remember what life felt like before Woodsdale.

But there are inevitable reminders, things that happen to yank me out of the surreal life I'm living and put me back in my place.

In the middle of the night, the phone rings from underneath a cashmere sweater draped specifically to muffle its noise. Mazzie hates having to climb out of bed, knowing that it takes a good thump to my face to wake me, and in my sleep I can sense her light feet padding across the carpet, the muffled *brr-ring* of the phone, her swears gurgling out in a hissed whisper, warped by her mouth guard.

She taps me on the face with the receiver. "It's for you, dummy." And she climbs back into bed and falls right back to sleep—at least I think she does—her jaw clicking faint vibrations into the mattress above me.

"Yeah?" I can't hear anyone. I'm holding the phone upside down. I turn it around, sitting up, trying to get my bearings.

The voice is raspy and tired and almost unrecognizable.

Almost. Immediately, I feel an ache in my chest that spreads to my belly and down my whole body. I feel lonely. I feel homesick. I feel scared.

"Katie." It's him. His voice sounds far away, like he's calling from someplace he's visiting with a time machine. It isn't the first time he's called since winter break, but it's the first time he's managed to catch me in my room.

I sit up, blinking to see better in the dark. "Hey, you. Where are you calling from?"

"I'm at home."

"Oh."

"Was that your roommate that answered?"

"Yes."

"I bet she's a rich girl, huh?"

". . ."

"So you like it up there?" His voice takes on a twinge of bitter sarcasm. "Up there at *prep school*?"

"Yes." I lean my head against the wall behind me, closing my eyes. There is an invisible thread connecting my brother and me, no matter how far apart we are—there always has been—but lately, whenever I sense its tug, it feels almost painful.

"Oh yeah?"

"Sure I do. Sure I like it. Why wouldn't I?"

He snorts. "You got some high-class boyfriend?"

"Cut it out. If you called me to be an asshole I'm going back to sleep."

"Come on . . . I'm just joking. Seriously, Mom tells me you got a boyfriend. What's his name?"

I hesitate. I only even mentioned Drew to my mom because she kept asking if I'd met any nice boys, and there was a part of me that couldn't contain my excitement over Drew—not even with her. "His name is Paul."

"Paul what?"

"Paul . . . my boyfriend Paul. Why do you want to know?" I imagine him calling directory assistance at three in the morning, hissing craziness over the line.

"And you like him?"

I sigh. "Of course I like him."

"You don't want to tell me his last name?"

"Hutton," I lie.

"Paul Hutton. Sounds like a rich boy."

"So?"

"So is he? One of them rich boys?"

"I guess so."

"You gonna marry him and live the high life? Eat bonbons and have babies and lie on your back for a living?"

"I'm going now." I start to hang up the phone, bringing it slowly away from my ear, waiting.

"Come on, I was kidding. Don't hang up on me, Katie." His voice is pleading. "Come on, man. I don't have anyone else to talk to."

"Well, it's the middle of the night. Why aren't you asleep?"

I can hear him puffing on a cigarette. I picture him in his bedroom, the window open, his head sticking out. He's on my parents' ancient cordless phone—that explains the poor connection. "I can't sleep here. It's impossible. I haven't slept in days."

"That's great," I murmur.

"You know I could have gone there. I could have gone anywhere I wanted to. I'm just as smart as you."

"Okay."

"What the hell's that supposed to mean?"

I sigh. "Well . . . you were always getting kicked out. Everywhere they sent you, you got kicked out."

"So?"

"So, you and I are different people. What I'm doing doesn't have anything to do with . . . what you're doing."

For a long time he doesn't say anything—at least it feels like a long time. I listen to Mazzie breathing in her sleep, her long, slow inhalations so calm that I can't help but relax a little bit.

Then he says, "Screw you, man. I didn't call to have you treat me like shit."

"Why did you call me, then?"

"I just wanted to talk."

"What do you want to talk about? It's almost four in the morning. I have to get up in an hour."

"They don't let you sleep late there? They don't come in and wake you up with feathers on your cheeks?"

"I have to get up for swimming practice. I have to be in the pool by five thirty."

"No kidding?"

"No kidding."

". . ."

". . ."

"You'll get kicked out too."

"I won't get kicked out, Will. I'm not stupid."

"Whatever. You think you're so much better than me?"

"I'm hanging up now."

"Fine. Hang up."

"Screw you, Will."

"Screw you too."

I lay the phone down and take a deep breath, trying to time my inhalations with Mazzie's. There's a pop as she slides her jaw back into place, and her face appears beside me, upside down, and before I know it she shimmies down her ladder and crawls into bed with me. She's been awake the whole time, listening. "Was that your dead brother?"

"Yes."

She slides down a little lower beside me, batting her eyelashes, seducing the truth right from my achy muscles. "Where's he at now? Another mental ward?"

"He's home, I guess. Were you eavesdropping?"

She pulls out her mouth guard, a thread of saliva stringing from her mouth, and lets it fall, wet, onto the rug. She is so quick—before I know it, she does a tiny, compact somersault onto the floor, pops upright, and arranges herself cross-legged on the carpet, rubbing her hands together with anticipation, ready to soak up my troubles. "What did he say? Is he going crazy again?"

"Aw, Mazzie, I have to get up in an hour."

"Like you'll get any sleep anyway."

"I'm serious, Mazzie."

"Why do you tell everyone he's dead?"

I lean my head against the wall, bumping it hard. "I don't know." It feels like we have had this conversation at least a hundred times before.

"You're ashamed of him."

"Well, yeah. Obviously. What's not to be ashamed of?"

She nods to herself, like it's something she's already thought of a long time ago. "That's understandable."

"You think?"

"Yeah." She presses an open palm to her mouth, as though she's just realizing something. "Oh my God. Can you imagine what Estella would do if she knew? And Drew? Everybody would hate you." She adds, as though I don't already know, "Because, you know, it's a terrible lie you've told."

"I have my reasons."

Mazzie yawns, bored. "Yeah, yeah. Whatever, I don't care."

I close my eyes. "I'm going to sleep. Will you please go back to bed?"

"What do you care?"

"I guess I don't." But I grasp a fistful of her hair, fine and straight; it will not hold a curl to save her life. It pulls between my fingers and falls across her face like water. I have to scrape her cheek with my fingernails just to get another grip.

I'm tired of talking about Will, even with Mazzie; I'm tired of worrying about him and lying about him and pretending everything is okay.

But Mazzie isn't moving. I know there's only one way for me to shut her up.

"How did your mother die?" I ask.

Her smile slips away. "Shut up."

"Come on, don't you want to talk about it?"

She shakes her head. "Shut up, Katie."

"Why are you so *secretive,* huh? Why can't you just open up for once? It's not like I'm going to tell anyone—" And before I know what I'm doing, it's obvious I've gone too far.

She looks me straight in the eye. "There was an accident," she says.

"Oh."

"I've never talked about it. Not even with my dad. He told me what happened, right after it happened, and that was it."

"Mazzie, I'm sorry. I was just trying to get you to leave me alone."

She shrugs, but she's obviously tense, her shoulders creeping toward her ears as she begins to fold into herself. "It's okay. Don't worry about it."

"I'm sorry, Mazzie. I really am."

She's quiet for a minute. Then she says, "Do you ever have nightmares?"

I shake my head. "I usually have dreams. About what things were like before we moved to Hillsburg."

"I have nightmares."

"I know you do." I pause. "You know—you aren't easy to live with sometimes, Mazzie."

She stares at me. For a second, I'm almost afraid she's going to reach out and punch me. "I'm not easy to live with? Katie . . . imagine how hard it is to live with me sometimes. Then imagine what it would be like if you could never get away from me. Imagine you were stuck inside my head all the time, even when I'm sleeping at night and all I can think about is my mother. I *know* I'm not easy to live with, Katie. I live with myself every second, every day."

"Okay," I say. "Calm down, okay? Everything's all right. Isn't it?"

She nods. "Right. Everything's fine."

But she doesn't get back into her own bed. Without a word about what she's doing, she tucks herself under the covers with me and curls up like a baby lima bean, so soft and little I can almost forget she's there.

"Can you hand me my mouth guard?"

I feel around on the floor until I find it, and push it back into her mouth. She grins at me in the dark, her speech slurred. "Shanks."

"No problem." I almost ask her what she's doing in my bed. But I want her to stay, so I don't mention it. Instead I ask, "Can we go back to sleep now?"

"Uh-huh."

". . ."

". . ."

Crunch-phee-crunch-phee-crunch-phee.

"Hey, Mazzie?"

"Hmm?"

"Do you love me?"

"God, no. I hate your guts."

I smile in the dark. "Well, I love you. I think you might be my best friend."

"Shut up, Katie. Really, before I puke. Just shut the hell up."

"I'm just telling you how I feel."

"Whatever."

Crunch-phee-crunch-phee-crunch-phee.

"You should let me take you someplace normal sometime," Drew says one night after we leave yet another party—this one at Dana Thomas's house. Dana is a junior and, like almost every other girl in school, is dying with envy that Drew Bailey is off the market. I make sure to hold his hand and stay by his side all night, especially when Grace and Leslie and Dana are looking.

"Like where?"

"Like somewhere other than a party. You don't have to drink to have fun. How about a movie?"

He takes me to see a Pixar movie. Leave it to Drew to take me to a cartoon. Afterward, we go back to his house. His mother is waiting up for us. I've seen her before at swim meets—she never misses one, even when they're hours away—but this is the first time we've been officially introduced.

Drew's mom's name is Patricia, but she tells me right away to call her Penny. "I'm so excited to see you without a swim cap," she breathes. "Oh, Drew honey, she's *adorable*!" And she reaches out to feel my hair. "Look at all that blond hair! Your mother must have put your hair in braids every morning." She takes a step back to look at me, beaming. "Am I right?"

"Oh, no. My mom always said my face was too round for braids."

Penny frowns. "Oh. I don't think so, honey." She sighs, giving Drew a sideward glance. "I always dreamed of having a little girl, but I suppose it wasn't in the good Lord's plan." She winks at me. "Maybe sometime you'd let me put those braids on you?"

We're standing in the kitchen, just the three of us, and I know that for the rest of my life I'll remember exactly the way this moment smells, like brownies and soap and Penny's perfume, which is called *Flirtation,* and which she tells me she's worn every day since the seventh grade. And I know I'll remember how Penny looks tonight: tired and hopeful and proud all at once. I'll remember how her fingers feel on my hair, and how she is wearing an actual *apron,* and how their fridge is full of nothing but real food and gallons of low-fat milk and fresh fruits and vegetables. At home, in my parents' fridge, there are mostly condiments and dietary supplements and wine.

That night, we spend four hours at the kitchen table with Penny, talking until almost midnight. At our next swim meet a few days later, she shows up early, tapping me on the shoulder as Drew and I sit on the bleachers together.

"I hope you don't mind," she says, "but I thought it might be more comfortable underneath that swim cap if . . ." She hesitates, her smile hopeful. Even though the air is thick with chlorine, I can smell her kitchen on her clothes. She smells like cookies and scalloped potatoes. Lucky Drew.

She holds up a hairbrush and ponytail holders. "I thought

maybe . . . we could give those braids a try? I mean, as long as your mother doesn't mind." She looks around. "Where is your mother?"

Penny is right: the braids feel great underneath my swim cap. After the meet, I let them dry in place. When I take them out the next day, my hair is wild and wavy.

"You look great," Drew tells me. "You should let my mom braid your hair all the time." We're in his car again, parked in Lindsey's driveway.

"My mom really likes you," he adds.

"She does?"

"Oh, yeah. She thinks you're wonderful." He lets his hand drift to my hair. Tucking a wave behind my ear, he says, "Tell me about your family." He pauses, suddenly remembering, and then says, "I mean, you don't have to talk about anything you don't want to . . . if you want."

I can't look at him. "Thanks."

"But what about your parents? You never mention them. What do they do? I want to meet them!"

"Drew . . ."

"My mom was thinking that maybe we could all go to dinner sometime soon. Maybe after OVACs."

A pizza delivery van pulls past Drew's car and comes to a stop at the bottom of the Maxwell-Hutton driveway. Beyond the sliding glass doors, I can see Mazzie building a house of cards while she sits alone at a table. Beside the pool, Lindsey, Estella, and a couple of other girls—Jenny Walker-Howard and Samantha Gray-Piper, who are both cheerleaders—are walking like Egyptians along the cement, arms bent in opposite directions. Their boyfriends watch from rafts in the pool.

Even from so far away, I can tell that everybody, even Mazzie, is laughing.

"Let's go inside," I say.

He frowns. "Why? We're talking out here."

"I'm starving. I want some pizza."

As we walk toward the house, our fingers laced together, he says, "You didn't answer my question. Your parents?"

My father is an apparition, and my mother is semiconscious. "My father is a psychiatrist," I say over my shoulder, "and my mother is an artist."

I step past the pizza deliveryman, into the thick, warm air of the pool room, pulling Drew along with me. Once we're inside, it's too loud for him to ask any more questions.

We haven't been at the party ten minutes when Drew takes me by the sleeve and pulls me inside Lindsey's house. As we pass everyone at the party, they give us knowing grins. We even get a wink from Stetson.

Drew leads me to one of the spare bedrooms on the third floor. He locks the door behind us. We sit down on the bed, and before he can say anything, I start kissing him, and he is kissing me back—everywhere—my lips, my cheeks, my neck. His body against me feels strong, not at all suffocating, and I wrap my arms around him and feel all the muscles in his back and along his arms. His touch is gentle and tentative at first, but then it becomes almost frantic. He takes one finger and draws a slow circle around my exposed belly button. I can feel every part of him against me. We've been dating for months now. Is this it? Is this how I'm going to lose my virginity? I'm nervous, sure, but it feels right. I feel ready. I wouldn't want it to be with anybody else but Drew.

He moves his hand from my belly to my cheek and tucks my hair behind my ear. "Katie," he says, "I love you."

I could melt into the mattress right now. I feel like my clothes could be pulled away with the tug of a single thread. He's so beautiful, so genuine.

"I love you, too," I murmur. I start to unbutton his shirt. My fingers are trembling; I've kissed boys before, sure, but never anything close to this. Since Drew is older, I'm sure he's a lot more experienced. I'm afraid to admit to him that I don't exactly know what I'm doing. Instead, I keep kissing him, aware of how excited he's getting as I continue to unbutton his shirt. He sits up and shrugs it off, tossing it onto the floor behind him.

I sit up and begin to take off my own shirt. He freezes. "Katie. We need to stop."

"What?" I'm out of breath. I lean back, resting on my elbows. "Why?"

"Because. We just do." Drew is breathing so heavily, I'm afraid he's going to hyperventilate. "I brought you up here to talk with you. I didn't mean for this to happen."

"What's happening? Drew . . . we love each other, don't we?"

He nods, still panting. He's sweating all over. "Yes."

"Well . . . what's the matter, then?"

He climbs off the bed, finds his shirt, and puts it back on in such a hurry that it's buttoned all crooked.

"Katie," he says, sitting beside me again, his breath more steady, "I don't want to have sex with you."

"Oh." I stare down at the bedspread, which is a silky cream color, thick and soft beneath me. All the warmth drains from my body in an instant. I feel cold, humiliated for being so stupid—to think that Drew Bailey would want to sleep with *me*.

"Katie," he continues, grasping my hands, "I've made a promise to—"

"To who?" I glare at him, willing myself not to cry.

"To God," he says. "I've made a promise to stay a virgin until I'm married."

All I can do is stare at him. "But what if you don't get married until you're forty? What if you *never* get married?"

Drew shakes his head, like he feels sorry for me. "There are ways to make love to a person without having sex. We can kiss and touch and . . ." He pauses, like something's occurring to him for the first time. "You *are* still a virgin, right?"

I nod.

"Oh. Good. Because if you weren't, we would have to break up."

I feel like the room is shrinking. "Why would we have to break up?"

"Because, Katie. You're *sixteen*."

"So?"

"Whatever. If you'd had sex already, that would make you . . . well, you know. I mean, you'd practically be like Estella."

I can't help but feel defensive for Estella. Drew barely knows her. "Estella's not so bad."

"She's not a Christian. She's unscrupulous. She's using Stetson, you know, and someday she'll be sorry. I've tried talking to her—"

"What do you mean, *someday she'll be sorry*?" I interrupt. "When will she be sorry?" I blink at him. My whole body throbs with the sting of rejection. "I'm sorry, I think I might be hallucinating. Are you telling me that everyone who isn't a good Christian is going to hell?"

He nods. "Of course."

"But Drew, *I'm* not a Christian. I'm an agnostic."

He puts his hands on my shoulders. He brings his face close to mine and gives me a kiss on the nose. I think he's trying to reassure me. "It's okay, Katie. I've told you, you're just lost. I love you. I want to stay with you and share our lives. You'll see how beautiful God can be."

I feel numb. "As long as we don't have sex before we're married?"

"Of course."

"But what about different religions? What about Mazzie? What about . . ." I stop myself before I say, *What about my brother?* "You think Mazzie is going to hell because she's a Buddhist? She's a good person! It doesn't make any sense, Drew."

He shakes his head. "It makes perfect sense. It's all in the Bible. Katie, I know it's hard. Sometimes I can't even think about it. But that's why it's so important to share God's word." He puts his arms all the way around me. "I love you, Katie. Everything will be okay."

I want to push him away. I can't believe he could be so *nice* to Mazzie's face—he's even been nice to Estella lately, now that she's my friend—all the time believing that everyone who doesn't think like him is going to burn in hell.

But then he starts to kiss me again. "I love you," he murmurs, in between kisses. "I love everything about you. You're so innocent and lost and beautiful. When I watch you in the water"—he moves his mouth to my neck, leaning me back on the bed again, lacing his fingers through mine—"you're the most beautiful thing I've ever seen."

I don't think anyone besides my parents has ever called me beautiful before. And I know Drew means well. He's just confused. He doesn't know Mazzie the way I do. And as far as sex is concerned, he can change his mind—he *will* change his mind. If there's one thing I've heard, over and over again from the Ghost and Mrs. Martin and pretty much every other adult, it's that teenage boys think about only one thing.

After practice one day, Solinger keeps me late. He takes me into his office and pushes a pamphlet across his desk for me to look at.

It's an application for Yale University.

"I'm only a sophomore," I remind him.

"I know that. But every summer they accept two hundred high school students—just two hundred—to study there." He adds, as though it isn't obvious, "It's a huge honor, Katie."

But I've been looking forward to spending the summer in Woodsdale with my friends, swimming at school every day for as long as I wanted, spending all my free time with Drew. I've already gotten the okay from my parents, and Mazzie and I have already claimed a room to share at Lindsey's house.

"I don't know," I say. "What does this have to do with swimming?"

Solinger leans back in his chair and clasps his hands behind his head. He's shirtless, wearing nothing but a pair of red swimming trunks and flip-flops. "It has *everything* to do with swimming. You know Yale has the largest college athletic center in the country. I've already talked to the coach. You can practice with the team." He adds, before I can ask, "They practice year-round, unofficially. So this will give you a head start at getting in. You do well there, you go back next summer and do even better, and you're in like Flynn."

He licks his lips, grinning at me, and gives me a wink.

"Come on, Kitrell. You want to be captain, right? You do this and you'll be the first junior captain we've ever had."

I smile. Grace will be seething with jealousy. And Drew can always come visit me.

But there's Mazzie, too—what is Mazzie going to do?

And there's so much else—will I even get in?

"You'll get in," Solinger assures me. "Trust me. I've made a few calls. You'll get in."

I pick up the application. It's never crossed my mind before that someone like me could end up going to an Ivy League school. Even though I've been at Woodsdale almost a full year, there is still a feeling of separateness. People from Hillsburg just don't get that far away, no matter how hard they try.

Estella has an expression that she loves to use around me, anytime she catches me doing something even slightly wrong, like forgetting to put my napkin in my lap as soon as we sit down for meals. "You can take the girl away from the white trash, but you can't take the white trash out of the girl."

Mazzie will be okay without me. I mean, she'll just *have* to be.

Solinger slides an envelope across the desk.

"What's that?"

"It's your letter of recommendation. You need two. Mrs. Martin has another one waiting for you, back at the dorm."

"I'll have to talk to my parents."

"I've already spoken with them." Solinger rocks in his chair. "Katie, don't you get it? You've got a *gift,* honey. Everything is going to happen for you. All you have to do is keep swimming."

part three

chapter 8

When I walk into my room on the first day of preseason, Mazzie is sitting on my bed, wearing a tank top and underwear, bouncing a tennis ball off the floor.

She doesn't so much as look at me. "It's you."

"Yep." I put my suitcases down. In the corner of the room, there's a tennis racket and several bottles of balls. "You're playing tennis now?"

"I've always played tennis," she lies. "How was Yale?"

"Amazing." And it was. I earned straight As in all of my classes, went swimming every day, and Drew came to see me every weekend. But Mazzie already knows this; she and I have been talking on the phone all summer.

"I was hoping you'd decide not to come back." She sighs, lying back in bed, her legs dangling over the side, toes barely grazing the floor.

I narrow my eyes, grinning. "That's why you've been sleeping in my bed? Because you can't stand the sight of me?"

"In case you haven't noticed," she says, "the top bunk doesn't have any sheets on it. That's yours now."

"Mazzie," I say, sitting down on the bottom bunk beside her, putting my head on her shoulder, "these are my sheets."

The big news on campus is that, just a few days earlier, Estella dumped Stetson. Fewer than twenty-four hours later, she was spotted holding hands with Jeremy Chase, who is also a senior.

Over the summer, Stetson was in a minor car accident that left him with a torn tendon in his right arm. He can still play water polo well enough to stay on varsity, but he isn't the captain anymore. The new captain is Jeremy Chase.

And I'm the new girls' varsity swimming captain.

"It's a big job, honey," Solinger says to me as we're sitting in his office. He hands me my new swimsuit that says "Captain" below my last name, and winks; he's always winking at the girls. "It'll be easy for you, right?"

"Absolutely," I say, staring at the swimsuit.

"I hear you did great this summer."

I grin. "Yep."

"You still dating Bailey?"

When I nod, Solinger says, "That's good. Drew is a little fussy, you know?"

I sure do.

"But he's the whole package: talent, good head on his shoulders, all the smarts he's ever gonna need . . ." He studies me for a moment, shakes his head a little bit. "You kids never fail to amaze me. You come in here and you know how to get things done." He glances at his watch, knocks on his desk, and says, "I have ultimate Frisbee in five minutes. Gotta go. But—hey Katie—you should stick with Drew. He's a good decision for you." Solinger seems to be struggling with his words. "That's part of what you're here to learn—how to make the right kind of decisions in life. Do you know what I'm saying?"

Life is good. Being captain is demanding—I have to come early and stay late at almost every practice—but since Drew is the captain of the boys' team, we get to be there together.

Things with Drew are great too. They're fine. It's funny—the more you get to know someone, the more you get to see how different they are from what everybody else thinks of them.

It's one of those rare Saturday evenings when there's nothing to do. Drew is out of town, visiting relatives with his mom. Lindsey has a bad cold and has gone home for the weekend to recuperate. The dorm is practically empty except for me and Mazzie. We're in our pj's, lying on the couch in the common room, watching a movie together. It feels like one of the first times I've been able to relax all year.

My eyelids are beginning to flutter, my body going limp as I fall asleep, when Estella barges into the room.

"Katie. *There* you are. I've been looking everywhere for you."

I glance over at Mazzie. She's asleep, or at least, her eyes are closed.

"Shh." I sit up. "What's the matter?"

"Do you have any condoms?" she asks.

I shake my head. "Sorry."

Estella scowls. "At least go *look.* You've got to have one in the back of your sock drawer or something."

"Estella . . . why don't you just go buy some?"

"Because I don't want to drive all the way to the store.

Come on, Katie, just go look." She clasps her hands together and gives me her sweetest grin. "Pretty please?"

I should just say I'm out, or that I'm on the pill. But I don't think fast enough. "We don't use condoms," I say.

Her hands go to her hips. "Then what do you use?"

"We don't use . . . anything." I lower my gaze. Mazzie is the only other person who knows that Drew and I don't have sex; I don't know why I'm telling Estella. I think it's because I'm just so *frustrated* by the whole situation. I want confirmation that there's something wrong with Drew, not me.

Estella's mouth drops open. Slowly, her lips curl into a grin. "Do you mean to tell me," she says, enjoying every word as it leaves her mouth, "that you and Drew haven't had sex yet?"

I just stare at her. I don't say anything.

"Oh. My. God. Katie, why haven't you *told* me this before?"

I shrug. "I don't know. It's a little embarrassing."

"Well . . . *yeah.* What's up with him?" She claps a hand to her mouth. "Oh my God. It's the religion thing, isn't it?"

Again, I don't answer, which tells her everything she needs to know.

Estella is excited, rising up and down on her tiptoes in front of the TV. "This is really interesting, Katie. You know, before you got here, Drew dated Amanda Hopwood for, like, a year. I was *certain* they were doing it. Even Stetson thought so."

"Why were you so sure?" I ask.

"Because she's *Amanda Hopwood.* She's like a revolving door."

I give Estella a blank look.

"You know," she says, annoyed, "*everybody gets a turn.*"

Estella speaks more quickly now, her voice rising as the truth unravels. "Amanda told me she and Drew broke up because she wouldn't sleep with him. I *knew* that didn't make any sense. And I was right. That's not why they broke up at all, is it? I bet . . ." Her eyes are practically glowing now. She smacks a palm to her forehead in epiphany. "I bet *she* broke up with *him* because he wouldn't sleep with *her.* And she didn't want to admit it because . . . well, because even a slut like Amanda's gotta have some pride."

I feel a little sick to my stomach. Estella rushes over to me, eyes still flashing with excitement, and presses both of her hands to my cheeks so hard that it hurts. Her fingernails dig into my skin. "Katie. I want to tell everybody."

I shake my head. "Please don't."

"Can I tell Lindsey?"

I hesitate. But there's no saying no to Estella. "Okay."

"Can I tell Jeremy?"

"Estella . . ."

"How the hell am I supposed to keep something like this a secret? Does he want to save himself for *marriage*?"

"Yes."

"Oh, God. Katie. They make *documentaries* about people like him."

"Estella, listen to me. Every time you feel tempted to tell somebody, I want you to find me. You can tell me all about how Drew Bailey is still a virgin. And every time you tell me, I'll pretend to be hearing it for the first time."

Estella nods to herself. "That's a good idea, Katie. Okay, I'll try it."

She gets up to leave, still shaking her head at the bombshell she's learned. When she reaches the door, she turns to look at me again. "Do you think Mazzie has any condoms?" she whispers.

I give her a smirk. "What do you think?"

"Right," she says. "Well . . ." She sighs, looking around the room. Her gaze lands on the kitchenette. "Do you think Saran wrap would work?"

As soon as Estella is gone, Mazzie opens her eyes. "Hi."

I don't say anything. I'm sitting on the sofa, my arms crossed against my chest.

"What's the matter?" she asks.

"You've been awake the whole time?"

She nods.

"It's just so *frustrating*. And now Estella knows . . ."

Mazzie nods. "It is a little weird, I guess."

Her response startles me. Of all people, I'd expect Mazzie to think Drew's reluctance wasn't such a big deal.

I nod to myself. "I know. It's like . . ."

"Like a monkey who doesn't want to eat bananas," she supplies.

"Exactly."

"So what are you going to do? Break up with him?"

Oddly enough, the thought hadn't even occurred to me. Because I *do* love Drew. He's kind and easy to be around, and we have a lot of fun together . . . when we're not being physical. Anytime we start to go beyond making out, there's an awkwardness that takes over and makes it hard for me to breathe around him.

I shake my head. "No," I tell Mazzie. "I don't want to do that."

She nods. "Look at you . . . my virginal roommate." She laughs out loud. "So *pure*."

"Mazzie?"

"What?"

"Go to hell."

It's a Friday afternoon, after swimming practice. I've just broken the school record for fastest 400-meter freestyle. The summer has just turned a sharp corner into fall. The air is cool and crisp, the leaves beginning to change colors, and as Drew and I walk back to our dorms together holding hands, I try to describe to him how happy I'm feeling.

"I think autumn is my favorite season," I say, taking a deep breath, my cheeks tingling against the cool air. "I don't know why. Even though everything is dying, it all makes me feel so *alive*, you know? Do you ever feel like that?"

Drew nods. "I do. It feels like a gift, doesn't it?"

"Yes!"

"Do you know who gave us this gift?" He doesn't wait for me to answer. "God," he says, beaming.

I'm in such a good mood that I don't want to argue with him about religion. "That's nice, Drew." As we reach my dorm, I stand on my tiptoes to kiss him on the nose. "Thank God for you, Drew Bailey."

My mother is in my room, talking to Mazzie like they're old friends. As I open the door, I can hear her saying, ". . . and of course Katie's dad is a mess, and our son is quite ill but he'll be coming home, too—"

"Mother." I shut the door, hard. "What are you doing here?"

Mazzie is leaning against her desk, throwing a tennis ball into the air.

"Oh, Katie." I can tell my mom has been crying. "I came to pick you up."

I shake my head. "No way. I have a scrimmage in the morning, I have a chem lab—"

"Katie," she interrupts.

My mom wouldn't drive down here without any notice just for a visit. Something's definitely wrong—things have been so good lately, it was only a matter of time before *something* bad happened. I don't want to hear whatever's coming, so I just press on, "—that's due on Monday that I haven't even started yet, and we're supposed to go look at homecoming dresses this weekend."

"Sweetie, it's your grandpa," my mom says.

Both of my maternal grandparents passed away years ago, so I know she's talking about the Ghost's father.

My mom's lower lip trembles. She doesn't say anything else.

I look at Mazzie, who is still throwing the tennis ball into the air, catching it with alternating hands. She stops for a moment, gives me a grave look, and says, "Dead."

The last time I saw my grandpa was months ago, but even so he'd seemed fine. His real name was Edward, but he always insisted that Will and I call him Effie. My whole life, he always had bubble gum for me, called me Kit-Kat, and seemed delighted when Will and I confided our nickname for the Ghost to him.

When his third wife died a few years ago, Effie moved to Miami. He used to send postcards of himself taken at the beach with his arm around a hot twentysomething in a bikini. It was easy to imagine him convincing them to take the picture;

he was sweet and ornery and nothing at all like the Ghost. More than once, after a visit with him, Will and I would remark on how impossible it seemed that someone as uptight as the Ghost could have a dad as cool as Effie.

"We have to leave right away," my mom says. I just sit there, my head down, feeling the panic as it spreads throughout my body. Mazzie watches both of us with a kind of detached, fascinated pity. "I'm sorry, honey, but you should get your things together. The funeral is tomorrow and your father is very upset and I'd like to get back."

"Come with me," I say, suddenly, to Mazzie.

She drops the tennis ball. "What? No."

"Mom, please, can she come? Mazzie is my best friend."

My mom is hesitant. I've never brought anybody home with me before. I've barely mentioned Mazzie to my parents. "I didn't even know you were roommates," she says. "I was just telling Mazzie I always thought your roommate was someone named Madeline."

"I told her it was a mix-up," Mazzie explains to me. "I was just telling her that Madeline never showed up."

"Maybe you'd want to bring your boyfriend?" my mom says.

All I can think about is getting my mother out of my dorm before anyone else sees her. If Drew knew what was happening right now, I know he'd want to come with me. But I have to get out of here before he has a chance to see my mom, or hear about what's going on—otherwise he might find out about Will, and then everything would be over.

"Please, Mom," I say. I give Mazzie a pleading look. I can't stand the idea of going home without her.

• • •

Mazzie and I barely say a word the whole way back to Hillsburg. I know she's imagining what Will might be like—she's never even seen a picture of him—and I keep my head against the window, my eyes closed, trying not to think about how the weekend will go.

Both of my parents are only children. With Effie gone—my mom tells me he had an aneurysm that killed him instantly, as he lay on the beach—it's only the four of us now: my mom and the Ghost, Will and me. Even though I rarely saw my grandpa, knowing that he's gone makes me terrified in a way that goes beyond my *feelings* about Effie. I *feel* like my family is connected now by a series of quickly disintegrating threads. I *feel* like it would take almost nothing for the whole thing to fall apart.

Mazzie and I take our things up to my room. "Where's Dad?" I ask my mom.

"He's at the funeral home. He'll be home later tonight." She smiles at Mazzie. "Well, it's wonderful to meet Katie's best friend, although the circumstances are pretty unfortunate."

"Where's Will?" I ask.

"He's in his room. Probably sleeping." Her gaze flickers to Mazzie. "He's very, very upset. You can imagine."

I nod.

"This is incredibly difficult for him. He's . . . sedated. I know you and Will loved your grandpa very much." My mom takes a deep breath, opens the fridge, and uncorks a bottle of white wine. "You should let your brother rest, Katie. He needs to rest."

"How's Dad?"

My mom takes her time pouring a very full glass of wine. She takes a long sip before answering, "You know your father had a very difficult childhood. Your grandpa was not always the way he was when you knew him."

We don't see the Ghost or Will until just before the funeral the next day. Right away it's obvious that the Ghost is annoyed my mom let me bring Mazzie home with me. She and I are eating a late breakfast in the dining room, sharing a stack of pancakes, when we hear my parents arguing in the library.

Their voices never rise above heated whispers. "Who the hell is this girl? What the hell were you thinking?"

"She says she's her best friend. I didn't want her to go through this alone—"

"Her whole damn *family* is here. This is my father's funeral we're talking about." There is a long pause. "We should have just called her. We didn't need to bring her home for this."

"William, I cannot let my own daughter miss—"

"What?" I can see the Ghost's expression in my mind: arms crossed, tall condescension, the same attitude of angry contempt that he always takes any time my grandpa comes up. "My father wouldn't have cared, you know. Maybe Katie thinks so—and maybe you do, too—but that's only because he practically duped women for a living."

"Can you believe this shit?" It's Will, standing behind us. We've been listening so closely to my parents, we didn't hear him approach.

Mazzie stares. I can't blame her. Will looks almost the same as he did the last time I saw him: far too thin, teeth yellow and more crooked than ever. But today he wears a suit and tie, instead of his usual jeans and white undershirt. Thank God, his arms are covered. The suit is at least two sizes too big for him. And Will's head is shaved, which he hasn't done in years. With no hair, he looks more gaunt than I remember, his head oddly shaped, a thick black tattoo of a lightning bolt jutting down the middle of his skull, all the way from the top of his forehead down to where his neck meets his shirt.

He's obviously on heavy meds. He gazes at Mazzie, rocking back and forth ever so slightly in his shoes, like he's on a boat.

"Listen to them in there," he continues, his voice a low monotone. "The Ghost is glad he's dead, you know."

"Will," I say, "no he isn't." Every few moments, I have a flicker of imagination, when I picture what it would be like if Drew were here with me instead of Mazzie. Just thinking about it makes it hard for me to breathe.

"Sure he is. Effie was cool. And you know the Ghost, man. He can't stand anything that ain't square as a dictionary." Even though he's been gazing at her for a while, Will suddenly straightens up, as though he's noticing Mazzie for the first time. "Katie? Who the hell is this chick?"

"This is my roommate, Mazzie."

He stares at her. She stares back, uncertain. Her expression is familiar, and I realize it's the same look she gets when she wakes up from her nightmares. She's afraid.

My immediate family, plus Mazzie, are the only people at Effie's funeral. It is a brief, closed-casket ceremony. Effie wasn't religious, so we don't have to go to a church or anything before the cemetery. Mazzie sits uncomfortably beside me while I lean my head on my mom's shoulder and cry for the first time since I learned my grandpa died. Will sits beside my father. Both of them stare straight ahead, glaring into the distance.

Mazzie and I are in my basement later that evening, quizzing each other on vocabulary words for English class. We hear heavy footsteps upstairs in the living room, two pairs, and I know it's my dad and Will, pacing around each other. My mother's walk is soft, almost soundless.

Will starts shouting. "How can you be so cold, man? You don't know how to love anything, do you? You're like an android! You aren't his son. You aren't part of him. He didn't love you. How could he? You're a monster. See your horns? See them? They sprouted from your brain, your tail came right from your ass, you're transforming into the devil right before everyone's eyes!"

"Shh." I put down the card for "nonplussed." I reach across the table to grab Mazzie's arm.

"Will, I want you to calm down now. Sit down. Your grandfather was complicated. My relationship with him was complicated. I want you to take some deep breaths, now—"

"I don't care what you want! I'm not doing what you want—that's what you want me to do! You think I'm stupid, right? You think you can tell me to calm down and I'll just do what I'm told? Go look in the mirror. Look at your horns, growing out of your skull."

It's like silent, invisible lightning, electricity crackling through the air. I can't hear as much as I can *feel* my father losing his temper. It's a mistake to lose control in front of Will. My dad, more than anyone, should know that by now. But I guess everyone has their limits, and the Ghost did bury his father just a few hours earlier.

"Will, your grandfather was a philanderer. I barely knew him until I was nineteen years old. He left my mother alone with a young son and didn't come back until she was very ill. I was very angry with him. But he is my father, and I loved him. Look at me, son. Please look at me. Take one deep breath. Just one deep breath."

A stillness seems to fall over the house then. For several moments we don't hear anything else. And then we hear footsteps—the Ghost's I think—stepping delicately upstairs, and I let out my breath, hoping that the trouble has passed. Mazzie defines "nonplussed," then "archetype," then "colloquial."

When it's my turn, I can't come up with the definition for "archaic," even though I've seen the word a million times before. I have felt this calm before in our house. Where are my parents? What is my brother doing?

"Katie. Are you defective? The word is 'archaic.'"

There is a flurry of light footsteps, my mother pattering across the floor, coming down the stairs so quickly that she slips on her way down, clutching the banister as she slides the last few steps and then stumbles over to us, car keys in her hand. Oh God, I've seen this face before—it's a wonder she isn't covered in blood already—and she grabs both of us, me by the sleeve, Mazzie by the neck of her shirt, and half hisses, half sobs, *"Go, girls, go, go, go!"* She pushes us in our bare feet toward the back door, pushes us through the backyard as splinters of bark and leaf mulch stick to the soles of our feet, her voice a little louder, saying, *"Hurry, babies, please hurry,"* until we get to the car and Mazzie jumps into the backseat and I get in the front beside my mother and stare up at the back of the house and can't even scream at what I see.

Will and my dad are in the guest room—the only room in the house with a lock on the door. The lights are on, the shades are up, and in the clear night we can see everything so perfectly: my brother pacing in circles, the Ghost standing in a corner, crying, begging. My brother holds a handgun, which he's pointing at himself, then at the Ghost, back and forth like he's not sure whom he wants to hurt more. He's screaming at my dad. When he lifts both arms, I see there's a screwdriver in his other hand. He probably used it to pry open the lock on the gun cabinet.

My mother tries to call 911 on her cell phone. She can't stop shaking or crying, she keeps pressing the wrong numbers, and while Mazzie huddles in the backseat, her body curled into a tiny ball like she wants to disappear, I take the phone from my mom and say, "Mommy, please go, please drive away." I dial 911 myself. My mother sobs while I'm trying to talk to dispatch, to give them our address, and finally she gets the car into reverse and backs down the driveway too fast with the lights off. We drive around the corner and sit at the first stop sign we come to, and my mother and I punch the dashboard and scream and claw at each other, and I know neither of us has ever felt so scared and helpless, and all the time in the back of my mind I know that we can't be silent for even a moment, scared to death of what sound might break through the darkness.

Will gives up the loaded gun to the police, who put him in handcuffs so tight that he yelps. As they're taking him out of the house, I run past him toward my father and put my arms around my daddy and sob into his beating chest while he holds me, then my mother with her arms around both of us, holding on to each other, Will staring as all the neighbors venture onto their porches to watch—four state police cars and two ambulances with lights all ablaze at ten o'clock at night—while Mazzie stays in the backseat of our car, staring at my family, taking it all in.

They don't take him right away. Once he's in handcuffs, my parents go to him. They try to speak to him, but he refuses to look at them.

"Katie!" he screams. I'm standing near the car, close to Mazzie, glaring at our neighbors. I want to scream at them to get back inside their shitty houses and just leave us alone. There are dozens of them now, porch lights on, standing on the street with their dumb mouths hanging open like they're watching a parade.

"Katie, come here," Will pleads. "Come here, Katie. Please come over here."

His pupils are big, flashing like an animal's beneath all the lights, no discernable color to his eyes but black and white and lightning bolts of red. Sweat drips from his face like he's just run a marathon. "I'll call you, Katie. Okay? I'll call you as soon as I can."

I shake my head. "Don't you ever call me again."

"Katie—Katie, no! That's what they want, Katie."

"I don't care." I'm crying again. I try to hit him and kick him; I want to hit him so hard that I kill him, but the Ghost and my mom and two of the policemen grab me and hold me back as soon as I begin to move. "I wish you would die," I say. The words come out with spit. "I hope you die in jail."

"Katie—don't you understand? That's what they want,

you're doing just what they want you to do. They sent you away to tear us apart, they want you to stop loving me. Katie it's me—it's *me,* Katie. I love you. You're my sister, Katie. Please, you're all I've got." He stares at me, breathless. "*Please.* Don't you understand that someone has to stop him?"

"No." I shake my head. I struggle in the grip of my parents and the cops. "He's not doing anything. You're doing it. You did all of it." I relax a little bit. "They love us. Everything would have been fine, but you got sick and you ruined everything," I say. And then I turn to our neighbors and raise my voice and scream, "It's your fault too! You did this to him too—just leave us alone!"

"Katie," the Ghost says, still holding me tightly, "shhh. It's okay, baby. Calm down. Go on inside now."

But before I go, I turn to look at Will one last time. "Don't call me. I won't be there."

And I turn my back on him. He screams while the police put him in the car and take him away. Our mom can't look; she goes inside and sits on the love seat in the foyer and puts her head between her knees and her fingers in her ears.

But the Ghost goes with him. On the same day that he buried his own father, his son almost killed him. But instead of falling apart, like any normal person would do, the Ghost goes into the house to get his car keys, gives my mother a kiss on the top of her head—she doesn't even look up—and lights a cigarette as he gets into his car, following my brother to the police station, to make sure things go the way they should.

The next morning I shuffle downstairs late, my bathrobe dragging on the floor while my parents' cat chases at its loose threads on the stairs. My parents' house has grandeur: the banister is thick and long and curved at just the right angle for sliding down, like they do in the movies. There are high ceilings, endless sunken rooms that make the structure more of a shell than a house, each few steps into the next room giving you the feeling of going deeper inside, and for a while it felt okay, for years it felt okay, until it started to seem like if you weren't careful, you'd never be able to find your way out again.

The Ghost sits at the table in the dining room, doing a crossword puzzle, drinking coffee that has undoubtedly been rewarmed in the microwave, holding a cigarette between his teeth. To look at him, you would think it was just another normal day.

"Where's Mazzie?" he asks without looking up from his puzzle.

"Upstairs. Still asleep."

He nods, still not looking at me. "She seems like a nice girl. I hope you bring her home with you more often."

"Well, after the fun we've had this weekend, I'm sure she can't wait to come back."

Finally, the Ghost looks at me. "Your brother won't come back this time," he tells me.

"I know that."

"Do you?" He studies me. "I know you're angry with him. Trust me, I know how it feels to be angry with someone you love. But Katie, when that anger goes away, you're going to love him again."

I shake my head. "No. Not after last night."

"You will. You'll love him because he's your brother, I know. But you can't talk to him. You have to let him go now. He's only going to get worse."

I've been hearing the same thing for years, always presented as a possibility rather than a definite. But now it seems certain that Will is never going to be my big brother again. At one point, years ago, somebody reached out and unlocked the cellar door in his head, and there he was: forever unhinged.

When I don't say anything, the Ghost puts down his crossword puzzle. "Come here."

I sit in his lap. He gives me a hug. I put my head on his shoulder and recognize the smell that is uniquely his. It occurs to me that he almost never says my brother's name out loud.

Had he been here at all, all these years, instead of working every day, the Ghost might have been a really great dad. I think it's better that I don't know him that well. Better not to really know what I'm missing and just swim away.

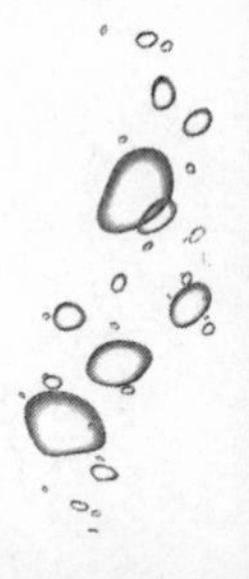

chapter 9

It's a long, silent ride back to school the following morning. All four of us go together: the Ghost, my mom, Mazzie, and me.

Before she goes inside, leaving me alone with my parents, Mazzie gives my mom a hug. She says to my dad, "I'm sorry about your father, Dr. Kitrell."

"Thank you," the Ghost says. He hesitates. "I'm so sorry about the weekend."

Mazzie only shrugs. "Shit happens. Right, sir?"

For once in his life, my father is speechless. Then—for the first time in as long as I can remember—he laughs.

I don't know what to say to Mazzie. How does someone apologize for something like this? For the rest of the afternoon, we continue to study vocab words on flash cards, quizzing each other. The only thing that's different from any other Sunday evening is that Mazzie is nicer than usual.

When Drew knocks at the window, interrupting me as I struggle to recall the definition for "phylogeny," I can tell

Mazzie and I are both grateful for the distraction. I open the window and give him a hand as he climbs in.

"What's going on?" he demands. "I couldn't find you, and then yesterday, Mrs. Martin finally told me your grandpa died." He glances at Mazzie, almost glaring at her. "The two of you went home? For the funeral?"

"My mom showed up out of nowhere, Drew. We had to hurry. It was a really emotional weekend, and I wanted to call you but I was so upset—"

"We've been dating for a *year,* Katie, and I've never even met your parents. I can't believe you would take—instead of—"

"I'm sorry, okay? It's a four-hour drive, Drew. *I* barely see my parents. Don't be mad, please—"

"I can't believe what a jerk you're being," Mazzie interrupts, startling us both.

Drew stares at her. His jaw drops. "Are you talking about me?"

"No, I'm talking about your mother. Of course I'm talking about you. Your *girlfriend* has to pack up and leave without any notice because her grandpa died, and she has a weekend that, let me tell you, was not pleasant in any sense of the word. And you come climbing in the window like a big angry giant and yell at her because she didn't think to bring you instead of me. Maybe she didn't want to bring you, Drew. Maybe she didn't think that her grandpa's funeral was the right time to play get-to-know-you with her boyfriend and her family." She whips "phylogeny" at him, nicking him on the forehead. "What would Jesus think of how you're acting, Drew?"

There is a long pause in which I know I cannot make eye contact with Mazzie without bursting out laughing.

"Oh, God," Drew says, "you're right." He puts his arms around me. "I'm so sorry, Katie. I'm acting so selfish."

As I look over Drew's shoulder, I can see Mazzie making a series of hand gestures in his direction, each one a little more obscene.

"I'll be here for you," he whispers.

I nod, unable to suppress my laughter, which I pretend is a sob. I bury my face in his shoulder and hold him tight.

A few weeks later, just after two in the morning, the phone rings in our bedroom. Mazzie and I both sit up; I wonder if she isn't sleeping well, either.

I've turned our answering machine off so that Will can't leave messages while I'm in class. The phone keeps ringing and ringing. Even though the volume is set to low, each ring feels like a smack that could startle the whole dorm awake.

I finally pick it up with every intention of hanging up immediately, but before I can put down the receiver, I hear an automated voice asking, "Will you accept a collect call from . . ." and then Will's voice, desperate, saying, "Please pick up, Katie, please talk to me."

I'm so tired that I can't think straight. I feel myself trembling at the sound of his voice. Where is he? Is he safe? Are they taking care of him? Why is he awake in the middle of the night?

Mazzie stands behind me. She puts her hand over mine on the receiver, and together we hang up on my brother.

The same weekend, Lindsey has a birthday party at her house for Estella. I feel exhausted from the week. Aside from everything else that's going on, swimming season is going to start in a few weeks, which means longer practices and less sleep. On Saturday morning, during a flip turn, I smack my big toe against the gutter and crack my toenail in half. A ribbon of blood dissolves in the water behind me as I swim to the opposite end, not realizing what has happened until Solinger is blowing hard on his whistle and Drew is wading over to me, his arms outstretched to pick me up and lead me to the edge.

The last place I want to be is at a party, but there's no getting out of it. When I tell Estella that my grandpa just died and I'm tired and sad and just not in the mood, she presses her lips together and says, "I didn't kill him, Katie. You're coming." When I don't say anything, her expression softens a twinge. "It will make you feel better to be around your friends," she assures me. "You'll see."

By ten o'clock, all I want to do is sleep. Drew holds my hand and takes me up to bed, on Lindsey's third floor, where there's one big room set up. It's like how I'd picture a nineteenth-century orphanage: there are eight twin beds, all made up with worn, matching sheets and blankets, in a row against the wall; a big bathroom; and bookshelves filled with all of Lindsey's and her sisters' old books. There are the complete Nancy Drew and Doctor Seuss series, and Woodsdale Academy yearbooks going all the way back to the eighties.

Drew and I go to sleep together in one of the twin beds, wearing nothing but our underwear. Mazzie is in the room with us, a few beds over, her nightstand light burning while she reads *Madame Bovary* for our women's lit class, and while I'm lying on my side trying to fall asleep, I focus on her little face, her jaw moving frantically back and forth, mouthing the words as she reads, her narrow shoulders hunched against a pillow, tiny hands holding the book up and far away from her face, almost out of the light.

Every time she goes to turn the page she takes a quick look at me, like she's checking to see if I'm asleep or not. I know for sure I'm awake because I can feel Drew's breath on the back of my neck. One of his hands is slung over my waist, his elbow digging into my hip.

I don't remember finally falling asleep, but when I wake up, in a blink, I'm on the floor and Mazzie is kneeling next to me with a towel in her lap, trying to fit her arms under my shoulders. At first I'm sure it's a dream because she isn't saying anything and all the lights are off except the bathroom light, which wasn't on when we went to bed. I can hear water running. It's the shower. Mazzie is in her underwear: a little white tank top stretched over her breasts, which are almost nothing; baggy white underpants; and white athletic socks. She isn't strong enough to pick me up, but she does it anyway, falling back onto her butt a few times until she finally props me up against the wall and puts the towel in my lap. I realize I'm all wet. My thighs are sticking together. Nothing makes sense.

"What's going on? What happened?" I whisper. My eyes burn as I blink, trying to get them adjusted to the dim lighting. Drew is still asleep. Mazzie has replaced my body with a pillow, and he doesn't seem to notice any difference. She shakes her head and puts a finger to her lips.

"It's okay," she mouths, and takes my hand to pull me up, holding the towel around my waist with her other hand. We go into the bathroom and shut the door. I notice that she's left another towel on the floor where I was lying.

"What's going on?" I ask again, looking down at my legs. My underwear is all wet. There's a smell.

She looks up at me. "You had a nightmare."

I'm still so confused. "Oh. Okay. Why am I all wet?"

"You were scared. You got out of bed."

"Why am I all wet?"

"Katie . . . you peed the bed. It's okay."

Oh, my God. "Oh, my God. Oh, shit." I realize that I have to pee, *now,* badly. I take off my underwear and sit down on the toilet, naked. Mazzie looks away. I'm so embarrassed that I start crying. I feel so dizzy that I have to lean forward and put my head against my knees. When I sit up, I ask, "Does Drew know? Did he wake up?"

"No. Don't worry, Katie, I'm not going to tell him. He won't find out."

Oh, shit. *Shit.* "What do you mean, he won't find out?" I'm crying so hard that I'm shaking. I'm so thirsty. "Did I pee all over him?"

"No. Be quiet, Katie. You'll wake him up."

"What happened, then? Did I pee on the floor?" I can't believe this. I haven't peed the bed since I was a little kid.

"No. You got into bed with me."

I don't understand. "I got into your bed? While I was sleeping?"

She nods, still looking away.

"Why would I do that?"

"I don't know. You wanted to."

"Did I pee in your bed?"

"Yes."

". . ."

". . ."

"I'm so sorry, Mazzie."

"It's okay, Katie. Get in the shower."

"Are you going to tell everybody?"

"I'm not going to tell anyone, Katie. Nobody has to know."

She's still in the bathroom with me, taking off her clothes now, and I realize that she's all wet, too. I wait for her to shower before I get in myself. When the water hits my face, it's too much. I lean over and gag into the drain, but nothing comes up. I have to sit down. The water hits me right on my stomach. Mazzie throws me a washcloth over the shower door. "I'm going to get the sheets off the bed," she says, wrapping herself in a clean towel. "I'll be right back." She shuts the door behind her.

We go down to the laundry room together, finally, both of us carrying an armload of dirty towels and sheets and our wet underwear. We're wearing nothing but oversized T-shirts, but at least we're clean.

Neither of us has any idea how to operate a washing machine. We stand in front of it, gazing at the control dial, contemplating the settings. I never imagined it could be so complicated.

"I think we should use hot water," she finally says.

"Why?"

"To rinse out any stains."

"I think you're supposed to use bleach for that."

"I don't think you can put whites and colors in together."

"Why not?"

"I think they bleed."

"Doesn't this thing have any freaking *directions*?" It does, underneath the lid. We do the sheets first, adding half a bottle of bleach for good measure. We watch the washer fill up with hot water and start running. Mazzie finds a garbage bag and stuffs the towels inside, then puts them behind a stack of boxes so nobody will find them before we get a chance to wash them. I sit on the washing machine and watch her pattering around, getting the bottoms of her feet black with basement dirt. She's wearing one of my Woodsdale Swimming T-shirts. It's about two sizes too big for her, and on the back somebody—probably Lindsey—has written *Club 813* in uneven bubble letters with white permanent marker. Lindsey's street address is 813; lately we've been writing it on everything, pretending we think it's a big joke, but deep down I know we all feel like we're genuinely part of an exclusive club. Mazzie is so petite, so skinny, that when she's bent over I can see each of her narrow ribs outlined beneath the fabric.

"How long do you think those are going to take?" She means the sheets.

"I don't know. I have no idea. Five minutes? Maybe ten?"

"Do you think we should wait here?"

"I guess so." I make some room for her on the washer. "You can sit up here with me."

We can feel the washer vibrating beneath us. Mazzie reaches up and turns out the light so it's like we're not even there.

"When I was a baby," I say, "my mom used to put my car seat on top of the washing machine when I wouldn't fall asleep. She says the vibration calmed me down."

Mazzie leans her head on my shoulder. "Do you feel better now?"

"I guess. I have to put some sheets back on the bed before anybody wakes up."

"I'll do it." Then she asks, "What was your nightmare about?"

I shake my head. "I don't remember."

"Not at all? You were trying to say something. You seemed so scared when you woke me up . . ."

In the dark, I think Mazzie might be crying.

"Mazzie," I say, closing my eyes even though it's already dark. "You're my best friend. You can talk to me, you know?"

I can feel her tense up. She doesn't say anything for a long time. The washing machine switches cycles underneath us.

We sit there for what feels like forever. I wonder what time it is. I am so thirsty that it's getting hard to swallow. Everything is warm. After a long time the washer gets louder, suddenly, and comes to a halt, and we relax against each other. Even my toes uncurl. I hadn't realized I was so tense.

She says, "You have to understand, Katie. It isn't personal. There are some things I'll never tell anyone."

"But you can trust me. You know that."

She reaches up and pulls the light cord. We squint at each other, the room suddenly bright. She looks pale and impossibly tired beneath the bare lightbulb, half moons of darkness beneath her eyes. "I don't know how you remember all these little details you're always talking about," she says. She almost sounds angry.

"What do you mean?"

"I mean, the way your mom used to put your car seat on top of the washing machine to get you to fall asleep. All the stories you tell, about when you lived in the woods and you'd help your mom make bread or pick blueberries or all those other happy things? I bet you remember all of it, don't you?"

We are both so silent for a moment, I can hear the house settling above us. "Yeah," I admit. "I remember everything.

But only because I don't want to forget the way things were, before my brother got sick. I want to remember when we were a family—"

"I *never* had a family. Not like yours. My parents both worked. Your father disappeared, slowly. You think it's funny to call him the Ghost, don't you? My parents were *always* ghosts." Her eyes are red. She won't look at me. "And now my mother isn't anything. She worked her whole life and went to school and did everything she knew how to do to succeed—my dad, too—and now my mom is just plain dead." She rubs the bottom of her nose, which is running all over the place. "And you know the worst part about all of it?"

I can barely force the word out. "What?"

"I'm going to do exactly what they did. Go to school, be a surgeon, work so hard that I don't have time for anything else." She shrugs. "I don't know any other way to be."

Before I can respond, she stands up and says, "We should put these sheets in the dryer. It's going to be morning soon."

The sheets don't look quite right to me, but at least they're clean. We sit on the dryer together, silent for a long time.

Finally, I can't stop myself. Maybe it's just morbid curiosity, but I don't think so. I remember how it felt when I told her about Will. I remember how good it felt to finally tell *someone*. "Mazzie," I press, "how did your mom die?"

She pulls her knees to her chest. Staring at the lightbulb, she says, "It doesn't matter how she died. She's dead, Katie. She's never coming back."

I want her to trust me, to spill herself into me the way I have for her. But I know her well enough to know that if I push any more, she'll only run away. I guess everybody deserves to have their own secrets, if they really want them that badly.

When we finally get back to the third floor (it takes the sheets *forever* to dry), I help her put clean sheets on her bed, in the dark. We go into the bathroom and shut the door, and sit on the edge of the tub and run warm water over our feet, watching dirt swirl down the drain, and then we wipe our feet against the bathmat and put on our clean underwear and go back to bed. It's starting to get light outside.

I have to rearrange myself against Drew so that he won't know I've been gone. It takes a few minutes. I wiggle myself against him and pull both of his arms around me. While I'm trying to get comfortable he gives a little moan in his sleep and wakes up a little bit.

Maybe he can tell something's different. He blinks in the almost-dark, confused. "Katie? Are you awake?" By now the sun is really beginning to come up, light slowly filling the room.

When I don't answer, he gives me a little shake. "Hey, Katie. You all right?"

"Drew," I whisper, almost hoarse from thirst, "will you *please, please, please* get me a glass of water? I'm so thirsty."

"Of course, baby." He strokes my hair. He frowns. "Your hair is wet."

"I was hot," I lie. "I splashed water on my face in the bathroom, and I got some in my hair."

"Are you still hot? Do you want me to open a window?"

"Sure. That would be nice."

He gives me a gentle kiss on the cheek. His breath is bad. "Did you get a good night's sleep?"

I nod.

"I bet you feel so much better now."

"Yes. Drew?"

"What is it, baby?"

"Will you open the window and get me some water?"

Once he goes downstairs, I turn to look at Mazzie. I know that she's still awake from the way she's breathing. She has her back turned to me. I get up and stand over her, just watching, until she finally opens her eyes and says, "What is it?"

I sit on the edge of her bed. "I just wanted to, you know, say thank you."

"No problem."

I don't move. She opens her eyes again. "*What,* Katie?"

"I don't know."

"Well, when you figure it out, tell me then. I'm trying to sleep."

"Sorry." I get into my own bed, waiting for Drew to come back with my water. I want to say more to her, but I know she'll only be annoyed. So all I say is, "Good night, Mazzie."

"Good night, asshole. Try not to pee the bed again."

Drew comes back with a coffee mug full of water and sits down beside me, giving me a shake. "Here you go. I'm up. I'm going home."

"Thank you."

"No problem. Hey, do you want to come to church with me later?"

Do I want to go to church with him? "No. Definitely not."

"All right. Don't come crying to me when you're burning in hell." He acts like he's only kidding, but we both know better.

"Don't worry, I won't."

He leans over and kisses my forehead. "I'll call you, sweet pea."

I do my best to smile. "I'll be counting the minutes."

He slams the door on his way out. I can hear his loafers pounding down the stairs, threatening to wake the whole house. Then it's quiet again. I'm so tired that my eyes are burning; maybe from thirst, too. I drink my water, then go to the bathroom and fill it up three more times before I start to feel better. Once I'm finally in bed again, I push a pillow between my legs and lay facing Mazzie, her back still turned to me.

I'm almost asleep when she says, "So Drew thinks you're going to hell, does he?"

"Yes." We're both so sleepy that our voices are barely more than murmurs. "He thinks you're going to hell too."

She doesn't say anything for a while, and my eyes begin to flutter shut. Then, just as I'm slipping into sleep, she says, "If we both end up in hell, at least we can still be roommates."

I smile. "Mmm-hmm."

"Doesn't sound so bad," she murmurs. And then she's out. I lay there for a while, listening to the sound of her breath, and finally fall asleep to the sound of tooth grinding against tooth through a thin layer of plastic, like a purr that I can feel in my whole body.

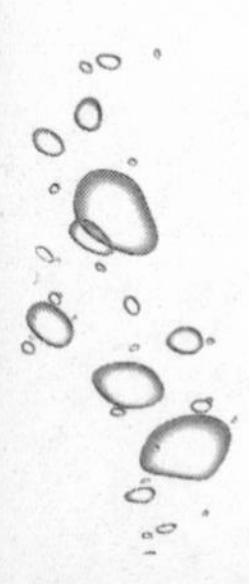

chapter 10

My parents don't protest at first when I tell them I'm not coming home for winter break. My mom is quiet on the phone, more quiet than usual, but I don't think much of it. A few days later, though, I get another call from the Ghost.

When I answer my phone, his receptionist says, "Please hold the line for Dr. Kitrell."

It's, like, five o'clock in the morning. If there were some kind of pill to let people go without sleep, the Ghost would be the first in line so he could work around the clock.

After a few seconds of Kenny G, my dad says, "Your mother is upset. She wants you to come home for Christmas."

"Dad, we talked about this, like, seventy-two hours ago and—"

"Just *Christmas*," he says. "Christmas Eve and Christmas Day. You don't understand what it means to her, Kathryn." I hear him take a swallow of something—I'm sure it's coffee. "She doesn't want a Christmas without children."

I know he must be serious; the Ghost is never this open.

I glance at Mazzie, pretending to be asleep in bed, her heavy Calc II textbook open on her chest.

"I take it my brother won't be home?"

"No. Not this year."

So I find myself sitting alone at the top of my parents' stairs on Christmas morning. Once the Ghost has made coffee, I'm allowed to come down and start opening my presents.

All the ornaments on our tree are handmade, either by me or Will or our mom. There are photos of us from elementary school glued to glittered plastic seashells, candy canes made from red and white pipe cleaners, garlands of old buttons and artificial pearls strung together on fishing line.

Mostly I get clothes, along with a new swimming bag (which I can't use because it isn't Woodsdale colors, but I don't mention that to my parents) and a new laptop and a whole stack of books with titles like *ACCEPTED! How to Get into Your Dream School* and *SAT Prep for the Advanced Student*.

On the other side of the tree, there is a small stack of presents that I know are for Will. My parents will visit him later in the day. I don't even bother asking; I know they won't let me come with them. Anyway, I don't want to see him.

Back at school, I give Mazzie a bag of gifts that my parents bought her.

"How thoughtful of them," she says, opening a box containing a sweater identical to mine, except for its monogram. Her voice is laced with saccharine sarcasm. "I should send your mother a nice thank-you card." She pulls the sweater over her head. "Did you explain to your parents that I'm a Buddhist? Do they understand I don't celebrate Christmas?"

I shake my head. "They'd already bought the presents."

She opens another package. It's a pair of pink footie pj's, patterned with tiny kittens playing with balls of yarn.

She looks at my own stack of presents, piled on my desk. "You got exactly the same pair."

"I know. I think she got us two of everything."

The collect calls continue, once a week, every Wednesday morning between two and three.

For over a month I stay up late on Tuesday nights, waiting for them. I don't know why. And every time the phone rings, I pick it up and listen to the same recording: "Will you accept the charges for a collect call from . . ." and then Will's voice, his message always similar.

"Katie, please talk to me. It's horrible in here, Katie, I need to talk to you. They're going to get you next, Katie, I can't—" *Beep.* He always gets cut off before he has a chance to finish.

One night the phone doesn't ring. I wait up until almost four in the morning, before I finally pass out against my will. When I get back from school the next day, I pick up the phone to call Drew. There's no dial tone. Mazzie has unplugged the phone.

I imagine my brother, trying to call, only to receive a message that my number has been disconnected or is not in service at the moment or whatever it might have said.

I plug the phone back into the wall and stand back, staring at it, willing it to ring.

But it doesn't. And even though I check and double check to make sure it's plugged in, it doesn't ring the following Wednesday morning, or the Wednesday after that, or the one after that. But I still lie awake on those nights—I don't know why, exactly—waiting, imagining my brother's sunken face, part of me hoping that he's staring at his own telephone miles away, the invisible thread between us still connected no matter what I do, tugging at me sometimes so hard that my whole body aches.

There are nightmares almost every night now. Terror winding across a field and down a highway, flattening itself like a tapeworm to wriggle through cracks in the windows, snaking under my covers, up my leg in a ribbon of slime and into my ear. Trying to wake myself up has become like trying to crawl up a down escalator on all fours. After almost two months without any calls from Will, when I can't stand the nightmares anymore, I get in the habit of staying awake and watching Mazzie. Since the collect calls from Will started, she sleeps in my bed most nights. She is like a doll, limp and flat, her face flawless and seeming to invite bright red circles of color drawn in lipstick on her cheeks, or bright plastic barrettes in her hair, the low *clackety-clack* of her jaw keeping time with the creeping of the lazy moon outside.

Even though I don't know how Mazzie's mother died, I wonder how it was ever a mystery to me that she is all alone in the world. Watching her sleep, it's obvious that she is a kind of orphan. Even though we're both almost grown-ups, Mazzie will probably look like a child forever. Maybe I will too. We are both so incomplete; it's like we were made to find each other someday. Every other friend I've had seems inconsequential compared to her.

Swimming season is brutal this year. My muscles ache all the time. We're well on our way to winning the OVACs, which wouldn't be happening if it weren't for me. I get up before the sun rises every day. When I am too tired to pull the straps up on my bathing suit, I let Mazzie do it for me. I lean against the bed while Mazzie sits on it, my head between her legs, letting my eyes flutter closed while she brushes my hair, and it's moments like these when I wonder what I will ever do without her once our time here is up.

For Drew, who is approaching the end of his senior year, his time *is* almost up. He gets into every school he applies to: Harvard, the University of Virginia, Rice, Notre Dame, and West Virginia University (his safety school). I know he wants to go to Harvard more than anything. The only problem he's got is that his mom—who is a nurse—doesn't have any way to pay for it. They've offered him a pretty substantial need-based scholarship, but it still isn't nearly enough. If he goes anyway, he'll be up to his eyeballs in student loan debt by the time he graduates.

We're sitting in his car, which is parked on a remote hillside in Oglebay Park. It's a few weeks before prom. I'm going back to Yale for the summer, and Drew is going to volunteer for Habitat for Humanity until late August, so he'll barely be able to visit on the weekends.

"I've been thinking a lot," he begins, and I know what's coming. I've understood for a while that this conversation is inevitable. And I've even tried to convince myself that I'm all right with it—but sitting here beside him, all of a sudden it's clear that I'm *not* all right.

I want to say, "Drew, it's okay, I understand. You're going to Harvard, and I'll still be here," but my eyes are getting wet; I can't help it after almost two years with him. Before I can stop myself, I start to panic. What will I do without Drew? He's always been so sweet to me. He's been my biggest swimming supporter, a better coach than Solinger in lots of ways. And he's so *genuine*. It's the thing about him that I love the most, even though it drives me crazy sometimes. So many people around us are phony, preoccupied with grades or their social lives and who's dating whom—with Drew, I always know that what he's feeling is real. I always know I can depend on him.

Drew watches me cry. He seems deeply interested in my emotion. "Katie," he says, so softly that I almost can't hear him.

I wipe my nose on my sleeve. I'm a mess. "What?"

"I talked with Dr. Waugh about some of my options," he says. In addition to being the admissions director, Dr. Waugh also functions as the college admissions counselor. "She had some interesting ideas."

I blink at him. "Like what?"

"She suggested I talk with the director of Habitat, which I did." He starts to smile. "And here's what I can do. If I delay college for a year and volunteer for them instead, they'll give me a grant for Harvard."

I'm stunned. I clap a hand to my mouth. "That's fantastic! Drew, I'm so happy for you!"

He nods. "I knew you would be. So, you know they're building homes all over the country, right?"

We're back to where we started. I can feel myself deflating a little. "Right."

"I don't have to go to any of those. I can stay right here in the Ohio Valley. We've got more than enough homeless." His grin is huge. "Isn't that wonderful?"

I don't know what to say. I'm happy, sure—but I'd been expecting us to break up, or at least agree that we'd have to break up at the end of the year—and now not only are we staying together, but surely everyone—Estella, Lindsey, and Grace and all of her nasty ilk—is going to think that a big part of why Drew's staying is because of me. Which, I guess, it kind of is. I'm actually surprised by how good—how *relieved*—I feel.

We start kissing, and immediately things go from warm to hot to heavy; we climb into the backseat and I unbutton the shirt of my uniform while Drew puts down the seats with two flicks of his wrist, like he's done so many times before.

I feel like I'm kissing him for the first time again, except now it's better, because I know we love each other. And God, he's beautiful. I can never decide where to touch him, because everywhere feels so good: his curly hair, which changes shades from dishwater blond to almost white, depending on the season; his sinewy muscles; his rippled tummy with that perfect *V* of definition at his hips.

We're both in our underwear, pieces of our uniforms scattered all over the backseat. Drew is still wearing his tie, which I grab and tug so that he falls on top of me.

We've never gone this far before, but I'm certain this is *it*. He doesn't seem like he wants to wait, and I know I don't.

"Katie," he breathes, panting through his open mouth, "wait, Katie, we should talk about this first."

He pulls away and leans against the opposite window, his body leaving a smear in the fog that has accumulated on the glass. "Katie, I love you."

"I love you, too, Drew." I crawl toward him. "I'm ready for this."

He's still panting. He seems genuinely torn.

"We can't do it—not all the way." *Pant, pant, pant.* "I told you I made a promise," *pant,* "to God."

"You have got to be kidding me," I mutter.

"No, I'm not, but," *pant, pant, pant*—his face is white and sweaty—"I'm ready to make love in a different way."

"Okay. How?"

He moves toward me and gives me a long kiss. He takes my hand and moves it down his body until I'm touching him so that his eyes close. "Katie," he says, looking at me gravely, as though God himself is supervising us from the front seat, "I'm ready for you to start giving me blow jobs."

As a senior prefect, Stetson McClure occasionally acts as a class supervisor when one of our teachers is out sick. So, when my chem professor breaks his leg in a bicycling accident a few weeks before school ends, my class gets Stetson for the whole week.

He doesn't even notice that I'm in the class at first. On his first day, he strolls to the blackboard and writes, *LESSON PLAN: HAVE FUN AND DON'T BLOW ANYTHING UP,* and then he takes a seat in our professor's cushy chair and proceeds to lean back and take a light nap for the remaining fifty minutes.

But later that week, as I'm sitting with my head down against my open book, my eyes closed, I hear someone clearing his throat beside me. When I look up, there's Stetson.

"We need to talk, Katie," he says.

We go into the deserted hallway. I'm almost sure it's the first time Stetson has ever called me by my name.

"You don't look good," he begins. "You look like you haven't slept in weeks. Have you?"

"I was trying to," I say. "But somebody interrupted me."

He shrugs, giving me an easy smirk. "It's my responsibility to make sure nobody misuses their class time. Okay—let me get to the point—I need you to talk to Estella for me."

The last time I saw Estella, earlier in the day in English class, she had thrown a balled-up piece of paper at my head while our professor had his back turned. When I opened it, I saw that she'd written, *If you don't have sex soon, your lady parts are going to grow shut.* Beneath the words, there was an illustration. I never should have told her and Lindsey about my experience with Drew in his car a few weeks earlier. But I mean, really—how could I *not* have told them? It was all just so . . . weird.

"Estella isn't going to listen to me," I tell Stetson. She and Jeremy Chase are still going out, and Drew has told me Stetson is sick about it. "You should ask Lindsey to talk to her."

"I already asked. She said no."

"Stetson?" I figure since she isn't even speaking to him, I've got nothing to lose. "Can I ask you a question? What's so great about Estella, anyway?"

He leans against the wall and raises one eyebrow at me. The look alone is enough to make my knees buckle. "Do I detect a hint of resentment, Captain Kitrell?"

I shake my head. "It's more like confusion. Estella is . . . well, *you* know."

"I don't. Please illuminate."

"She's a bitch," I blurt.

Stetson touches the tip of his tongue to his upper lip, grinning. "Katie, haven't two years of gender studies taught you anything?" He recites one of Dr. George's favorite feminist maxims, which has been written at the top of the chalkboard for as long as I've been at Woodsdale: "Women who degrade other women are a male-dominated society's most powerful tool for continued oppression."

"She's a bitch," I repeat, "and you know it. She broke up with you because of a *minor injury*." I don't think it's necessary to mention that, for at least a few months before she dumped Stetson, Estella was already seeing Jeremy on the side.

Stetson only shrugs. "The girl likes to get what she wants. It's one of the things I admire about her. Just because she isn't timid or quiet and says what's on her mind doesn't make her a bitch. And even if it does"—he grins at me again—"she's the most perfect-looking girl I've ever seen."

When I don't say anything, he says, "Come on, Katie. You can admit it. If you could trade places with a girl like that, you'd do it in a second. Everything that people want, Estella's got." And he takes me by the wrist and presses a note into my palm. "Make sure she gets this, okay?" He leans a little closer, his voice almost a whisper. "By the way, I know all about you and Drew. He tells me everything, you know."

I close my fist over the note. "What do you know?"

"Everything." He holds my gaze, tonguing the side of his mouth real slow, so I can't miss what he's doing. "You're a bad girl, Katie."

A few days after I give the note to Estella, I notice her and Stetson talking in the hallway for the first time all year. Her arms are crossed, chin pointed toward the ceiling. I told him he wouldn't get anywhere with her.

Estella, Lindsey, Mazzie, and I have Russian lit together this year. Aside from gender studies, which I mostly like because of Dr. "Please Call Me Evan" George, our lit courses are my favorite classes. Sometimes, when I'm reading a really interesting book or short story, it's the only time outside the water when my mind can focus on something without all my other, noisy thoughts bursting through.

We are spending the last part of the year studying Chekhov, starting with one of his first plays, *The Bear,* and ending with *The Cherry Orchard.*

Estella, who is usually chatty to the point of distraction throughout class, sits down before the bell without a word to me or Mazzie. The four of us are in the back two rows, where we can easily pass notes back and forth undetected by our teacher. Dr. Silva is a brilliant, elderly woman who has been teaching at Woodsdale for something like fifty years. She has a humpback and a thick Russian accent. She doesn't hear that well anymore, but *man* can she deconstruct literature.

Estella is quiet throughout the beginning of the lecture.

"Now you spleet into pairs and finish ze worksheet," Dr. Silva says.

Behind me, in a low voice, Estella mutters to Dr. Silva, "Why don't you come back here and read me a story, Grandma?" Then she says, to Lindsey, "I haven't read any of this crap yet, so you're going to have to do all the work, okay?" And as she turns her chair to face Lindsey, she kicks me in the shin so hard that it brings tears to my eyes.

Mazzie notices. She gives me a questioning look. I only shake my head, my whole body tensing, and we put our heads close together and pretend to start the worksheet.

After a few minutes, Estella raises her voice pointedly in my direction. "Hey, Linds," she says, "did you know that I'm a bitch?"

"Yes," Lindsey says. She probably doesn't even look up from the worksheet.

I can feel my eyes stinging as I try to stare straight ahead, my gaze fixed on Dr. Silva's hump as she copies a Chekhov quote onto the chalkboard in her shaky cursive handwriting.

"Listen to me," Estella snaps. "Guess who I talked to today?"

"Stetson," Lindsey murmurs, still probably not looking up. Even though I'm staring forward I can imagine her looking bored, used to Estella and all the drama that comes with being her friend. And Stetson did tell me that he'd tried talking to Lindsey about Estella first.

"That's right." She raises her voice just a little higher. From the corner of my eye, I see Mazzie glancing at me, her mouth slightly open, unsure of what to do.

"He wants to take me to the prom," Estella continues. "He told me he's still in *love* with me. Can you believe that?"

"Mmm-hmm."

"Of course I told him I can't go, since things are getting serious with me and Jeremy. But I'm still glad we talked. He had *sooooo* many interesting things to tell me."

Lindsey, sighing deeply, cracks her neck. There's no air-conditioning in the main academic building, and we're all sweating and rubbing our eyes in the heavily pollinated air, a general sense of weariness and constant fatigue and headache having caped the school for weeks. "Like what?" Lindsey asks.

"What I just told you. That I'm a bitch. He says even some of my Very. Best. Friends think so." She kicks me again, this time so hard that my chair moves a little, forcing my tummy against the desk. "Can you believe someone would say that to him? I mean, how could anybody be so stupid? Of course he's going to tell me about it."

Dr. Silva takes a step back to admire her handwriting, which is barely legible. "Here"—she gestures with a bony arm to the board—"is Anton Chekhov's most famous piece of wisdom. True in life eez well eez art, I beleef."

I have to squint at the board to see what she's written.

"I can't read that," Estella shouts at Dr. Silva. At the same time, she leans forward and flicks me *hard* on the back of the head.

The board reads, *If a gun is on the mantel in the first act, it must go off in the third.*

I rub at my eyes with my fists.

"Poor baby. Look at the poor little crybaby," Estella murmurs. Lindsey, confused, says nothing.

I get to my feet and move toward the door; I can't breathe, I need air. I walk fast down the hallway, not quite sure where I'm going. Estella won't follow me; I'm certain she's satisfied enough already.

The girls' bathroom is deserted. I splash water on my face and take deep breaths. Every time I close my eyes, I see Will and the Ghost through the upstairs window, my brother pacing in those tight crazy circles like a wild animal. I see the Ghost crying. I see my own father, begging his son not to shoot him or himself. Without another thought, I crouch down and open the cabinet door beneath the bathroom sink. The space looks impossibly small, half-filled with winding pipes, and I can't imagine I'll ever fit.

But I do. And as soon as I'm settled, I know why Mazzie comes here sometimes. The space evokes the same claustrophobic feeling as sharing a twin-sized bed with another person or being underwater: so suffocating that it winds all the way to the other side of the spectrum to feel liberating.

I pull my knees tightly against my chest. It's cool under here, quiet as can be, and I let myself breathe and cry.

But I freeze when I hear the bathroom door open. I hold my breath.

Mazzie opens the door to the cupboard. She shakes her head. "That's my spot."

And before I can respond, she closes the door, opens the second door on the farther end of the sink, and climbs in with expert, almost acrobatic grace. It takes her only a few seconds. She rests her head atop her knees, legs folded, and smiles. "It's nice," she whispers, "isn't it?"

I nod.

"You're upset."

"No, Mazzie. I just wanted to be as close as possible to human waste."

She nods. "Estella probably forgot already," she says. "She was just being . . . you know. A bitch."

I shake my head. "That's not all."

"It's what Dr. Silva wrote, isn't it?"

I nod again.

Mazzie appears at a loss for words. We sit together in silence for a long while. We listen as a handful of different girls come into the bathroom, the sounds of the toilets flushing loudly. And then, when they wash their hands, I notice that one side of the pipe nearest my legs has a slow leak. The pipe itself is cool and damp with condensation. Beneath it, a small puddle of water has accumulated on the cabinet floor.

"Mazzie," I whisper once we're alone again.

Her eyes are closed, head against the wall. She probably naps in here sometimes.

"Can you reach my shoes and socks? Can you take them off?"

She reaches toward me—she's so much smaller that there's

wiggle room for her—and removes my shoes, tucking them into the space between her thighs and heels. Then she rolls my knee socks down, one at a time, and slides them off to reveal my bare feet.

I put both feet in the puddle of water between us. I smile at her. "Thank you."

She reaches toward me again with both arms and puts her tiny hands over my own long fingers. She squeezes my hand and whispers, "We can turn the phone on at night, if you want."

"It's been on," I say. "He hasn't called."

I expect her to let go of my hands after a few moments, but she doesn't. I expect her to get up, to go back to class, but she stays put. We stay there like that for the rest of the hour, together under the sink, with my bare feet loving the feel of cool water against their soles, until the bell signaling the end of the period rings, and we have no choice but to go our separate ways.

part four

chapter 11

Everything is different my second summer at Yale. I'm a year older, sure, but it's more than that. For one thing, Drew is so busy working for Habitat that he'll be able to visit only a few times, if that. But there's something else—something Drew doesn't know about. His name is Eddie.

It's a couple of weeks into the summer. This year, on top of all the swimming, I'm taking two classes, Romantic lit and early British lit. Even though I love to read, they're tough; I can already tell it will be a struggle for me to get all my work done, especially if I want to have any fun.

I'm leaving class on a Thursday afternoon, thinking about the nap I'm going to take as soon as I get back to my dorm. It's so hot and humid outside that it might as well be raining already. I'm standing at the corner of Chapel Street, waiting for the light to change. My mouth is open, and I'm staring up at these big gray clouds, kind of waiting for a raindrop to hit my tongue, when somebody tugs at my sleeve. It's Eddie. He's in my Romantic lit class, and he's a *real* student at Yale. He sits a few seats over from me in class. Half the time, he's either asleep or on the verge of unconsciousness.

I stare down at his hand on my sleeve. "Can I help you?"

"I know who you are," he says. He's a little out of breath; he must have run to catch up with me. "My buddy Sam is on the swim team. He told me there's a high school girl who gets in the pool with him every morning and tries to keep up."

He's still holding on to my sleeve. I yank my arm away. "I don't *try* to keep up. I *do* keep up." But this isn't exactly true. In addition to all the homework I've had to do, I've been going out to parties with my roommate, Renee, almost every night. Why shouldn't I get the chance to have some fun? I've been drinking a lot, and smoking too much, and Eddie's friend Sam is right: the past few days, it's been a struggle to keep up in the water. But I'll be fine; my body just needs time to adjust.

Annoyed as I am to have to delay my nap, I can't stop looking at Eddie. He's what Estella would describe as "empirically good-looking." As in, it isn't a matter of opinion. He looks a lot like Drew, except he has straight blond hair instead of curly. But there are other things, too.

As we're standing there together, it starts to rain—hard. Without saying a word, Eddie takes my arm again and rushes right into the crosswalk, holding up his free hand so all the traffic will stop for us. He leads me down the street into a little deli, both of us running with our full backpacks smacking in rhythm against our bodies. By the time we get inside, we're soaked.

We stand there dripping, breathless. Eddie grins at me. "Wow."

"What?" I ask, wringing my hair out over the doormat.

His smile gets so big that I can see his top gums. "I feel like we just took a shower together."

Eddie gets two hand towels from a waiter so we can dry off. Then he asks if he can buy me lunch.

"I don't even know you," I say. "Why do you want to talk to me?"

"I told you. My buddy Sam—"

"What does that matter?" But I sit down at the counter beside him anyway, almost without realizing what I'm doing. "Do you swim?" I ask. "I haven't seen you at the pool."

He shakes his head. "I play soccer. And I like to talk to interesting . . . women." He looks me in the eyes the whole time he talks to me. It isn't like talking to high school boys, with their eyes looking all over the place and their dumb flirty lines. It isn't like being with Drew, who I'm so comfortable around that sometimes he feels more like a friend than a boyfriend. Eddie seems obviously interested in me, and just looking at him makes me feel like there's electricity dripping down my spine. I can't help but want to stay and talk to him.

He orders lox for lunch.

"That's salmon, isn't it?" I ask.

He nods. "You've never had it before?"

"I've had salmon, sure. How is lox different?"

Eddie licks his lips. He leans toward me, until our faces are only a few inches apart. His complexion is flawless except for a single, tiny mole in the center of his chin. "Where are you from, Katie?"

For some reason—even though he's an honest-to-goodness Yalie, even though he's probably the son of a senator from Westchester or something like that—I don't feel embarrassed to tell him, "I'm from a little town in Pennsylvania."

"A little town?" he repeats. "That's super. I grew up in this little town in upstate New York. We had only one traffic light. People here call me a country boy, but it had its charms."

I shake my head. "Mine didn't."

"Well . . . you're here now, aren't you?"

I nod. "Sure. I guess I am."

"Then you'll probably never have to go back."

"I wish," I tell him. "Sometimes I feel like, no matter where I go, I'll never be able to completely *leave*." It's crazy—I don't know why I'm telling him all this. But he doesn't seem to mind. For the first time since we've been talking, his eyes flicker down the length of my body. "That's interesting," he says. "I know exactly what you mean."

We watch as the waiter brings our food. I ordered a chicken salad, which looks almost embarrassing—*very* small-town—compared to what's on Eddie's plate.

"Want to try some?" he asks.

I nod.

"Okay. Wait a second—close your eyes first. Open your mouth."

And right there at the deli bar, with people all around us, Eddie takes his bare fingers and places a piece of lox on my tongue. I keep my eyes closed while I chew. When I open them, he's staring at me—his eyes are the same shade of blue as Drew's—and I swear to God, I could slide right off my seat and onto the floor if I weren't holding on to the counter.

"I have a boyfriend," I blurt.

Eddie picks up another piece of lox. "Who said anything about boyfriends, Katie? I just want to get to know you a little better."

He brings the lox to my lips. I can't stop myself; I close my eyes and open my mouth again.

• • •

When I get back to my dorm, Renee—another high school student here for the summer—is sitting on the floor, smoking a cigarette and reading a play for her drama class. Renee's mother is a famous actress from New York City. Renee goes to a boarding school in Connecticut, and she has this confidence that I've never seen in anyone else. I know her family has money, but she's so *dirty.* She wears long skirts that swish against her ankles when she walks, and she goes barefoot almost everywhere. Girls aren't supposed to walk *anywhere* after dark without a guy, because there's so much crime in New Haven, but Renee does it all the time. Plus, when any boy tries to talk to her—and plenty of them do—she just kind of nods, listening to everything he says, and then giggles in a way that probably makes him feel ridiculous for expecting her to care. It isn't that she's trying to be mean or make them feel insignificant, it's just that she doesn't crave acceptance the way everyone else seems to.

When I tell her about Eddie, she puts her book aside and sits up straight. "Oh, Katie. You don't believe that he just wants to be friends, do you?" Her long black hair hangs over her shoulders in two loose braids.

I shrug. "I don't know. It's *possible,* isn't it? That a boy could be interested in a girl for something other than sex?"

She already knows about Drew and his commitment to virginity. "I guess it's *possible*—I mean, you know it is. But I know Eddie—he's a Phi Gamma Delta," she says. Their frat house is right around the corner from our dorm. "He's gorgeous, Katie—hell, even I'd like to sleep with him. And you know, I'm very selective." She crosses her legs. The bottoms of her feet are so dirty, they're almost black. Our room is a mess of clothes and books and makeshift ashtrays.

"Drew is gorgeous too," I say.

"Right." She nods matter-of-factly. "And Drew barely wants to touch you."

"What are you getting at?"

"Well . . ." She chews at the edge of her thumbnail, considering. "Are you going to tell Drew about Eddie?"

I shake my head no.

"Why not? I mean, if you aren't doing anything wrong, then why keep it a secret?"

I try to come up with a good answer. I don't have one. I know what she's getting at—if I'm not doing anything wrong, then there shouldn't be any reason why I can't tell Drew about it. And I know I probably shouldn't get to know Eddie any more than I already have. I also know I might not be able to help myself.

It's funny what you remember about people sometimes. As I'm standing there talking to Renee, I remember how, the first time she and I ever went out together at night, we were walking back to the dorm when she decided she had to pee. Instead of waiting until we got back, or trying to find a real bathroom, she just ducked into an alley, hiked up her skirt, and squatted in the dimness while I stood there waiting for her.

"People are going to think you're homeless," I said.

She just kind of shrugged as she stood up. "So?" Then she smoothed her skirt and kept walking, like nothing had happened.

I think that's the thing I'll remember most about her once the summer is over. Renee is smart and pretty and has money and everything else people are supposed to want. But she isn't preoccupied all the time with making sure everybody notices, like Estella. She doesn't seem embarrassed by her shortcomings, either—like the way her nose is a little big, and she's so pale despite all the sunshine this summer. I can't imagine how good it would feel to be so confident—how easy and free she must be, even in her sleep.

Over the next couple of weeks, Eddie and I start spending a lot of time together. He takes me to a few parties at his frat house, and he always makes sure I have a drink and that the music isn't too loud for me, and then afterward he walks me back to my dorm and we sit outside for a while and talk. Sometimes we talk all night. And every time we're together, he does little things that make it clear he doesn't just want to be friends. Like, he keeps his hand on my waist and stands a little too close while we're talking at parties, or else he puts his arm around me while we walk back to my dorm. I know I shouldn't let him, but it all feels so good, so *exciting,* that I keep telling myself I'm not doing anything all that wrong.

One afternoon before class, we're watching TV in the attic of his frat house. As he's flipping through the channels, he stops at a rerun of *Sesame Street.* "Hey! That's me!" He points to the screen, where there's a little boy singing a duet with Oscar the Grouch.

I can tell from the blond hair that it's definitely Eddie. He looks about six years old. He sings with his thumbs hooked in the straps of his overalls and has a sweet, high voice.

"Oh my God," I say, leaning forward to get a closer look. "It *is* you!" I shake my head. "You were a child star!"

"Aw, no, it was nothing like that. My mom was a producer for PBS. They're always using staff kids for extras."

"How many episodes were you on?" I can feel my heart beating faster.

Eddie grins. "Ten."

On-screen, he and Oscar finish their song, and a few of the other characters come into frame. Little Eddie, his smile wide and familiar and sweet as pie, does his best to wrap his arms around Oscar, Elmo, and Big Bird, all at the same time. "I love you, my friends!" he says.

I look at the grown-up Eddie. He opens his arms wide. "Come here, my friend," he says, giving me the same sweet grin. That's when I know I'm in trouble.

I should stop seeing him, but I just can't. Instead, I keep pretending there's nothing going on. One night, as I'm getting ready to meet Eddie in the lobby of my dorm, I notice that Renee is just lying on the floor, tossing a rubber stress ball into the air, trying to catch it with one hand.

"What are you doing tonight?" I ask.

She misses the ball. It rolls across the floor and lands at my feet. Sitting up to reach for it, she says, "Not much. I'm kind of tired."

"Why don't you come out with us? It's fun."

She shrugs. "I'm not really into frat boys." She pauses. "Well, maybe I'd be into someone like Eddie."

"You should come," I urge. "I could set the two of you up."

She smirks at me and throws the ball at my head. It hits me right between the eyes. "Katie, I get the feeling he wouldn't be interested."

• • •

It seems like I stay out later and later every night. Either I'm talking to Eddie until sunrise, or out drinking with him or Renee. No matter what night of the week it is, there's always something to do. I've started chain-smoking, too. It's hard not to; I'm either at a party, where it's nearly impossible not to smoke while I'm drinking, or else I'm in my room with Renee, who smokes constantly.

I'm not keeping up with the reading in either of my classes. I'm at a slight advantage because I've read most of the material before, at Woodsdale, but I'll be lucky if I can still pull off As.

And then there's swimming. Most mornings, by the time I get to the pool, I've barely slept at all. For a while, I figure it's okay; as soon as I get in the water and start moving, I feel the exhaustion slipping away. I still finish drills before lots of the other swimmers, even on the mornings when I show up late.

But one morning I'm not so lucky. It's mid-July, and I haven't had more than eight hours of sleep all week combined. Even Renee seems concerned.

As I'm leaving for the pool, she puts her hands on my shoulders and studies my face. "Jesus, Katie. You look like hell."

"I'm just tired," I tell her.

"You mean exhausted."

"Yeah," I admit. "But it's fine. I'm going to bed early tonight."

She wrinkles her nose. "You smell like a frat house sofa."

"That's funny," I say, grinning, "because that's where I've been all night."

She raises her eyebrows. "Still not cheating on your boyfriend?"

I nod. "Eddie just likes to flirt. We have fun together."

In reality, there's a little more to it than that; I know it, and so does Renee. But I haven't done anything I should feel guilty about. I've lain beside Eddie on a sofa and let him wrap his arms around me. I've held his hand, the same way I've held Lindsey's or Mazzie's—or even Estella's—a thousand times before. I've fallen asleep beside him, both of us fully clothed, and slept that way all night. But I've never kissed him. I've never let him touch me in any of the ways I might *want* him to touch me. I know I'm lucky to have someone like Drew, and I'm not going to do anything that will make it hard for me to look him in the eye.

When I explain this to Renee, she asks, "So what if Drew were doing the same kind of thing with another girl? Would you think he was cheating on you?"

I still feel drunk from the night before. I haven't eaten yet this morning. "That's not fair," I tell her. I don't know why she's so concerned about my relationship with Drew. I get the feeling that she's disappointed in me somehow.

"It isn't?" She shakes her head. "Whatever. You need to go. You're already late."

I don't make it past my first 400 yards of freestyle before I have to stop swimming, hoist myself over the edge of the pool, and throw up into the gutter. It's nothing but straight booze coming out of me, and everyone around me knows it; the smell is enough to make me sick again.

One of the coaches—his name is Paul Goodman—hurries over to me. "Out," he says.

"I'm okay," I insist, trying to catch my breath, unwilling

to look at him. For the first time in my life, I feel like if I let go of the gutter, I might sink to the bottom of the pool. "I'm just tired. I didn't sleep last night. I just need to get warmed up—" But I gag on the sentence, leaning over to throw up again.

"Who kept you up all night?" Goodman asks. "Let me guess—it was a boy, right?"

My vision is blurry, my thoughts jumbled. "Uh, yeah."

"And I bet I even know his name," he says. "Let's see, who could it have been? Jim Beam? No . . . he's a little out of your league. I'm guessing it was Sam Adams." He doesn't wait for me to respond. "Get out," he says. "Rinse your mouth out, put some clothes on, and come to my office."

Sitting across from him, I want to cry. He leans back in his chair, gazing at me with a look I can't quite identify. Is it anger? Pity?

"You're screwing up," he says.

I shake my head, panicked. "I'm just overwhelmed. My classes are hard, and I'm not used to having so much work. And, okay, I admit, I've been to a few parties." Before he can respond, I say, "I'll stop. I'm done. I know I messed up, and I know how to fix it."

"You've been late almost all summer," he says. "It doesn't matter how fast you are. If you want to be part of our team when you're a freshman here, you have to act like you're part of it now."

I nod. "Okay. I'll be on time. I'll be *early*. Please, just give me another chance."

He narrows his gaze, considering.

I can't help it; I start to cry. "Please. Swimming is the only thing I'm good at."

"Okay, Katie, you don't need to cry. It's okay. You can come back."

I wipe my eyes. "Thank you. I promise I'll do better."

"Good. I hope so." He stands up. "I should make you clean up the mess you made, but I think you'd be better off going back to bed."

I look down. "Thank you."

"You've got one more chance, Katie. I'm giving it to you because you deserve it, and I know you're sorry."

I nod.

"All right. Go back to your dorm. Go to bed. Don't get up until tomorrow morning."

For the rest of the summer, I don't so much as look at a beer. I stop smoking during the week, and I even convince Renee to go outside to smoke. I show up at least ten minutes early to every practice.

But I don't stop spending time with Eddie. By the end of August, we're together almost every night.

Two days before the end of the summer semester, Eddie asks me to come over and watch a movie. Instead of lying on the sofa in the common room of the frat house, we go to his bedroom.

For a while, everything seems normal. We're lying on his bed, watching the movie, our bodies barely touching. But after a few minutes, for no discernible reason, Eddie reaches over and turns off the light. A few minutes after that, he reaches out to hold my hand.

This is okay, I tell myself. *We've held hands before . . . like friends.*

He turns onto his side, tugging my body against his.

"I can't see the movie," I complain.

"Shh." And he tucks my hair behind my ear and starts to kiss my neck.

"Eddie," I murmur, "what are you doing?"

He doesn't answer me. He turns his body so he's lying above me, and before I know what's happening, he slides one hand up my shirt and cups my face with his other hand, kissing me on the mouth, wrapping his body around mine.

I can't move. I can't breathe. And as much as I don't want him to stop—as much as I feel like I've been waiting for him to do this all summer—I imagine what Renee might say, and how Drew would feel if he knew what I was doing.

It takes all my willpower, but I push Eddie off of me and sit up. I'm almost gasping for breath.

"I can't," I tell him. "It's not that I don't want to, Eddie . . . I just can't."

He doesn't say anything for a while. He's breathing just as hard as I am.

He stares at the ceiling. Finally, he asks, "Can I try again?"

I can't help but smile. "No." I get off the bed. "I should leave."

He grabs my hand. His expression is frustrated, but there's also a trace of the grin that I've grown so crazy about, like he thinks he still has a chance. "Come on, Katie. Nobody has to know about this."

I shake my head. "*I'll* know."

"Katie, there's a *rule* about this kind of thing, when you've got a long-distance relationship."

"What rule?" I cross my arms. "There isn't any *rule*."

"Yes, there is." He tugs at his hair with both fists, his grin slipping away. "If you're in a whole different state than your boyfriend, it's okay to sleep with someone else. Everybody knows that," he says. "It's practically in the Bible." He rolls his eyes, and for the first time since I've known him, I feel like a little kid.

"Sleep with you?" The words come out in a shriek. "I was never going to *sleep* with you, Eddie." I feel almost panicked, like I'm suddenly in way over my head. I'm so used to taking things slow with Drew, it genuinely hadn't occurred to me that Eddie would expect to have sex.

"Why not? At first, sure, you might have been just a piece of ass." He takes a deep breath. "But I really *like* you. I've been hoping all summer that you get accepted next year, that maybe we can even . . . Oh, Christ." He pauses. "Katie—are you a virgin?"

"Eddie, I have to go." I don't wait for him to try and grab me this time. I just leave his room and get to the door as fast as I can, ignoring him as he calls after me. When I reach the sidewalk, I run.

Classes end two days later. Drew comes to pick me up. I haven't seen him in over a month, and when we're finally together again I stand on my tiptoes in the courtyard outside my dorm and kiss him, so long and hard that he eventually nudges me away. "Katie," he whispers, "control yourself. There are people around." He stares at me, only half smiling. "What's gotten into you?"

"Nothing," I say, a little too quickly. "I missed you, that's all."

"I missed you, too. Can you just wait a little bit? You're hanging all over me."

I feel more than a twinge annoyed. "Can't I even kiss you?"

"Of course you can. Look, I'm sorry. Let's just get your stuff. We've got a long drive."

We're sliding my last suitcase into the back of Drew's SUV when a voice behind us booms, "Katie! You weren't going to leave without saying good-bye, were you?"

It's about eighty degrees outside, but I feel my whole body go cold. "Eddie," I say, turning around, forcing a smile. "Of course I wasn't."

Eddie gives Drew a wide grin. "Let me guess. You're Drew, right?"

Drew nods. He doesn't smile. "Who are you?"

"I'm Eddie." He licks his lips. I can tell he's doing his best not to smirk. "Didn't Katie tell you about me?"

"No. She didn't." Drew gives me a confused look.

"Oh, well then, let me tell you myself. Katie and I have been like two peas in a pod all summer! Haven't we, Katie?"

I want to die. Even from a few feet away, I can smell booze on Eddie's breath. It's not even noon. "Right," I say, "we're friends. And Eddie knows all about you, Drew. Eddie, haven't I been telling you all summer how much I miss him?"

"She has indeed," Eddie says. He reaches out to shake Drew's hand. "You are one lucky man," he tells him. "Girls like Katie are one in a million, and she is *very* devoted to you."

I make a gesture over Eddie's shoulder like I'm chugging from a bottle, and mouth, *"Drunk."*

"Well . . . thanks," Drew says. "It was nice meeting you."

"The pleasure was all mine," Eddie says.

The three of us stand there for a moment in awkward silence.

Drew clears his throat. "I guess we'd better get going, Katie."

"Right!" Eddie blurts. "You have to go . . . back to Pennsylvania?"

"West Virginia," Drew says. "She's going back to school." He looks from me to Eddie, then back to me, and finally says, "I'll let you two say your good-byes. Okay?" And he walks around the car and climbs into the driver's side.

Before I can hurry away, Eddie pulls me into a tight hug. "I'm sorry," he whispers, suddenly sober.

Thank God Drew can't hear us. "So am I," I whisper back. As we stand there holding each other, I realize how hard I've fallen for him. I want to stay here in his arms, instead of getting into the car with Drew. All of a sudden it's obvious: I want Eddie *because.* I love Drew *despite.*

Eddie gives me a kiss on the forehead. We pull apart. I notice that Drew is watching us in the rearview mirror.

"I hope I see you again," Eddie says.

I feel like crying. "Me too."

Drew is quiet as we make our way out of New Haven. Once we're on the interstate, he says, "You must have spent a lot of time with Eddie. He seemed really attached to you."

"We were just friends," I say. "I mean, you don't have to be suspicious or anything. I would never—"

"Don't worry about it," he interrupts, closing his hand over mine. "I trust you completely, Katie." He winks at me. "You're my girl."

"Oh." I bite my bottom lip. "Good. I just didn't want you to get the wrong idea."

"Katie, come on. I know you better than that. Besides, it was obvious you two were just friends."

"It was?"

"Sure." He fiddles with the radio dial, trying to find good reception. "I can spot gays from a mile away."

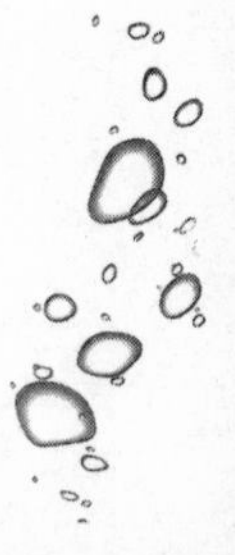

chapter 12

From the highest point of the steepest hill that winds down into Woodsdale, West Virginia, tonight you can see the lights of Oglebay—the state's oldest national park—caped in translucent ice crystals that cough gobs of wetness from the sky and slick the hills, filling the valleys. At the edge of the city, up a narrow unpaved road and through a curtain of pine trees, the entrance to Woodsdale Academy is gated and well lit and attended to at night by Papa Rosedaddy and Puff—a sweet Saint Bernard with late-stage canine arthritis.

Papa Rosedaddy is also the bus driver and the groundskeeper and the school's sole security guard, and he has been here longer than any of the students, longer even than most of the faculty. Tonight he and Puff walk by flashlight, slowly so as not to fall on the ice that has covered the sidewalks and all but snuffed out the streetlights, taking one long trek across campus for the last time before they go to bed, earlier than usual because of the storm. The evening has crept up on campus, through the weather; there are only a few lights still on in the dorms, persisting against the evening so that the silhouettes through the windows seem like ghosts moving behind a thick frost.

Merriweather Hall sits on the farthest corner of campus, between the headmaster's house and the maintenance barn, a three-story maze of antique construction with luxury updates: a few new rooms added here and there, which spill out on three of its sides, the bell tower boarded shut to prevent secret cigarette smoking.

Merriweather is for prefect senior girls only. It has seven bedrooms, which are enough for fourteen girls, and a large downstairs apartment for the house mother, Mrs. Christianson, and her husband. It has always been Papa Rosedaddy's last stop before bed.

For people who live at Woodsdale Academy, it becomes their world, and tonight the world has become almost silent under the ice and rain, which have been falling for days and have crusted over Woodsdale, nearly erasing the skyline. Even the lights inside the houses can hardly be seen from outside. It isn't October yet, but already the weather is too cold. This year, there won't be an Indian summer.

Papa Rosedaddy keeps one hand on Puff's thick neck, as if comforted by the dog's breath gathering in clusters of moisture. Puff's panting is the only sign of warmth in the night. Papa Rosedaddy looks at the sky and squints into the wet. He seems to listen for a moment, then shuts off his flashlight and follows Puff toward the barn with his head down, leaving no tracks on the frozen ground.

As I watch Papa Rosedaddy from the window of my room, I think about how I've been here for two years now, and it has become the only home I know anymore. When I'm away from Hillsburg, I don't remember it really—I remember more than anything how ugly it is. The way people there dislike anything different out of sheer stupidity, never realizing how pathetic their own lives are. I remember neighbors standing on their porches as my brother screamed at me to help him, to love him, all the ignorance surrounding us like a dizzying funnel that sucked our family inside and whirled it to bits. Every time I go back—for a weekend here or there, always at the Ghost's insistence, for things like my mom's birthday or their twenty-fifth anniversary party—I always try to bring Mazzie with me. Ever since the last time I saw my brother, I don't want to go home without her.

Tonight it's freezing in our room. There is ice on the insides of the windows. Mazzie and I are wearing our matching pj's, covered in small puffy kittens, that my mom bought us for Christmas last year.

I climb into the lower bunk, beside Mazzie. "I can't believe it's so freaking *cold*," I say. I cup my hands to my mouth and blow warm air against my palms.

She leans forward so that I can feel her breath in my face. It smells like fresh toothpaste. She pinches my cheek, digging into my flesh with her fingernails. "Does Drew think it's a sign of the apocalypse? Does he think it's going to start raining frogs soon?"

The longer I know her, Mazzie only gets meaner.

"Stop that," I say, swatting her hands away. "And no." What I don't tell her is that he thinks this cold snap is good evidence that global warming is a liberal hoax.

Mazzie wrinkles her nose at me. "You smell like chlorine and barf."

"There's a surprise."

"It makes me want to puke. I might have to go sleep downstairs. You're repulsive, you know that?" I don't think she knows how to be any other way. She rests her head on my shoulder and says, "Oh, Katie. I hate you with every shred of my being."

"That's funny," I tell her, "because you've signed up to be my roommate again for the last two years in a row. Why would you do that?"

"Because I feel sorry for you."

"The more you hate me," I add, "the more I love you, you know."

She sighs. "I know. It's a lose-lose situation. I might as well give up."

Mazzie's tongue is like the kittens' on our pj's, small and delicate as she sticks the tip of it out at me right now. With her pinky finger, she scratches unabashedly at the edge of her nose, probing up into the nostril.

The storm outside is violent; along with the ice, there's thunder and lightning, which occasionally makes our lights flicker. We've laid towels along the window frames so they won't rattle in their tracks all night, like something's coming for us, shaking chains in its fists.

We're up later than usual, operating on the assumption there won't be school tomorrow because of the ice storm. After lights out, we're going to get drunk.

I shuffle my legs and produce a pint of coconut rum from under the covers.

Her finger is still up her nose. Her mouth opens in surprise. "Did you just pull that out of your vagina?"

"Let's do a shot," I say. "Quit picking your nose."

When it's just the two of us, Mazzie becomes a completely different girl than the one whom everyone else knows. In public, she has never had so much as a sip of a drink. She has never taken a drag from a cigarette or a joint at a party.

But when it's the two of us, alone, she's up for almost anything. It's like whatever happens when our door is closed is part of a different world where we can finally relax.

We pull my comforter up to our hips and sit with our backs bowed against the wall, legs splayed and overlapping under the covers. Mazzie's feet barely reach my knees.

Even in her slippers we can hear Mrs. Christianson—who is on her second marriage and a lot younger and more laid back than Mrs. Martin ever was—from the other end of the dorm, her ratty bathrobe dragging against the floor as she opens each door after a quick knock. She pokes her head through each room's crack to say good night, turns out the lights, and moves to the next room.

Here's what I love most about this place: even though it is so far from home for so many of us, Woodsdale has a way of being better than home ever was. I have explained it nicely in the Berkeley application that I wrote for Mazzie, which is in an envelope in the mailbox downstairs: students come here expecting to get into a good college and make some friends. Not only do we have that, but living on campus is practically like getting a hundred brothers and sisters. Having faculty living in the same building is like a few extra sets of parents at the ready, should we need them for any reason. It's not like we love every single person—actually, I can't stand most of them—but they're always here. Like a family.

Okay, it isn't exactly like that, not all the time. But I'm sure the admission staff at Berkeley would like to think so.

When I was writing the essay, I almost started to believe it myself. There are times when this place seems perfect, as though we are living in a tiny diorama of the Real World. It gives me a sense of relief to know there are worlds outside southwestern Pennsylvania. These other worlds are the places where people don't look at you sideways when they hear that you go to prep school, where everyone—even me, now—owns a pair of white gloves, just in case, and knows which fork to use for each course and how to dress for each of the seasons. I like the rules here; I like knowing which ones it is okay to break, as long as everybody else is doing it, and which ones mark a person as being Trouble. I like the sense I get sometimes that other people are pretending just as much as I am. Like maybe I'm not the only one with a secret brother, miles away, whose name I haven't said out loud in months.

Mrs. Christianson knocks twice at our door, so softly that an untrained ear would never notice. I shove the bottle underneath my pillow. Light triangles against the floor as the door opens.

She trusts us 110 percent. It's amazing how, as long as you keep your grades up, you can get away with pretty much anything. She hardly looks into the room at first. "Good night, ladies."

"Good night, Mrs. Christianson."

"Good night, Mrs. Christianson."

After a second's pause, she squints her eyes at us, peering across the huge room into the dark. "Why are you girls in the same bed?"

Mazzie pinches my side underneath my shirt, trying to make me squirm.

I wait three, four seconds for her to answer for us before I say, "We're just talking."

Mrs. Christianson taps a manicured nail against the door frame. Her cat, Wonka, stands beside her, looking upward, impatient for her to move on. "Okay. That's fine. But you girls need to go to sleep soon."

"All right. We will," I say.

"Good." And she shuts the door.

We wait without talking, without even moving, until we hear her knocking, saying good night four more times at different rooms until she changes direction and heads back down the hall for the last time tonight, down the carpeted stairs, across the foyer, and we hear the click of the deadbolt in the front door. A few seconds more and then the Christiansons' own door shuts, and the late news from the television in their apartment filters up through the ceiling. If we press our ears to the floor in a few minutes we'll be able to hear the latest weather forecast: *Stay indoors. Keep your babies close and your kitchens stocked. Everything is about to get covered in ice.*

Anybody could get the wrong idea. After almost three years in the same room, you get comfortable in ways you wouldn't guess. The girls here get relaxed with each other in the same ways that boys on a football team do; it becomes second nature to touch each other, letting your bodies overlap without really meaning to, the same way your living space does. Without real families here, we all learn to improvise in ways that are tough to explain unless you're here, living through it.

I rest my head on Mazzie's shoulder. It is, for our purposes, the middle of the night—the windows are so thick with ice we can barely see outside. There is no reason to go to sleep. There will not be school tomorrow. In the dark, on nights like these, even our memories can seem like dreams if we want it badly enough.

In the morning—through my blurred, stinging vision I see my alarm clock switch from 4:59 to 5:00—Mrs. Christianson knocks at our door again, opens it just a crack, and I see that she's still in her pajamas. I pull up the covers to hide Mazzie, who's sleeping beside me, and start gearing myself up to swim. I start by curling and relaxing my toes, feeling the sleep slip away.

"Ladies," Mrs. C.'s sweet voice lilts with clear pleasure, "school is canceled. Go back to bed." This time, she doesn't even turn her head in our direction. She's still in her nightgown, no robe, no slippers. She'll be back to sleep like the rest of the house in no time.

But there are things that need to be accomplished, no matter what the weather is like. I take a few minutes to stay in bed with my eyes closed, awake, wiggling my fingers and toes. Beside me, with her head covered by the blanket, Mazzie is curled into a tiny ball, almost invisible. When she breathes in and out, light and delicate, I can smell liquor on her breath. She looks so angelic like that, I don't want to wake her up. So I get up as slowly as possible, placing one foot on the floor at a time, wincing as the floorboards creak beneath me. Almost without making any sound, I pull on my swimsuit and warm-up clothes, slip my bare feet into snow boots, pull one of Mazzie's ski hats—it barely fits my head—over my ears, and tiptoe out the door, down the wide curved staircase, and into the coldest October day I've ever felt.

Aside from Papa Rosedaddy, who raises a gloved hand at me from across the street, I'm the only person outside on campus. Papa Rosedaddy and I are used to meeting this way. He doesn't say anything as I trudge past, keeping my head down. Campus is still dark. The streetlights are no help at all, their brightness dimmed by the thick layer of ice that has accumulated on the glass. I make my way uphill, unsteady on my feet, and he pauses in his work to watch me, making sure I'm okay. I can't imagine when the guy sleeps.

The side door to the natatorium is always kept unlocked specially for me, but even if someone forgets, I have my own key. I spend the next two hours swimming, loving the feeling of water rushing past my body, and not thinking about anything at all.

That's not exactly true. I think about Will when I'm swimming sometimes—in fact, I think about him almost all the time, both in and out of the water, no matter how much I try to stop. He's there in the faces of strangers, in my every memory of home, his absence always taking up space inside me.

Thoughts like these can make you crazy if you don't find a way to keep them out. In our humanities class, we're doing a whole unit on philosophy. We've been talking about things like morality and the meaning of it all and human codes of conduct, and it's enough to make me dizzy sometimes when I think about it too much. I wouldn't be here if things hadn't happened with Will the way they did, which begs the question: would he be where he is, if it weren't for me somehow? Did my very existence do something to damage him that I don't know about? And could I have prevented it in some way, if I had known or tried?

But how could I have known? How could I have tried? Even in the water, sometimes, when I open my eyes to look forward, I see his face for just a second. But it's not Will like the last time I saw him. It is Will at maybe fourteen, kind of chubby, his teeth in braces for the first time. Back then, his eyes still had some hopeful color to them; he still laughed and told us he loved us, and there were more good times than bad. I tell myself that it's because there's so much water between us—not just the water I'm under, but all the rivers and clouds between us—that this is the reason I can't get a clear picture of what he looks like now.

I'm in the locker room, pulling on my warm-up suit, wet hair still wrapped in a towel, when Solinger taps at the door, tilting it open a crack before I can say "come in."

"Hold *on*. I'm not even dressed."

"It's okay," he says from the other side of the door, "I'm a doctor."

"You're a doctor of sports medicine, not a gynecologist." I yank a sweatshirt over my head.

Once I'm dressed, I go to his office. I've been in here so many times—even sitting on his side of the desk, looking at racing times and merchandise catalogues and whatever—that I go ahead and perch my butt on the edge of the desk, waiting as he finishes some paperwork.

"Freshman intramurals," he says, shoving the papers into a drawer. "They're gonna drive me to drink. How many games of Frisbee golf can one man referee before he loses his mind?" Moving on, he asks, "How are your applications coming?"

He means my college applications. "Great," I say.

He leans back in his chair. Despite the ice outside, he's wearing a threadbare Dave Matthews T-shirt and swimming trunks. "Tell me again where you're applying."

"Brown. Penn. Harvard. And, obviously, Yale."

He narrows his eyes. "No safety school?"

I return the look. "Do you think I need one?"

Even though we're alone, he leans closer to me, resting a hand on my knee. He's like that with all the girls. If this were public school, he'd be fired in a second, but at Woodsdale he's just the flirty swimming coach.

When he doesn't say anything, I say, "I could apply to WVU, but it wouldn't matter. I won't have to go there."

He still doesn't say anything. "Right?" I ask. "I'm getting into Yale for sure, aren't I?"

"Don't see why you wouldn't." He sits up and leans back in his chair, clasping his hands behind his head. "Do you think the cafeteria has any brownies left over from last night?"

I shrug, staring at the floor. "Probably."

"How were your grades last summer?"

"One A, one B."

"And how were your times?" He means my swimming times.

I hesitate. "They were good. You know me."

"Uh-huh. Katie? Is there something you want to tell me?"

I shrug again. I've known this conversation was coming, and I've been trying to avoid it for weeks.

"I got a call a few weeks ago from Paul Goodman. You had some trouble this summer, didn't you?"

"It's complicated."

"Oh, it always is." He pats my knee again. "A bunch of high school kids, unsupervised on a college campus . . . Come on. I want to hear all about it."

"Okay," I say. "I screwed up. I met this boy. You can't say anything to Drew."

His eyes twinkle with interest. "Right-o."

"We were just friends," I say, a little too defensively, "but he was in a frat and he started taking me to parties all the time, and . . . I overdid it. After Goodman talked to me, it wasn't an issue anymore."

Solinger nods. He licks his lips. "Oh, the *drama* of it all. What I wouldn't give to be eighteen again."

"Do you think I'll still get in?" I ask.

He shrugs. "Sure. I don't see why not. It's just . . ."

"What?" I feel cold all over, even though it's almost too warm in his office. "What's the matter?"

"Swimming was your ace in the hole, that's all."

"But I have almost straight As. I missed only one question on my SAT verbal. I'm a *prefect.*" I cross my arms. I can feel my shoulders rising in tension toward my ears. Half-kidding, I say, "If you rearrange two letters in the word, it spells *perfect.*" It's something I've heard Estella say a hundred times—except she's not kidding.

"Right." He nods. "You've got a lot going in your favor. You and every other kid who applies to the Ivy Leagues." He leans back in his chair, stretching. "There's one other thing, though, in addition to all of that. You've got the whole rags-to-riches story. Places like Yale *love* that."

I blink at him a few times, confused. "What do you mean, rags to riches? My father is a doctor."

He shrugs. "Katie, you're from a little town in Pennsylvania. These other kids . . . you're talking about kids of senators, CEOs, people whose families have *legacies* at places like Yale." He looks around the room. "And between you and me, Woodsdale might be a nice fancy prep school, but it ain't Exeter."

"I'm not poor," I tell him.

"I know you're not—not compared to a lot of people. But you're going for the big leagues, kid. Hey—don't get all upset on me. Everything will be fine. I'm sure you'll get in, no problem." He stands up, walks around the desk, and tugs me out of my seat. "Come on. Let's go see about those brownies."

Campus is still deserted as I make my way back to Merriweather Hall, my wet hair wrapped in a towel. As I'm coming down the hill toward my dorm, I brace myself against the ice and just let my body slide all the way down, like I'm on skis.

Mazzie is still sleeping; she looks like she hasn't moved since I left her a few hours ago. I take off my clothes and put my pj's back on. I tiptoe down the hallway, into the empty bathroom, to blow-dry my hair, which is frozen in parts just from walking back from the pool. And then I slip back into bed beside Mazzie, wriggling close to let her body warm me up again.

chapter 13

Estella, who lives two doors down the hall, with Lindsey, wakes us up a little after noon by pounding on our door with her fist.

"Get dressed," she says, glancing past me at Mazzie, who is sitting up, rubbing her eyes with closed fists, sweet as a little child.

I know Estella has noticed before that we sleep in the same bed sometimes. But I figure she knows personal space takes on a different meaning when you live with someone for so long. She's never said anything to us about it.

Normally, anytime school is closed for weather, nobody is supposed to leave campus for anything. But because our grades are good, we're allowed to go off campus for the day to Lindsey's house. Besides that, there's a kind of mild insanity that seems to have settled on campus because of the ice storm. Normally we'd still be wearing shorts this time of year, and nobody—not even the maintenance staff—is prepared for something like this, so everything is improvised.

The four of us glide down National Road on skis borrowed

from the field house, each of us wearing maroon jackets that have been embroidered over the left breast with the words "Club 813." Other people like to pretend they think it's stupid, but that doesn't stop them from coming to all of Lindsey's parties.

Lindsey's house—specifically her indoor pool—is the kind of atmosphere where we can do anything we want: we can drink and smoke and peel away our clothes and swear and scream just to hear the echoes of our own voices against the cement walls. The boys are always taking advantage of the chaos to cop quick feels of so many tangled legs, or better, under the water. We intertwine ourselves and make sloppy business of socialization, learning how to hold a cigarette in the air while swimming across the pool, or to keep a bottle of liquor from being contaminated by pool water.

Being so used to the water puts me at an advantage; I am able to maintain my composure long after other girls have lost theirs. There have been plenty of nights when someone has gotten sick enough that we end up folding them over an inner tube and casting them into a corner or laying them on a beach towel to be supervised by Mazzie. But it never happens to me. Almost never.

Once in a while, when I've had way too much and the room starts to move without my approval, Mazzie and I catch each other's gaze across the room, or brush past each other's shoulders, and sometimes I think I can feel her getting angry that I'll do these things with so many other people—even strangers—when she will do them only with me. But I think she needs to get over it. Everyone just wants to fit in, and doesn't she know this is just what people *do* in high school?

All the kids who are in the know are here, many of them spinning in fat black inner tubes on this frozen afternoon in the Maxwell-Hutton family pool, which is crowded and stinky from too many bodies bumping into each other and has stray cigarette ashes collecting in scummy half moons around the overworked filters. The water feels thick and suspicious, as though it has collected a slick of mucus from God knows what. There are panels of recessed lighting in the ceiling, turned off today in favor of a half-dozen tacky tiki lanterns positioned around the room: Lindsey's dumb idea. The room is a shade too dark to make out everybody's faces. The cement deck is littered with oversized white bath towels monogrammed with the Hutton family crest and acting as a patchwork picnic blanket for scattered plates of half-eaten cucumber sandwiches and wineglasses swimming with cigarette butts.

Most of the girls have cocktail tans, which require an investment of a few hundred dollars to get right. They are available by appointment only from the area's premiere tanning salon, When a Tan Loves a Woman. A cocktail is a combination of light-bed tanning, achieved a few minutes at a time over a three- to four-week period, enhanced by spray-on tan applied by a trained professional with an airbrush gun. Aside from Mazzie, I'm the only girl in the room without one. I tried it once and was left with patches of pasty skin, like a flesh-eating disease working backward, when the chlorine ate its way through the spray-on.

With so many dyed bodies in slow motion, the spray-on chemicals leak into the water as the girls move, the subtly different shades of reddish bronze spreading out on the surface like a hundred open veins. These girls all have long hair cut into smart layers and painted with creamy highlights. Behind their inner tubes, they trail long wet tendrils that puddle around them, sticking like glossy seaweed against the rubber, fanning atop the water. The girls—my friends, all of them, even the ones I don't really like—are circling the boys like sharks, nestled into their inner tubes with their flat bellies folded into small, exposed rolls of skin, rowing themselves around with cupped palms. From above, I imagine our group looks like a cluster of bumblebees moving clumsily through steam.

Estella is perched on the edge of the swimming pool, splashing whoever happens to pass her, laughing loudly when she manages to get their hair wet enough to ruin their style. She wears an ivory one-piece swimsuit covered in red polka dots, cut low to show off her cleavage. Her right breast is pushed so far up and outward that I think I see the edge of a nipple—but she's quite tan, so it's hard to say. Her eyes are hidden behind a huge pair of sunglasses with heart-shaped rhinestone detailing at their outer corners. She has gathered her long red hair into a high ponytail and tied a red ribbon around it. Her fingernails and toenails are manicured to match the pattern of her bathing suit. She looks trashy, yet like perfect meringue—and she's both of these things, for sure—but the whole effect is so *expensive.* There's a big difference between trashy poor and trashy rich.

She lowers her sunglasses to look at me. Her lips spread into a grin that's so moist and lovely, it sends a shudder of warmth through me; that's how good her attention feels. Estella has applied to Yale too, and she'll probably get in; both her mother and stepfather are alumni. Behind her back, I tell everyone that I'm praying she gets rejected (her grades are good but not great; her SAT scores were above average but not quite as high as they should be). Secretly, though, there's a big part of me that hopes she gets in, that we can be roommates, at least for the first year. I don't want to be all alone, and I know Estella will always be a good person to know.

At the opposite end of the pool from Estella, I'm sitting on the edge, wiggling my toes in the water, bored, when I notice a few of the girls around me getting quiet, gazing past me and upward, batting their damp eyelashes at the presence that has come up behind me and is invading my personal space.

I feel big hands on my shoulders. They slide down to my arms and hook around my waist.

The hush in the girls' conversation is ripe with envy. I press my lips together into a smile, feeling a tug of satisfaction.

"Would you mind telling me," Drew says, kissing my neck, nipping the strap of my swimsuit, "where the hell you've been all morning? I thought I'd go nuts without you."

"Oh, really?" We both slide into the water. I turn around to face him, our hips pressed together. "Are you okay now?" I gather a fistful of his curls, which have grown long over the summer and hang almost past his eyes. "I'd hate for you to suffer because of me."

He pretends to pout. "I think I'll live. Wait—you'd better—oh God, I need CPR." And he cups my face in his hands, pulling me onto my tiptoes for a kiss.

He pulls away after a few seconds. Even though we know everyone here, he still gets embarrassed by public displays of affection.

I slide my hand down to his butt, walking him backward

until we hit the wall of the pool. I give him another kiss on the mouth, pressing my hips against his, *forcing* him to keep kissing me.

When he finally wriggles free, he says, "Katie, come on. What the hell's gotten into you?"

"It's the storm," I say. "It's making me crazy." I reach around to pinch his butt, but he jumps out of the way before I have a chance.

He's wearing green swimming trunks and a white T-shirt over his thick swimmer's build, along with a woven hemp necklace that asks, "WWJD?" in square ceramic letters. He takes me by the hand and guides me as we weave through the inner tubes to the shallow end of the pool. We hop out beside a cooler filled with Budweiser and sit on the edge to dangle our feet in the water.

In a lot of ways, being with Drew for so long has created a constant feeling of mild disappointment in pretty much every aspect of his personality. I wish he still seemed perfect, like he used to, and like he still does to everybody else. But after so long together, he's just Drew: smart, but only because he studies for hours upon hours. Fast in the water, mostly because of all the time he spends in the pool and the gym, not to mention the dozens of supplements he takes every day, and all the salmon he eats. For a while, he was having it for breakfast, lunch, and dinner. It got to be so his sweat even stank like fish.

As much as I try to avoid it, I find myself thinking about Eddie all the time. I wonder what he's doing and whether he has a girlfriend. Sometimes, when I'm by myself in the dorm, I even turn on PBS, looking for old episodes of *Sesame Street.*

Drew snaps his fingers in front of my face. "Earth to Katie."

I smile at him. "What? I'm right here, baby."

"Hey," he begins, "my youth group is having kind of a Halloween party tomorrow. Do you want to come?"

"Halloween is weeks away," I say, avoiding the real question.

He weaves his fingers through mine, his tone hopeful. When I don't say anything else, he adds, "You'd have fun, Katie. Everybody brings food, and there's music . . ."

In the past few months, Drew has become more concerned than ever about my lack of faith. He's told me about conversations he and his priest have had regarding my salvation.

But it isn't Drew's religion that has started to bother me so much. It's how absolutely certain he is that Mazzie is going to hell. Lately, the more obvious it's become to him that she and I are close friends, the more vocal he is about her eternal damnation. And it's not just her—it's her and everyone else who isn't exactly like Drew. A couple of years ago, I couldn't stand to hear about it. Now, the more he tries to force his values on me, the more I feel sorry for him. But that's just Drew, and there's nothing I can do about it, so I've stopped trying.

"Drew, no. You know I don't want to go."

He pretends to be confused by my lack of interest. "Why not?"

"Drew. Stop it."

"Okay. *Sorry.*"

"Thank you."

Drew tightens his arm around my waist. His entire body is tense. "Can I just say one more thing? Please?"

"What?"

"I'm just worried about you. I have nightmares sometimes."

"Nightmares about what?"

He keeps his voice low. "You know. About you . . . in hell."

I imagine how Mazzie might respond, if she were in my place. *And I have nightmares about you . . . being elected to public office.*

Instead I say, "That's fine. Feel free to be concerned." I turn to look at him. "But while we're talking about it, aren't you getting a little bit old for youth group? You're nineteen, for Christ's sake."

"Katie." His voice is low, hurt. "Please. Don't say 'Christ's sake.' And I'm not a member of the group anymore—I'm a *leader.*" He tries a different angle. "You don't have to be a Christian to come to youth group. It's a bunch of people just like you and me, trying to do good things to help the less fortunate."

"I go to the soup kitchen every Saturday."

He and I both know this isn't true. Since signing up to volunteer at the soup kitchen at the beginning of sophomore year, I've gone exactly twice. It isn't my fault that I always have swimming meets or scrimmages or practice or *something* that prevents me from going. Nevertheless, nobody says anything when I put it on all of my college applications.

"You don't go enough," Drew says. He puts his forehead against mine. "I know you're a good person, Katie."

I look across the room at Mazzie, who wears a plain red bathing suit and sits cross-legged against a wall, staring into nowhere. With one hand, she reaches into a bag of Cheetos, mindlessly eating them, her mouth stained bright orange. She catches my gaze and rolls her eyes.

I put my hands in Drew's hair, holding his curls with my fists, trying to feel the way I used to about him. But all I can think about is Eddie's hair, and how much softer it was. I don't understand what I'm even doing with Drew.

As the night wears on and everybody continues drinking, we come to overlap in the water, Lindsey and Estella and me, our inner tubes bumping together, each of us sipping directly from a bottle and holding our cigarettes high in the air, rubbing each other's calves with our painted toenails, murmuring a private conversation below all the noise. Estella's knuckles are loose around the neck of her wine bottle. She takes delicate sips from a straw, looking around distractedly. She seems bored. In the moment, she thinks everything is lame.

Lindsey has a polo shirt with "Club 813" embroidered on it covering her bathing suit. She's self-conscious about her weight, which has climbed a few pounds over the summer. She elbows me sloppily as we bump together, and says, "We all have to promise each other, guys." She gets like this from drinking—one of *those* girls. She'll tell us we're her best friends in the world. She's so desperate for approval that it's hard to watch sometimes. In college, I imagine she'll be the girl who has too much to drink and starts taking off her clothes.

Estella narrows her eyes, emits a low burp, and a small green bubble rises between her perky lips. Somehow her lipstick is still bright and even. "What is it, Linds? What do we all have to promise each other?"

Lindsey gives my arm an urgent shake and says, "If any of us are famous someday, we all have to use our power to bring everyone else up. We all have to support one another. Okay?"

Estella snorts. "What if one of us doesn't deserve it?" And she does a careless spin in the water, splashing me with her feet so I'll know exactly who she's talking about.

"Don't worry," I say, "you can just sleep your way to the top." Estella is the only person who I talk to this way, because Estella is the only person I know who doesn't get offended.

She points her tongue and runs it across her upper lip. But she doesn't say anything.

Then, changing the subject without taking her gaze off of me, she says, "Hey, Linds? You're having a Halloween party, aren't you?"

"Oh, that's right, I am! It's going to be a costume party." She raises her voice. "Everybody hear that? Halloween, costume party, right here."

Estella, shouting louder than Lindsey, adds, "Seniors only!"

A girl in the corner, whom I don't recognize, claps a hand to her mouth and points at the four of us: me, Lindsey, Estella, and a senior named Matilda Ashton, who happens to be standing nearby. "You should be the Beatles," she suggests. Turning, she points across the room at Mazzie. "And you could be Yoko!"

When I take a closer look at this strange girl, I see that she's got piercings all over her face, eyebrow and nose rings and even a stud going through her chin like a bulbous silver zit. She obviously doesn't go to Woodsdale, because we aren't allowed to have any piercings except for our ears.

I pinch Drew lightly in his side and he pinches me back as if to say, *I know.* My gaze moves quickly—from Estella to Lindsey to Mazzie—each of us exchanging a flicker of a glance that means *Who is this girl?* Only Estella has the nerve to say anything right away, so she doggy-paddles herself over and demands, "Who are you?"

The girl blinks. "Who are you?"

"It doesn't matter who I am." Estella's posture improves.

Silence. I look at the water, tapping my toes. It's almost too awkward to stand.

"Did somebody invite you?" Estella asks, and now everybody looks at them, and a part of me feels bad, but at the same time, I mean, *come on.* How does she expect anyone to take her seriously with all that garbage on her face?

"You guys," Lindsey says, shifting uncomfortably, "leave her alone."

"Do you know her?" Estella asks.

"Not really."

Estella paddles herself closer to the girl, leisurely, and stops when their faces are inches apart, pronouncing her words pleasantly enough, her lips lovely and full around their sound. "Why don't you get out of here? Okay? You're getting everything scummy." She pauses, pretends to realize something she hadn't considered yet, then says, "Oh my God. Do you go to the public school?"

Silence. I can feel the adrenaline pumping into my fingertips, the tips of my toes, as the girl gets up and leaves.

"You guys," Lindsey says after she's gone, fiddling anxiously with her cigarette, shaking her head at us. "She brought dope. You shouldn't have just kicked her out like that."

Estella splashes water in Lindsey's face. "Smarten up, dummy. Just because somebody is providing you with a service, that doesn't mean you invite them to the party." Estella snorts. "Why don't you call the pizza delivery guy and have him hang out with us? Huh? Maybe *he* can get us some pot." She glares at Lindsey. "God, you're dumb sometimes."

Drew rubs my shoulders, wrapping his arms across my chest. "Are you okay?"

I'm tense. "I'm fine. Where's Mazzie?"

She's in the corner again, drinking a can of Hawaiian Punch. Now there's a red mustache to go with her orange mouth.

"Good." He squeezes my shoulders. "I'm sorry you had to see that, baby." He gives me an extra squeeze. "Sometimes, in this world, we see things we don't want to see."

Oh my God. I am *dying* to get out of here. "Thank you, Drew."

"Are you sure you're all right?"

"Well, maybe."

"What's the matter?"

"Can you just do one thing for me?"

He turns me around to face him. "Anything, Katie."

"Can you please, please, please shut up?"

Back at the dorms that night, Mazzie and I have shut ourselves in our room to finish the homework that would have been due that day had school not been canceled. As quickly as the ice storm arrived, it's gone; the temperature is above freezing and there's no doubt we'll have class tomorrow.

Studying is a halfhearted effort on both our parts; I watch Mazzie as she looks around the room, distracted, and chews so hard at the end of her pen that I'm afraid she'll break it.

After a while, she says, "Did you know girls like that?"

"Girls like what?"

"Like that girl at Lindsey's today. From the public school."

I shrug. "My brother is a lot worse. He's got that tattoo."

She nods in agreement. "And he's criminally insane."

"Well, sure, that too." Will hasn't been in touch since the end of last year. Once we started plugging the phone in at night again, it was too late—I guess he'd given up. I feel almost wholly detached from him now. For the first time in my life, I'm doing everything the Ghost always wanted me to do, and in a lot of ways it's freeing. But sometimes I wake up in the middle of the night and find myself asleep on the floor, and I don't remember how I got there. Or else Mazzie will wake me up to tell me I've been squeezing her arms and muttering to myself while we sleep. And she'll push up her sleeve to prove it, showing me the fingernail marks I've left in her skin.

"You could have ended up like that girl," she says.

I shake my head. "No. I wouldn't have."

Mazzie shrugs. "You know what Estella says. You can take the girl away from the white trash, but you can't take the white trash out of the girl."

"Estella is a bitch."

"I know that. But that doesn't make her—"

"Mazzie, shut up. I'm nothing like that girl. She didn't know what she was doing. Who just shows up at a party without being invited?"

There's a tap at our door. It's Mrs. Christianson.

"You girls are being loud," she says. "What's the matter?" Her gaze flickers back and forth between us. "You aren't fighting, are you?"

We both shake our heads, sullen.

"You'll have to get in bed soon," she says. When neither of us moves, she presses us. "Come on. Somebody tell me what's the matter."

"Katie is mad about . . . something Estella said," Mazzie supplies.

"Oh? What did Estella say?"

"It's not important," I tell her.

"I'm sure it's not," she says. And she comes all the way into our room, shutting the door behind her. "Let me tell you something about girls like Estella," she says, helping herself to the free chair in our room. "Everybody knows someone like her in high school." Her gaze grows cloudy. "Mine was Angela Caruso. Her father was an Italian grocer, and her mother used to pick her up from school in these ridiculous floor-length fur coats. Of course, then, every time Mrs. Caruso got a new one, she'd give Angela her hand-me-down, and so Angela would march into school wearing her own mink, while the rest of us were— Oh, you're not paying any attention, are you?"

Mazzie and I both shake our heads.

"Okay. Let me put it to you this way." She stands up. "People tend to grow into their personalities as they get older. It's like Kafka said: 'By middle age, pretty much everyone has the face they deserve.' "

When we still don't say anything, she rolls her eyes. "And so will Estella. Trust me. At my last class reunion, Angela Caruso was on her third marriage, and she was still wearing her mother's old fur. High school is almost over, girls. Things will be different for everyone soon. Nobody is going to care who Estella's stepfather is."

I want to believe Mrs. Christianson—I really do. But she just doesn't get it. It's like, sometime after college, it seems like people wake up and all of a sudden they're adults, and they forget everything that matters about being a teenager. They start recycling and listening to talk radio. How can Mrs. Christianson be so dumb, when she lives with teenagers every day? What does it matter if things won't always be this way? All that matters is what things are like *now.*

"Right," I say to Mazzie, once Mrs. Christianson is gone.

"I'm sure it won't matter a bit that Estella's stepdad donated a Wallace Hall to Yale, too."

Mazzie closes her chem textbook and chucks it across the room. It whips past me, just a few inches from my face, and lands in the middle of the floor. "I am so tired of this." She rubs her temples. "I just want to graduate and go to college."

I know what she means. Since I'm feeling so sure of where I'm going to school, everything about our classes seems meaningless. All I have to do until graduation is tread water: keep my grades up, win OVACs again, and make it to May.

By the middle of the year, between being swimming captain and studying for AP exams and waiting to hear back from colleges, I start to feel exhausted almost all the time. The only class I have even the slightest interest in anymore is our senior-year gender studies class. Dr. George—Evan—has been my favorite professor for three years. He tells us he's trying to give us the ability to "function as intellectuals and better understand our personal humanity as we prepare to navigate the adult world."

One day in class, just before winter break, he draws a number line, which goes from 1 to 10, across the dry-erase board. "Sexuality is a continuum," he tells us. "You don't have to be gay or straight. There's a lot of in-between." He leans against his desk, his wedding band flashing beneath the fluorescent lights. "For example, if one is completely straight, and ten is completely gay, then I'm about a two and a half."

The guys in the class all groan. Nathan Boyer, who is a well-known pervert, raises his hand. "So, can environmental factors affect where someone is on the continuum?"

"That depends," Evan says. "Can you give me a specific example?"

"Sure I can. Like, all the ladies who live in the dorms together. I mean, if all these chicks are seeing each other naked all the time, walking around in their panties with their hair all wet"—he starts talking real fast—"you'd think even the straight ones would get a little curious from time to time and maybe want to start touching each other. Right?"

"Maybe so." Evan nods. "I'm sure it's possible. You're a boarding student, too, aren't you?" he asks Nathan, who nods.

"Well, you tell me." Evan winks at the rest of us. "Does being around all your naked guy friends ever make you feel curious?"

"Helllll, no!" Nathan roars. "I'm no *two and a half.* I'm a *one.*" He nods at the rest of the class, mostly girls, and says, "You ladies feel free to experiment, though. I'd like to encourage you to explore all those feelings you have late at night. Preferably with your blinds open."

Nathan couldn't have things more backward. Even Evan doesn't really get it. When I'm with Drew, sex is always an issue. The fact that we're not having it drives me crazy. And no matter how much Drew talks about religion and virginity and all the other reasons why he wants to wait, I can't help but feel rejected. But with Mazzie, we both know that all we want is to be close to each other. There is no awkwardness, no expectations, no tension. We can just relax.

Out of the corner of my eye, I see Estella. She's in the front row—Evan's class is the *only* one where she sits in front and pays attention and takes perfect notes the whole time—and she's turned around in her seat, looking around the room. I can tell she's looking at Mazzie, then at me, watching the two of us with a casual scrutiny, and I can only imagine where her mind's going, and what she could possibly be thinking that makes her lean back in her chair and cross her arms and crack her knuckles, like she could turn the whole world on its side with a flick of her wrist.

chapter 14

I can't stand the idea of another Halloween party at Lindsey's house. I don't want to dress up like JFK and Marilyn or Romeo and Juliet or Bonnie and Clyde with Drew. It's like I feel this slight tug, and even I am surprised when I ask Mazzie, "Do you want to come home with me for Halloween weekend?"

She's eating a pile of chocolate chip cookies smuggled back to our room in her blazer pockets from the cafeteria. The corners of her mouth are covered in chocolaty crumbs. "That depends. Can you guarantee my safety?"

I roll my eyes. "You've been there with me half a dozen times since last year. You know Will isn't home."

I feel a pang just saying his name.

Mazzie shrugs. "Whatever. It's better than being forced to dress up like Yoko Ono for another year."

My parents have grown to love Mazzie. My mother typically has her camera on hand all the time, ready to take candid photos of Mazzie doing the most everyday kinds of things, and in her studio there is a series of really beautiful pastel portraits collecting dust in a corner: Mazzie washing her hands in the kitchen sink, the running water catching the light of sunset that came through the window at her back; Mazzie winding spaghetti around a fork that seems too big for her small hands; Mazzie tinkering a few bars of Tchaikovsky on the piano; Mazzie leaning over a Monopoly board, fingers pressed to her temples, making her move to build a cluster of condos on Atlantic Avenue and drive me into bankruptcy. I was in each of these photos, too, but my mother always chose to paint Mazzie alone.

We take our time on the way to Hillsburg, stopping a lot to stretch our legs and take bathroom breaks, collecting a stack of postcards from the gas stations along I-84. ("Greetings from Beautiful Bridgeville!" "Hello from Historic Hannastown!")

"Oh my God," she remarks as we're coming down the valley into town, "I still can't believe how much *corn* there is everywhere."

"Isn't there corn in Connecticut?"

She glares at me, puts her window down all the way, slides the top half of her body outside, and spreads her arms out, her legs balanced delicately against the door, and yells, *"Corn!"* over and over again, until I yank her inside by her shirt collar. We're both giggling so hard that we have tears in our eyes.

"Good old Hillsburg," she says as we're coming down the street my parents live on. "What a shithole. You'd better get out of here and never come back."

"Yeah, well, that's kind of my plan."

"What do people *do* here?"

"They get high and have sex."

"What else?"

I pretend to think about it. "That's it."

My parents are not home when we arrive, but all the doors are unlocked, the security system is off, the water is running in the kitchen sink. The whole house seems to be in motion. We look at each other.

"Freaky," Mazzie says, turning off the kitchen faucet.

I shrug. "Well, my parents are freaks."

But there are other things: my parents' cat is lying on the dining room table, shredding a bunch of lilies, the vase tipped on its side, water running in a crooked trickle over the edge and seeping into the Oriental rug like it just happened a few seconds before we walked through the door.

Mazzie brushes past me, dropping her bags on the floor, heading back downstairs.

"Where are you going?"

"Bathroom. Turn some lights on, would you? This place is giving me the creeps."

While she's gone I walk through the rooms, looking for anything else out of place. The piano—a baby grand that nobody in the family ever learned how to play—is closed, its lid covered with family photographs. At one point while he was home, last year I guess, Will cut himself from each of the photos and replaced them in their frames without him. So in each formal pose—though all of the pictures are more than a few years old, taken when we still got together and stood close enough to really touch each other—there is my mother, the Ghost, me, and a white outline of somebody else, in the center of our cluster, so that, in addition to his own removal from the scenes, he has removed slivers from the rest of us. It's funny—the photos have clearly been dusted recently, and rearranged on the piano to allow for the placement of new photos from my parents' trip to Greece last year—but nobody has bothered to correct Will's work.

Mazzie and I are eating pork rinds we picked up on the way and playing a cutthroat game of Uno in the basement when my parents get home a few hours later. We hear their footsteps before their voices; they seem to be taking their time upstairs, whispering to each other, and then one of them turns on the television, turning up the volume much louder than necessary—we hear bits and pieces of conversation from a rerun of *The Tonight Show*—while they remain upstairs, probably having a top secret conversation about something I couldn't care less about. They're like that. Everything always has to be just between the two of them.

My mother comes downstairs, her shoes *clackety-clack*ing against the floor. She rushes over to us, putting her arms around our shoulders and kissing us both on the tops of our heads.

"Oh, girls! It's so nice to see you both!" She musses our hair. "Look at you two, all grown up and ready for college. I can hardly believe it." She glides her fingertips down the back of Mazzie's head and dances them along the couch, over to me, leaning over to hug me from behind. "Hi, baby." I get another kiss on the cheek. "It's so *good* to have you home for once." She peeks over my shoulder, looking at my cards. Her fingers are trembling against my face.

She gets this way around Mazzie. It's embarrassing the way she tries to appear maternal. Last time Mazzie came home with me, my mother—exhausted by the end of the weekend from her efforts to be nurturing—fell asleep drunk on the living room sofa with a book called *Hot Monogamy* open on her chest and her mouth wide open, her silver fillings reflecting light from the chandelier. Mazzie and I stuffed her mouth full of marshmallows and took Polaroid pictures of her, which we taped all over the house in discreet places (under the toilet lid in the guest bathroom, on the back of a box of Wheaties) for her to find after we'd gone back to school.

"Hi, Mom. Hey, don't look at my cards."

She heads right over to the bar and bends out of eyesight, reappearing with a bottle of wine cradled like an infant in her arms. "Well, I'm just exhausted. I'm going to fix myself a little drink.

"You two didn't spoil your appetites, did you?" she asks. "Your father and I brought home some Kung Pao chicken from the Wokery."

That's another thing: every time Mazzie comes to visit, my parents assume that she wants to eat Chinese food, even though I've told them a hundred times that she's Korean, even though she's *allergic* to MSG. It's almost like they're unable to stop themselves. Ridiculous.

My mother comes over to the couch with three glasses of red wine. "You girls can have some, too," she whispers. "Don't tell anybody."

I drink my wine very quickly while Mazzie leaves hers untouched after a polite sip. "Where were you earlier?" I ask. "You said you'd be here."

"Ohhh . . . we weren't anywhere. We had a meeting to go to. It was last-minute." She peers down at her wine, squinting as she swirls it in the glass. She extends her index finger and reaches carefully into the liquid, drawing her finger slowly back and forth, finally raising it to her eyes and nodding in satisfaction. I see a single, almost invisible piece of dust on the tip of her pointer finger.

My parents go to bed early, around midnight. Mazzie and I have moved on to playing Monopoly. Once we're certain they're asleep, we dig in to their liquor collection and mix up a couple of whiskey sours, which we pretend to sip like good Southern women, counting our Monopoly money and exchanging subtle insults across the coffee table.

After a while, I have the sense that somebody is still awake upstairs. It could be the cat, flopping around on the living room carpet, wrestling with bits of flowers, but it sure sounds like somebody pacing up and down the hall. I'm used to strange sounds in this house—it's over a hundred years old, so it has to settle now and then. But there are all the little things from earlier this evening—the feeling that my parents had left in a rush, as though they were pulled away for some reason. I can't shake the feeling that something is wrong.

Mazzie and I pause in our game, listening to the noises upstairs, our eyes bloodshot and locked together.

"I think it's just the cat," I whisper.

Mazzie nods, slowly, and then her gaze shifts toward the stairs. I turn my head and see Priscilla pattering into the basement, her ears back, just as nervous as we are.

"Hello?" I call.

Priscilla jumps into Mazzie's lap and begins licking her face. Mazzie hates cats. She swats her away, sending her a few feet across the room.

"Go up there and see who it is," she says.

"I'm scared."

She rolls her eyes. "Don't be a baby."

Eventually we agree on a compromise: we'll stay downstairs and turn the television up loud enough to muffle any noises coming from upstairs. Mazzie falls asleep before I know it in the middle of a *Quantum Leap* rerun, her empty glass tilting toward the edge of the sofa, her mouth open and jaw relaxed against a goose-down pillow.

I'm out of cigarettes, so all that's left is to go on a search for the Ghost's ultralights. Holding Priscilla like a baby, I tiptoe up the stairs to find his stash, which is probably on top of the refrigerator.

There are voices coming from the second floor: my parents. It's past two in the morning. The Ghost *never* stays up this late.

For a second, as I'm heading toward their bedroom to eavesdrop, it occurs to me—what if they're having sex? I stop and listen. I hear the murmur of my father's voice, low and calm. It sounds like my mother is either laughing or crying.

My parents do not have sex, I tell myself.

Once I get within a few feet of their closed door, their voices pause. They hear me.

Whispers. I squeeze my eyes shut.

The Ghost appears in the doorway. I open my eyes and stare at him. "Why are you still dressed like that?"

He's still in his work clothes. He looks down at himself. All he says is, "Oh."

And my mother is still in her outfit from earlier, too; she's even still wearing her earrings, which dangle close to her shoulders, her earlobes sagging. Her lipstick has been rubbed away so all that remains is a thin line of crimson liner around her mouth. Her hair is pulled into a sloppy ponytail. She sits on the mattress, her back against the headboard, and she appears to be half-drunk. Her mascara has smudged into raccoonish half moons below her eyes. She looks terrible.

This is one of the first times I can remember ever seeing my mother so disorderly; even when she drinks too much, even when she spends long hours painting in her studio, she always has an almost eerie sense of calm to her.

But I can't forget how the two of them look tonight: my mother seems somehow stripped, her clothes too wrinkled for the amount of time she's been wearing them, and she looks like she's lost ten pounds since I last saw her just a few hours earlier. The Ghost looks the same as always, except his tie has been loosened, his collar unbuttoned to reveal his undershirt.

I don't think I've been in my parents' room in years. Little memories are everywhere: my mother used to cut the Ghost's old undershirts into long strips of cloth and wind my wet hair around them before bed, and I'd wake up with a mop of golden curls. We called them Daddy curls. My dad's guitar case sits covered in dust in a corner. Before we moved to Hillsburg, he used to play for me and Will sometimes before bed. I remember his gentle singing voice, his callused fingers on the guitar strings, the way I'd stare at him while he played, his face the last thing I saw before I fell asleep. I was always so happy when he was home.

"Katie. What are you doing up here?" My mother hardly seems to recognize me.

"I heard voices. Why are you still awake?" Priscilla struggles in my arms, and I let her jump onto their bed.

"Dad?" I glance back and forth between them. "What is it?"

He sits down beside my mother, and they glance at each other, neither of them saying anything. They don't have to talk in order to communicate.

"Sit down, Kathryn," my father says.

I feel awkward sitting on their bed. My mother leans her head back and keeps her hands on Priscilla, who has curled up in her lap. She closes her eyes while my father begins to speak, and shortly after he begins she gets up and goes into their bathroom, shutting the door behind her. A few minutes later we hear the bath water running at full blast, as though she can't bear to hear the story again.

The Ghost can't look at me while he talks.

"We weren't just out getting Chinese food earlier," he says. "We were at the hospital."

"With Will? What's the matter?"

He clears his throat. He clutches a handful of the bedspread in his fist, his knuckles white. "Early this morning, an orderly at the hospital where Will is staying was killed. In your brother's room. He was stomped to death by someone wearing a pair of heavy boots." The Ghost finally looks at me. "They were your brother's boots," he says. "They have video surveillance of the orderly walking down the hall and going into the room. A nurse found him this morning. His body was in the bathtub." The Ghost swallows hard. "There were shoeprints all over his neck and face. Will and his roommate were fast asleep, or at least pretending to be, when the nurse started screaming and woke them up. Neither of them will talk. They both claim to have slept through the night." Then my dad adds—and I can almost detect a note of hope in his voice, his expression strong as he gazes past me—"They wear the same shoe size."

"Will couldn't have done that," I insist. "When has he ever hurt anybody? He's never hurt anyone."

My father puts his arms around me. He starts to cry. "Oh, baby," he says, the smells on him—cigarettes, maybe a little booze, fatigue, and sweat—curling into my nostrils and turning my stomach. "I love you." He looks at me with cloudy eyes. Even in the shade of their bedroom, the lenses in his eyeglasses have darkened. Maybe it's the heat from his face. "You're just a little girl."

"Do they think he did it?"

The Ghost covers his eyes. Tiny splashes sound from the bathroom. "I think so, honey."

"He couldn't have—I have to talk to him. Daddy, I have to talk to him!" I feel a stab as I recall hanging up on those desperate collect calls last year.

My father just stares.

"*Dad*. Come on, you know he couldn't have done anything to anybody."

"Kathryn—"

"*No.* Nobody knows him better than I do. He wouldn't hurt anyone."

The Ghost shakes his head. "He did. He has. Remember, honey—last year. And the year before."

"He didn't hurt that cat. It was an accident, I tried to *tell* you . . ."

"But he hurt himself. He almost killed himself twice. He almost killed me." The logic stops me, my mouth open, poised to speak. "Didn't he?"

When I don't say anything, the Ghost continues. "Baby, listen." He puts his arms around me. "He's gone, honey. He isn't here anymore. We've lost him." He strokes the hair on my forehead, tries to calm me as I start to feel panic rising in my chest. "I'm sorry, baby. I'm sorry we let you down. We tried so hard."

"I want to talk to him," I whisper.

"You can't."

"I want to write him."

"You can't."

"*Yes, I can.* I have to talk to him, there's something I have to say to him—please tell him to write me. Please?"

There's a click, and the bathtub drain begins to gurgle behind the door.

"Okay," the Ghost says, reluctant. "I'll tell him."

My mother has wrapped herself in a bathrobe. Without makeup, her face looks like worn paper, a million tiny blood vessels burst in a flush of deep red below her skin. She has removed her contacts and squints at us from behind a pair of glasses.

My mother looks at my father and me in bed. It's one of those high mattresses, two box springs beneath a California king. It's so high that my mom needs a stepstool to climb in. Instead of getting into bed, she leans against the wall and slides toward the floor. She spreads her arms and says, "Come here, honey."

We sit on the floor together for a few minutes, the fan circling above our heads, repeating its aggressive *swish, swish, swish.*

My mom takes a few long, deep breaths, which the Ghost has taught us to do when we need to calm down. She says, "He had a family."

"Who did?"

"The man who was killed. He had a wife and parents and people who loved him."

The Ghost removes his glasses and begins to clean the lenses on a corner of his shirt. "Sweetie," he says to my mother, "now listen to me—"

"What about us?" I interrupt. "What about my brother? What about *our* family?"

My mother grips my arm so tightly that I'll have faint bruises the next day. "This is no family," she says.

"Honey . . ."

"This is important," she tells my father. "I want Katie to hear this." She presses our foreheads together. She has the breath of someone who hasn't slept. "I don't know what we did wrong," she says, "but I'm sorry. Katie, I am so sorry. We tried so hard. You kids were everything to us."

"It's okay, Mom." We are all crying, and I've never been so thankful to have my mommy beside me.

"No, it isn't. Listen to me. I want to tell you something."

"What?"

She pulls back. She continues to squeeze my arm. I try to wiggle away, but it's no use. "Never have children," she says. "Never have babies. It will break your heart."

Things slow down after that. I go downstairs to make myself a drink, digging through the fridge behind several half-empty varieties of all-natural peanut butter and a plastic bag full of rotting turnips until I come across a six-pack with four cans missing.

I drink one right there in the kitchen, standing in front of the open refrigerator all by myself, and have just crumpled the can in my fist and tossed it into the sink, when my mother pushes through the swinging door, nearly hitting me in the face.

She begins searching through the cabinet above the sink, where she keeps the medicine, paying no attention to me. The lights are off.

"What are you looking for?"

"Oh, I don't know." She goes to the fridge and opens the last beer for herself, holding the plastic six-rings for a moment, looking at it with uncertainty. She opens the cabinet under the sink and pulls out a plastic garbage bag, which is half-filled with something I can't see. She opens the bag and places the six-rings inside, laying it carefully on top of the contents.

"What are you doing?" I ask.

"Oh, you don't remember? You can make a hammock out of six-pack plastic." She smiles at me. "You need five hundred of them."

"We never made a hammock."

"I know. I've been saving them since you were little. I thought it would make a nice project for you and me and Willie some afternoon."

"Oh."

". . ."

". . ."

"But not anymore," she says.

"I guess not."

"I can always do it by myself. I think I must have more than five hundred by now."

"Mom?"

"Yes?"

"Why don't you just buy a hammock?"

She opens her mouth, as if to answer right away, closes it, opens it again. She looks like she has no idea where she even is. "I've been saving these for so long." It seems like the thought has never occurred to her. She frowns, puts her empty beer can on the counter. "I have to go check on your father."

"What were you looking for?"

"Where?"

"In the medicine cabinet."

"Oh. Nothing. Something to help me sleep. I don't think it matters, though."

"Take some nighttime cold medicine."

She shakes her head. "You can't mix those things with alcohol, honey. It'll kill you."

My mother's problem, I realize, isn't that she's a drunk, or that she's cold or uncaring. I have an idea of who she is, of the kind of mom she tried to be when I was a kid. I imagine that she woke up one day, looked around at her life as a parent, and realized that it was not anything like she'd expected. It was our fault, I know. Will was so sick, and the two of us were just so *bad*.

Downstairs, Mazzie is curled in a ball in the crook of my parents' sofa, her hands pressed together as though in prayer and slid between her upper thighs. Her mouth hangs open slightly.

I stand over her for a while, just watching, and then I tap her on the shoulder with one finger.

She opens her eyes a sliver. When she begins to speak, the spit that has pooled in her cheek spills over onto her pillow.

"What do you want?"

I say the first thing that comes to mind. "I have to get out of here. Right now."

She sits up. "What, you mean *now*? It's the middle of the night. I was asleep."

"We have to go back."

She can sense the urgency in my voice. She moves slowly at first, gathering up her things, and then faster as she sees me shoving my clothes into my duffel bag, not even bothering to change out of my pj's.

"Should we say good-bye to your parents?" she asks.

I shake my head. "It's done."

Since we haven't even been gone twenty-four hours, nobody at the dorms seems to notice we ever left. We have to sneak up the fire escape and into our room through the window, since it's the middle of the night. At least we missed Lindsey's Halloween party.

The dorm is deserted; aside from Mr. and Mrs. Christianson downstairs, Mazzie and I are the only students left for the weekend.

While we were driving home, I told her what happened with my brother.

"Do you think he did it?" she asked.

I didn't answer her for a while. As I was driving, the highway stretching out in a long straight line before me, I remembered so many things about my big brother: the way he trained our first dog, Wags, to sit and stay and roll over. The time Will saved a baby bird that had fallen out of its nest and tried to nurse it back to health. Will was devastated when it died. I remember my brother as such a gentle and loving child, the best big brother a girl could hope for, but I remember when I started to sense our family's world tilting on its axis, the kaleidoscope turning, when things started to go wrong. From then on, it was like we were still ourselves, but our lives played out as though reflected back to us from a funhouse mirror. But I know it's real: it happened, it's still happening, and eventually it will be over. Maybe it already is.

"I think it was his roommate," I said. "I can't imagine my own brother—"

"Katie," Mazzie interrupted, "that's just it. You can't imagine your own brother, period. You have no idea what he's like now."

"But I remember what he *was* like," I insisted. "And there still must be a part of the old Will somewhere inside, right?"

Mazzie shrugged. "Whatever you want to believe."

I expect everyone to know. I expect it to be on the news, to be the absolute talk of the school. But nobody treats me any differently. Actually, that's not true. People are happy for me. On the bulletin board in the cafeteria, Mrs. Waugh has posted a list of all the seniors and all the colleges they've been admitted to so far. Beneath my name, in twelve-point font, it says, "Yale University."

"I haven't gotten my letter yet," I tell her.

She gives me a wide smile. "Katie, you should be more confident. You were there for *two* summers, correct?"

I nod.

"And both summers, you went to swimming practice every morning."

"Yes."

"Beyond that, you have an impeccable record here, you have great SAT scores, you're in AP classes, you've been scouted by coaches all over the country, and you have letters of recommendation from your professors at Yale."

I nod again.

"Why wouldn't you get in? How could that possibly happen?"

I lick my lips and give her the biggest smile I can muster. "You're right," I say. "I'm sure I'll get in." Apparently she hasn't talked to Solinger lately.

chapter 15

Because it's the last weekend before everybody goes home for Christmas break, we've all decided to do something really special together by heading down to Virginia for the weekend. Our plan is to visit some of last year's seniors who go to college now at the University of Virginia. According to the social grapevine, there's supposed to be some really superb marijuana available. Some *college-grade* marijuana.

It's a relief to get away. Despite the letter I wrote him, which I don't even know if he ever got, I haven't heard from Will, and it's killing me. My parents don't like to talk about him, or what's going to happen next. I have nightmares again almost every time I close my eyes for more than a few seconds. When sleep takes hold of me, I feel my insides coming undone, my whole self unglued and whirring like goo in a centrifuge. I feel a near-constant tingling in my fingertips, and I start to have difficulty breathing again—I can't relax knowing that he's all alone somewhere, probably scared and confused, and even if he isn't the brother I knew, there will always be a part of him who's still my brother, somehow, in some way.

Ordinarily, none of the boarding students would *ever* have permission to visit a college campus without an adult chaperone. Getting out of town this weekend has taken a complex web of lies—lying to Mrs. Christianson, lying to Lindsey's parents, lying to Estella's parents. So we are totally disregarding the Woodsdale Academy honor code in order to spend a weekend at college. I don't feel that guilty. Seniors are *supposed* to do things like this.

Once we get to UVA, I make a conscious decision to try to forget about Will and have a good time. It's an odd mix of people this weekend: of course there's me, Drew, Mazzie, Lindsey, Estella—but then there's the people we're staying with: Stetson McClure and Jeremy Chase. Despite all the drama over Estella, they're roommates. And this weekend the rest of their crew from high school is visiting, too.

The second I see Stetson, it's obvious that college has only made him cooler. He takes us down the hall in his bathrobe, drinking a forty of malt liquor in a paper bag, to show us the signs that he's made and posted all over the dorm. They say:

Do you find yourself feeling alone at college?
Is it difficult for you to make friends?
Do you feel like nobody understands you?

(And then, all the way at the bottom of the page)

IF SO, THEN YOU ARE A LOSER.

We all agree that it's the funniest thing any of us has ever seen. Stetson catches my eye while I'm laughing and winks at me.

For a second, I don't know how to respond—where's Drew? Did he notice what Stetson just did?

But I have some experience with college boys now; I'm not as freaked as I would have been, say, a year ago. When I look back at Stetson, intending to smile, he's talking to Lindsey—he's telling her she's really "filled out in all the right places"—and everyone has turned around to head back to his room.

Stetson lives in a suite, which is as big as an apartment. The whole setup feels very grown-up. He and Jeremy live with another guy from Woodsdale whom I don't know very well, John Whitaker.

When we get to the suite, the boys show us how they've taken all the shelves out of their refrigerator in order to make room for a keg. In the bathroom tub, several bags of ice have been spread out to hold the contents of the fridge that wouldn't fit around the keg: a few gallons of whole milk, half a case of Schlitz, a package of American cheese, and what looks like a lifetime supply of ketchup and soy sauce packets from take-out restaurants.

Stetson sits down next to me on the sofa and gives me a tap on the shoulder "So . . . Katie," he says while everybody else talks and drinks and looks around, "how do you like the place?"

"Are you kidding? It's awesome." I stare at the walls, plastered with band posters, the coffee table covered in ashtrays and beer bottles and college-level textbooks and a few porno DVDs. "It's just so . . . man, it's like you're a real grown-up."

"How's the swimming coming?" he asks.

"Pretty good," I say. I'm lying. We only took second place at OVACs this year, and since I'm the captain, everyone thinks it was my fault. They don't understand that I can't breathe, not even underwater anymore. They don't know that I barely sleep at night, waiting for the phone to ring. Most mornings, my arms and legs are so achy from lack of sleep, I can barely force myself to move through the water.

"Do you know where you're going to college yet?" Stetson asks.

I nod. "I think I'm going to Yale."

His perfect mouth forms an O. "Yale. Really?"

"Uh-huh."

"Wow, that's great. Did you apply early admission, or what?"

I try to give him a coy grin. "No. But I'm not worried."

"Well, if you change your mind . . ." He kind of tilts his head to one side and grins. "You can always come here. I'll swim with you."

Is he trying to be sexy? Is Stetson trying to flirt with me?

"That would be fun," I say.

Then he reaches over and puts his *hand* on my *leg*.

"It sure would." He doesn't seem at all fazed by all the people around us—not even Drew, who is only a few feet away. Nobody is paying attention to our conversation—but even if they were, I don't think he'd care. Guys like Stetson—they're the kind of guys who could start their own religion if they wanted to.

I'm drinking a lukewarm beer—the keg still isn't chilled—and my body has sunk deeply into the couch, which is probably several decades old and has more threadbare spots on the upholstery than I can count. "Good," I say, "then we should do that sometime." I have no idea why he's paying so much attention to me, and I don't really care. I already feel so out of control inside, I can't help myself from wanting to get a little bit reckless.

Besides, if Drew were paying any attention to me, I wouldn't be talking to Stetson.

He nods, smiling some more. "Good."

"Good."

"Good."

Drew and Mazzie are in the kitchenette. I think they're talking about some type of biblical theory. I watch Drew drinking a beer and shaking his head, disagreeing with her about something. Mazzie looks bored. John Whitaker has decided that we should all watch *Beetlejuice* while we break into this half pound of reefer that he's produced for us from underneath a sofa cushion.

"Do you want another beer?" Stetson asks me.

"Sure."

"I'll get you one." He gets up and heads toward the kitchenette, then stops, twirls around, and points his finger at me. "Do you want a glass, too?"

What a gentleman. What a fox. "That's okay. Just a beer." He didn't ask anybody *else* if they wanted a beer. He just asked *me.* I light up a cigarette and cross my legs, exhaling delicately to showcase my sexy smoke.

I've been saying for a long time that I'm going to stop smoking cigarettes *now,* but the plan is constantly getting postponed. I can give them up for a few weeks, and then I start again. And every time I start telling people that I'm going to quit smoking for good, they all tell me that I can't—that I won't be me if I quit smoking. And everybody else smokes, so what would be the point, really? But most mornings when I jump in the water, I can feel my lungs getting full too soon. I know it isn't just the stress of Will that's been slowing me down. If I don't quit smoking soon, I'll have full-blown asthma. When

I fall asleep above Mazzie, in our room, we are a two-woman symphony: she grinds her teeth, wearing through one mouth guard after another, while I wheeze. We have our rhythm: *crunch-phee, crunch-phee*—it goes like that all night. She pushes in and I push out, each separate noise competing for space, and in the morning she rubs her jaw in the mirror while I cough over the sink, and we both wonder what the hell is wrong with us. Why we can't just relax, for once.

By three a.m., everybody in the suite has fallen asleep. Mazzie is out on the sofa, a trickle of drool working its way into the foam upholstery, her forehead sweaty. Lindsey lies bowed over an armchair, and Drew is asleep facedown on the floor in a sleeping bag, which I'm supposed to be sharing with him. Estella is in Jeremy's bedroom. There are Schlitz cans covering the countertops in the kitchen and the living room coffee table. There are ashtrays overflowing everywhere. Cigarette butts are ground into the hardwood floor. The ceiling is cloaked in fat gray swabs of smoke.

Stetson and I are the only ones still awake, determined to drink all the beer in the keg.

"It was a plan to save money," he explains, referring to the keg. "We figured that, if we invested in the keg, it would last us a lot longer than a case or two of beer. As it is, our alcohol budget pretty much breaks us."

The keg is almost kicked; a few more drinks and it will be gone. "How long ago did you get the keg?" I ask.

He grins. "Yesterday."

I can feel myself growing more and more dehydrated; when I wake up in the morning I'll go into the bathroom and my pee will come out like dark yellow syrup, no matter how much water I drink tonight.

We both fall silent. It's strange to be the only two people awake in the room, trying to have a conversation while everyone around us is unconscious. We both watch as, in her sleep, Mazzie rubs a finger back and forth across the bottom of her nose. I know it's probably the smoke bothering her. Finally she sneezes. The sneeze sets off a small chain of motion in the room: Lindsey opens her eyes for a moment, looks around in suspended panic before falling back asleep almost immediately. Drew rolls onto his back, kicking over several empty beer cans in the process. One of them rolls along the uneven hardwood floor, across the room, coming to a halt when it makes contact with Stetson's foot.

He turns his head, looking at me. "Are you tired?"

I am. I am so, so tired. "Not really."

"Me neither." He licks his lips. "We should go somewhere else and talk. I don't want to wake everyone up."

The common area of the suite is big, big enough that we can move to the other side of the room, behind the sofa, and it's almost like we're somewhere else entirely. I don't know why we don't go into his bedroom. The thought crosses my mind that I've completely misunderstood his intentions. Maybe he really does just want to talk.

I figure out soon enough that I haven't misunderstood at all. We sit in a corner of the room, where Stetson moves close enough that his head is almost touching mine. "Shh," he whispers, putting a finger to his lips. "We should still be quiet, okay? Quiet like mice." He pauses. "It's really hot in here, isn't it?"

Before I can respond, he reaches behind his head and pulls his shirt off. Then he leans over and tugs off his socks.

He leans against the wall, takes a long sip of beer, and smiles. "There. That's better." He doesn't have any chest hair. His hair is just long enough so that it's growing into small yellow curls, just below his neck. I give the curls a little tug and his shoulders go up. He elbows me and says, "Hey, that tickles," so I do it some more.

We're positioned in such a way that I can see Drew's sleeping form—at least, from the shoulders down—from where I'm sitting. His free hand reaches outward, in my direction, palm up. His fingers are callused from building houses all year for Habitat.

In contrast, Stetson's fingers are smooth and boyish. They're sweaty on my neck. We start kissing and I feel tingles in my whole body, partly because it feels good to kiss him, and partly because I've got one eye open, looking at Drew, trying to figure out how it feels to hurt him. It feels awful, worse than I could have imagined, but I don't stop.

"Let's go into the bathroom," Stetson whispers.

I hesitate. But only for a second. I'm so tired of being the one trying to convince someone—my own *boyfriend,* for godsakes—to want me. I missed my opportunity with Eddie. I'm not going to miss it again. What does it matter? Drew already thinks I'm going to hell. Right now, I feel like he's probably right, and I don't even care. At least I'll get to see my brother.

As soon as the door is closed, Stetson pushes his hands up my shirt, down my pants, rubbing against me, tugging my clothes off.

I am leaning against the wall, self-conscious as Stetson stands a few feet away, gazing down at my body. All that's left are my underwear. He nods at them. They are pink with tiny images of Tweetie Bird printed on them. "Take those off."

Drew would never tell me what to do like this. But that's

why I'm here: I don't *want* Drew. "Why?" I ask. Even as the word leaves my lips, I can see the mildest hint of annoyance in Stetson's expression. Before it has a chance to surface, though, he covers it up with his usual, easygoing smile, as though he's amused by my naiveté.

"You're still a virgin. Aren't you, Katie?"

I nod.

He stands so close to me that our lips are touching. "Drew doesn't deserve you. He's going to end up in a monastery someday, and you'll be left with a bunch of memories that don't mean a damn thing."

I flinch, so imperceptibly that Stetson doesn't even notice. I can't believe what he's doing to his best friend. What we're *both* doing.

I could walk away now and everything would be okay. But I don't. I just stand there, almost unable to move, and whisper, "I couldn't have put it better myself."

It seems to last forever, but I know it hasn't been more than five or ten minutes at most. We're sitting on the floor next to each other when Stetson cups my chin, tilts my face upward, and looks into my eyes. "Hey," he whispers, giving me a kiss on the tip of my nose, "this is our secret. Right?"

I nod. "Sure. Sure it is."

He smiles at me. "You're a great girl, Katie. You should visit again sometime."

And then he shimmies back into his boxer shorts and stands up, handing me my shirt.

I feel hollow and sick. I can't wait for Stetson to leave the room so that I can gag into the sink.

We are both almost dressed when someone knocks lightly at the door. "Stetson? Hey, hurry up, I have to pee."

We stand perfectly still. Stetson holds up a finger. "Hold

on, Estella." He stares at me while I hurry to finish getting dressed.

But Estella can't wait, and we have forgotten to lock the door. All of a sudden she's just there, staring at us. She chews on the inside of her cheek, taking in the whole grisly sight.

"What's going on in here?" she asks. Her voice is soft, beautiful rage.

I shake my head. "Nothing."

Before I have a chance to continue—God, what can I possibly even say?—Stetson interrupts. "We were just talking. We didn't want to wake anyone up."

Estella nods. "Just talking," she murmurs. "Right." And then, without any warning, her voice rises to a screech. *"Drew!"*

Suddenly we have an audience. Everyone stands around us, staring at me and Stetson in the bathroom. We are both fully dressed, but I'm sure we look tousled. Stetson is relaxed, sitting on the closed toilet seat, his arms crossed behind his head.

"Estella, cut the drama. We were just having a conversation"—he points to Drew—"about you, man."

Drew is looking at me in a way that I've never seen before. It's a combination of hurt and hopefulness and wariness and contempt, all at once. "Katie," he says, his voice trembling and hopeful, "is that true?"

"Yes." I go to Drew, take his hands in mine, and kiss him. "Of course it's true." I still feel sick to my stomach, and I know it's not the beer.

"What were you saying about me?"

I shrug. "Lots of things. I'm going to graduate soon. We were talking about you and me and the future . . ."

"And you didn't think to have that conversation with *me*?" Drew sounds bitter, doubtful.

"Man, you were asleep. Katie just wanted some advice." Stetson stands up, walks over to Drew, and puts both hands on his shoulders. "I swear to you, nothing happened. I would never do that to you."

Estella is furious. "I know what I saw," she says. "You two were in here for a long time, and you sure as hell weren't *talking.*" She glares at everyone.

"Would you shut up?" Stetson snaps. "Just because you're jealous doesn't make it okay for you to go making things up."

"Jealous?" she sputters. "What exactly am I jealous of, Stetson? I dumped *you,* remember?"

"Not me—Katie," Stetson says simply. "You're jealous of Katie."

"Oh, don't make me laugh. Little miss small-town Pennsylvania here, with her magical gift for swimming and absolutely nothing else?"

"Shut up, Estella!" Drew says. "I'm so tired of hearing you *talk.* Nobody believes you. Katie and Stetson—my girlfriend and my best friend—fooling around ten feet away from me?" Drew shakes his head and glares at her. "Even for you, that's ridiculous."

The whole time we've been having this conversation, I notice Mazzie hasn't said a word. After it's over, Drew and I go to his sleeping bag and lie there together while Estella and Jeremy go back to his room. Stetson goes to his own room. Mazzie goes into the bathroom.

I lie awake all night, trying to fall asleep. For a while I can hear Estella in Jeremy's room, insisting that something was going on between Stetson and me in the bathroom. Eventually they quiet down, and for a while I believe I'm the only one who's still awake.

But then Mazzie comes out of the bathroom, pattering almost soundlessly across the hardwood floor in her bare feet, and slips into her own sleeping bag, which is not far from Drew's and mine.

In the almost-dark, we gaze at each other, and I know that she knows.

I've heard from plenty of my friends that, after you have sex with a boy, you feel full and alive and like a woman for the first time. But I don't feel that way at all. Instead, I feel like something inside me died. I think I'm supposed to feel like things are coming together, like I'm finally a grown-up. Instead, everything feels like it's falling apart. And I have no idea how to fix any of it.

It's an awkward ride back to campus on Sunday; Estella won't talk to anyone, so we all try to carry on a conversation while ignoring her. But Estella isn't an easy girl to ignore.

That Monday, I know I can't face her in gender studies. When I peek into the room, I see that Mazzie isn't there either. I'm pretty sure I know where she's at.

I tuck myself under the sink across from her.

"Aren't you going to miss class?" she asks. We're finishing the semester with a close reading of *The Awakening.*

I shrug. "Aren't you?"

She shakes her head. "I read that freshman year at my old school. I can't believe we don't cover it here until senior year. Pathetic."

After a pause, she says, "You had sex with Stetson, didn't you?"

She's taken my shoes and socks off for me, automatically,

so I can rest my feet in the puddle of water beneath the pipes. "Why would you think that?"

"Because after everyone left the bathroom, I stayed to pee. There was a condom in the toilet."

". . ."

". . ."

"Oh."

"Why would you do that, Katie? Even if you don't like Drew anymore—why would you do something so awful?"

I shrug. "Maybe I wanted to feel awful."

"Did it hurt?"

I nod. "Yes."

"Did you cry?"

"Almost."

Mazzie sucks in a deep breath. "I always knew he was a jerk. Cool, sure—but still a jerk."

"I know. Me too. Hey, Mazzie, you won't say anything to Drew, will you?"

She stares at me for a long time. Underneath the sink, it's so dark that almost all we can see of each other are our pupils. I love being here with her. I can't imagine what she must think of me, but I hope she knows I was telling the truth: I wanted to feel bad. I *deserved* to feel bad.

Mazzie doesn't say a word. She presses her thumb and forefinger together, holds them at the edge of her lips, and pantomimes zipping her mouth shut and locking it. Then she opens the door to the cabinet—just a crack—and tosses the imaginary key onto the dirty ceramic tile floor.

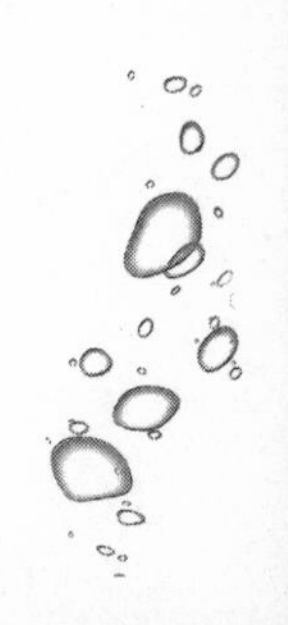

chapter 16

Christmas break of my senior year is the first Christmas where there is no trace of Will in our house. There are no presents for him under the tree. His stocking is not hanging beside mine on the mantel. His bedroom door is locked.

It all seems too cruel to bear. On Christmas morning, it takes me over an hour to open a mountain of presents (new clothes, a new luggage set, and a thousand dollars—cash). There's also a ton of stuff that my mother says is for me to "give to Mazzie, if she wants them, or just keep them for yourself."

When the last present is opened (an emerald tennis bracelet), I turn to my parents and demand, "What about Will? Are we going to see him?"

They glance at each other, like they knew this was coming.

"Kathryn . . . I thought we talked about this," the Ghost says.

"You aren't going to visit your son on Christmas?"

"Of course we are," my mom says. "But honey, it's not a good idea for you to come. You would be upset."

"Why? Because of where he's staying? Because of what he looks like?" I shake my head. "I don't care. I want to see him. It's *Christmas,* for godsakes."

The Ghost can't help himself. "What does it matter if it's Christmas? You and Will don't believe in God, anyway."

"That's right." I glare at him. "Maybe you should take all these presents back."

My mom starts to cry. Immediately, I wish I'd kept my mouth shut.

"Let's all take a deep breath. Katie, I'm sorry." My dad closes his eyes, and I notice how the deep wrinkles on his face never go away, no matter what his expression is. "We need to love each other right now. It's more important than ever."

But they still won't let me come. The only thing I can get the Ghost to promise as they're getting ready to go is that he'll make sure Will has my new phone number at school.

"He doesn't get to use the phone very often, Katie," he says to me, "and I don't want you to be upset, but it's been almost a year since you've seen him. He's different now." The Ghost and my mom both have their coats on. Outside it's snowing lightly. It's Christmas, and these people—a doctor, a painter, people whose house has a library and a swimming pool and everything most other people could ever dream of wanting—are going to visit their only son in jail on Christmas Day. Who'd have ever thought our lives would unfold like this? Certainly not my parents—I know that much.

"He might not want to call you," the Ghost says. "I don't want you to be upset if you don't hear from him."

"Promise me," I say. "Promise on my whole life that you'll give him my phone number."

He hesitates. My mother looks back and forth at both of us.

She's wearing a ridiculous faux fur coat and is overdressed for a jailhouse visit, even on Christmas Day.

"I promise," the Ghost says. And I believe him. I think he's so certain that Will will never call me, not in a million years, that he figures, what the hell? I'll give him her number.

But I know he'll call, no matter what shape he's in. Even when I hate him, I love him. Even when he stops calling, I hear his voice. Will is my only brother. Without each other—without the invisible thread that binds us together, no matter how weak or frayed it becomes—we are simply drifting, all alone, without anything like a compass to know where we're headed.

Two weeks into the spring semester, people start hearing back from colleges. Mazzie gets into Berkeley—the only college she bothered applying to. This is no surprise.

The mail system at Woodsdale is slow and disorganized, so even though all the Ivy League schools are supposed to mail their letters on the same day, the letters trickle into our boxes as the mailroom staff deals with the overload. The first school I hear from is Brown. Of course, they're pleased to offer me a spot in the fall. After that, there's Harvard, followed by Penn. I get in everywhere, and I even get nice scholarships from all of them.

But all I want is my letter from Yale. "Can't I just go to the mailroom and *ask* for it?" I'm sitting in my room, chewing on my bottom lip while Mazzie combs my wet hair. She is perched on the bottom bunk, and I am on the floor, my head back, flipping through Harvard pamphlets.

"Lindsey already tried. They won't let anyone in." She tugs

hard at a knot in my hair. "Don't worry so much. I'm tired of hearing about it."

Mazzie is still annoyed by Woodsdale's poor Ivy League matriculation rate. In Hillsburg, I'd never even *heard* of someone going to an Ivy League school. It will definitely be in the local paper.

"Berkeley isn't an Ivy League school. You realize that, don't you?"

She yanks harder on my hair.

"Ouch!"

"Oh, I'm sorry. Did I hurt you?" She does it again. "Oh, my mistake. Mea culpa."

I try to wrestle the comb away from her. She's just secured me in a vicious headlock on the carpet when our phone rings.

Once. Twice. Three times.

"It's probably just Drew," she says.

But I know for a fact that Drew is busy all day.

"Answer it," Mazzie says.

Will's voice is far away, as always. The connection is poor. "Katie," he says. He sounds eager, almost high. "How are you?"

"I'm okay. How are *you*?"

". . ."

"You don't have to say anything—"

"No, I'm okay. I mean, considering everything. I'm kind of incarcerated." He pauses. "How was Christmas? Did Mom put toothbrushes in our stockings? Remember how she always does that? Who needs a toothbrush for *Christmas,* right?"

I almost drop the phone. I start to wheeze a little bit. I can't bear to tell him they didn't put up his stocking.

"Will." My voice is pleading. "Please tell me you didn't do what they think you did."

"Katie, I have so much to tell you—only you. But I can't tell you over the phone. Can you visit me?"

"What? Where are you?"

"I'm in Pittsburgh. It's like an hour and a half from where you are."

"When?"

"Next weekend? Between one and five?"

There's a party next weekend at Amanda Hopwood's house—I'll be glad to skip it. "I'll be there," I tell him.

His voice becomes a shaky whisper. "Promise? Mom and Dad never visit, and it's so lonely and I'm scared, Katie, and there's something I need to tell you, okay? I can only tell you. You're the only one who can know the truth."

"Will, just please tell me you didn't—"

"Next week. I'll tell you next week. Hey, Katie?"

"What?"

"I love you. I love you so much."

I close my eyes. I'm crying without making any noise. "I love you too, Will. I'm sorry I didn't take your calls last year."

We're at an honest-to-goodness prison, Mazzie and me, right here in downtown Pittsburgh. There's a separate visiting area for psychiatric patients. While Mazzie waits in the car, I go through the whole process of having my purse searched and my ID checked. Then there are all the stares from the guards and inmates that make me feel like they're trying to undress me with their eyes. The whole place smells like bodily fluids and cleaning solution. Fluorescent lights burn overhead, dead bugs trapped in the plastic panes that cover the bulbs, the barely noticeable hum of the lights becoming deafening if you focus on it for too long. Lying awake at night in a place like this could drive you crazy, if you listened closely enough to all the background sound that isn't really sound at all.

After a few minutes, they bring out my brother. I've seen him in handcuffs before, but never like this. He's wearing a bright orange jumpsuit and his head is still shaved. He's smoking. It's a pathetic gesture, trying to smoke with handcuffs on. We aren't allowed to touch each other.

What is there to say? There isn't any small talk, no questions about how I'm doing or what he's been up to in prison or anything like that; it would be too depressing.

"Will," I say, leaning across the flat metal table, "what did you want to tell me?"

"I'm so happy you came, Katie. Will you come again? Before my trial?"

"I thought Dad said there wasn't going to be any trial."

He shrugged. "That was before I learned what I know now. There has to be a trial so I can make my case."

I hesitate. "Okay."

"And afterward, when I get out of here, will you come visit me all the time?"

He looks so hopeful. He's so glad to see me. Everything from the year before is forgotten, at least on his end.

"Will." I lower my voice to a whisper. "What did you do? You said you would tell me. What happened that night?"

He's still smoking, right down to the filter. With his other hand, he makes a *come here* motion. I lean in.

He whispers to me. When I sit back again, all I can do is stare at him.

"So you see—it all makes sense, doesn't it? I started doing some reading while I was here, and it all makes sense now.

You be careful, Katie. Be careful the same thing doesn't happen to you, because that's what they *want* to happen, you know? And we can't let it. You can't let it. You keep your head low and go to school and just promise you'll come visit me as much as you can. Promise."

I wish I could hold him. It makes me ache inside to be able to see him but not to touch him.

Back in my car, Mazzie is waiting with her bare feet on the dashboard. She's reading *King Lear.*

"That was fast," she says, closing the book and tossing it into the backseat.

I nod.

"What did he say?"

"He made me promise not to tell anyone."

"Oh . . ."

I'm suddenly more tired than I've ever felt in my whole life. I know I'll remember his words for as long as I live. And Mazzie is the only person in the world I can tell them to.

I close my eyes. "He said, 'I am Icarus, son of Daedalus. I will plunge to my death in the sea. It is your fault, Minos, for keeping us imprisoned. I will come back and eat the meat from your bones.' "

Mazzie says, "That doesn't make any sense. I mean, it's kind of the Icarus myth, but he's got it all mixed up . . ."

"He did it, Mazzie. He doesn't know what he's saying. He said he'd been doing a lot of reading. He must have come across Greek mythology in the library and felt connected to it for some reason." I put my head on her shoulder. "He did it," I whisper again.

She presses her palm to my cheek. "It's okay. You can still love him."

I nod. "I know."

"Or not. You can walk away and never come back and forget all about him. You can do whatever you want, Katie. You're free."

But I'm not—I'll never be, not as long as I've got Will. That's one thing Mazzie doesn't understand. If I walk away from him now, it's almost like Will never existed at all—not even the good parts of him, so many years ago, before he began to melt away.

When we get back to the dorm, there's a letter waiting for me from Yale.

"Here it is," I say, weighing it in my hand. It feels suspiciously thin. But then, my letter from Penn was just one page.

We sit on the bottom bunk. "I can't open it," I say to Mazzie, handing her the envelope. "Here."

"Katie, don't be stupid. You know you got in. Just *open* it already."

I shake my head. "I can't. Will you please do it?"

"Oh, fine." She rips open the envelope, scanning the letter. There is a prolonged silence. And then she says, "Oh . . . my God."

"What?" My eyes are closed. "What is it? Did I get a full scholarship? Please tell me I got some good money."

Her voice is flat. "Katie. You didn't get in."

"Shut up. Come on—what did I get? I got a full scholarship, didn't I?"

But her tone doesn't change. I feel her press the letter into my hands. "Here. See for yourself." I've never seen Mazzie look so embarrassed or sorry.

When I tell Solinger, he takes a deep breath, leaning back in his chair to stare at me as I sit there crying.

"You knew this could happen, Katie."

"You told me I shouldn't worry! You told me everything would be fine!"

"And it will," he says. He shrugs. "So you didn't get into Yale. Big deal. Where else did you get in?"

I try to take deep breaths to calm myself down, just like the Ghost always taught me.

"Everywhere else," I tell him.

"And you got some scholarships?"

I nod, sniffing the air. Since his office is adjacent to the pool, it smells strongly of chlorine in here.

"Everything feels like it's ending," I say, "and I don't want it to. I'm not ready yet."

He shakes his head. "What's ending?"

"A *lot.* OVACs are over—I screwed those up—swimming season is almost over, and pretty soon you'll make me turn in my key to the pool. Then what do I have?" I pull my knees to my chest, still crying despite the deep breaths. I feel close to hyperventilating. "*Nothing.* I don't have anything."

"Oh, for godsakes, Katie. You're still going to an Ivy League school on a great scholarship. You've got your entire life ahead of you." He pauses, considering his next words carefully. "There are kids in this school for whom high school will be the high point of their whole lives. Trust me, Katie. You do not want to be one of those kids." He reaches across the desk to pat me on the knee. "I know it feels like everything is ending, but it's not. Things are just beginning for you, kiddo. You can have everything you want. All you have to do is go out and take it."

I don't say anything. I want to get in the water and let the rest of the world disappear.

"Feel any better?" Solinger asks.

I shrug. "I'm gonna go for a swim."

"Hey, I can do you one better than that." He reaches into a desk drawer, pulls out a tattered three-ring binder, and slides it across the desk. "Aquatic freshman intramurals. We've got the final, uh, *competitions* coming up next week. I'll be honest with you, Katie—I don't want to go it alone. Fifty fourteen-year-olds playing water polo, water volleyball, and"—he rolls his eyes—"Marco Polo."

I flip through the pages. "So? What do you want me to do?"

"Want to be my assistant coach?"

"Really?"

He nods. "Absolutely. And Katie, nobody's going to make you hand in your key. You keep it as long as you want."

I jump up, run around the desk, and give him a hug. "You're my favorite coach," I say.

"I'd better be. Okay, now—that's enough. We wouldn't want anyone to walk in on this love-fest, would we?"

I take the binder in my arms and hold it close to my chest. "I'm going to organize this tonight."

"Good for you. I'm sure as hell not gonna do it."

He rifles through his desk drawer, pulls out a bottle of Wite-Out. "I'm off, then."

"Where are you going?"

He shrugs. "I have to go Wite-Out 'Yale' from the list of college acceptances in the cafeteria. Never had to do that before for *anyone*."

When he sees me start to frown, he holds up a hand. "Katie, I told you—it's just the beginning. Especially for someone like you."

Even though I've got intramurals, and Solinger managed to cheer me up a little bit, I don't want to call my parents and tell them I didn't get into Yale; not yet. They're already happy that I've gotten into all my other schools, so it won't be as big of a letdown for them as it is for me. They won't understand how embarrassed I am. All I can think about is getting drunk and forgetting about everything that's happened today: my brother, Yale's rejection—and as much as I hate to admit it, the fact that I'll probably never see Eddie again.

Despite how tired I'm getting of parties, I'm grateful that Estella is planning a get-together at her house tonight. Estella's house has been the same for as long as I've known her: perfect. Even the mess we're making seems lovely against the colorful background of her living room, the wallpaper matched perfectly to the upholstery on the sofa, the curtains crafted from hand-woven silk. And tonight has been the same as any other weekend night in high school. By midnight, our group is one barrel of drunk monkeys.

Drew is always the last to show up, especially at Estella's house. He's told me he doesn't want to risk getting stuck alone with her. When he walks through the front door, keys still in hand, he makes a beeline toward me on the sofa.

"Where the hell have you been? I couldn't get you on the phone, you weren't at the pool . . ." He shakes his head. "Are you avoiding me? I don't understand how you make it impossible to track you down sometimes."

Mazzie leans over the back of the sofa, resting her elbows on my shoulders. "We were studying all day," she tells him.

Drew doesn't even look at her. "I called and called, Mazzie. Nobody answered."

"We had the ringer turned off, genius."

Drew scowls. "Didn't you think to call me? Didn't you think I'd be worried when I couldn't get through to you?"

I nod, looking at him, right into his blue eyes, which are so desperate and sad that I've forgotten about him all day. I put my hands on his shoulders, trying to find some sense of affection for him—*there.* He feels warm, his neck in need of a shave.

Looking around the room—at Estella, Lindsey, Mazzie, Drew—what do we all have in common that brings us together? I don't know any of them, not entirely, and maybe even they can't tell me the whole truth about themselves. Even while I watch it happening, I know I'll remember these evenings forever—the chance to be a part of something that matters, not just in one room to a few people, but to everyone. We are the ones who matter. We are going places. I am part of them. Things are happening for us.

Well, mostly. "I didn't get into Yale," I blurt, louder than I'd meant to.

Prior to my announcement, Estella and Lindsey had been playing a game of pool. Drew was drawing a gentle figure eight on my bare thigh. Mazzie was, as usual, eating from a bag of Cheetos, her lips and fingertips stained neon orange. Everyone stops what they're doing except Mazzie.

"You didn't get in? But I thought there was no question. I mean, you already *went,* and you did great," Drew says.

I nod. "Plus I had letters of recommendation from two of my professors *at* Yale. I'm a National Merit Scholar. I get all As here. I'm a prefect."

"And you didn't get in," Lindsey says, awed.

"Nope."

"I got in." Estella leans against her pool stick, giving me a special look of contempt. "I got my letter today too."

"That's nice," Drew says, refusing to look at her, his voice flat.

"Yeah, nice timing," Lindsey adds.

"Katie," Estella begins, "have you thought about why you didn't get in? I mean, can you come up with any conceivable reason why they would reject you?"

I shake my head. "I don't know," I lie.

She licks her lips. "I have an idea. You know my mom's second husband is an attorney. He's licensed to practice law in Ohio and Pennsylvania, too, because it's such a small area, and because he used to live outside Pittsburgh with his old family. He's still friends with lots of judges around there."

I feel a heavy coolness spreading throughout my insides. "And he heard about a case a few months ago," Estella continues. "Well, normally he would have just forgotten, but there was something about the last name that seemed familiar to him."

This can't be happening. Not now, not so close to graduation when I've almost made it. Not here in front of everybody who matters to me. I give her a pleading look, but I know it's too late; she decided she was going to *get me* the night she caught me in the bathroom with Stetson. We've barely spoken since then, and I knew it might be stupid for me to come here tonight. She's probably been planning this for weeks, waiting for exactly the right moment to drop her bomb.

The whole room is quiet. I can tell Estella is loving every minute.

"We all know about Katie's dead brother, right? The one who died in a terrible accident a few years ago?"

"Estella. You're a bitch," Mazzie pronounces.

"Well, as it turns out, he isn't dead at all! He's just *crazy*. He's been in and out of jail and mental hospitals his whole life. And it gets better—a few months ago, he actually *murdered* someone. So, the whole time Katie has been here, pretending to be one of us and having a good old time, her brother has been institutionalized, pretty much constantly, losing his mind while his sister parties and cheats on her boyfriend and . . . sleeps in the same bed as her roommate."

I'm crying. Drew still has his arm around me, but I think I can feel his grip loosening. The room is still silent, aside from my sobs. My head is down; I can't bear to look at anyone.

"Let me ask you something, Katie," Estella continues. "Why do you *really* think you didn't get into Yale? You got into all your other schools. I mean, Harvard is even better than Yale, isn't it? So what is it about Yale? Why don't they want you?"

She doesn't wait for me to answer. "I'll tell you what I think. I think it's because you were *there*. I think that they saw—just like I can see—something defective deep inside your core. You can swim as fast as you want and you can pretend to be classy and get good grades and date the right boy, but deep down you know you'll always be poor white trash, no matter how dressed up you get. I think they saw that, when you were there, and they knew they didn't want you. And I think you know the same thing. It's true, isn't it? You know I'm right. Come on! You know it's true—"

"Shut up!"

I look up just in time to see Mazzie shoving Estella—*hard*—against a wall. "You don't have any right to say that to her. Who knows why Katie didn't get into Yale? Maybe it was because she partied too much her second summer there. Maybe they'd already filled their quota for West Virginia boarding school kids. But it's not because she's trash. Estella, a person can have more money than God, and they can know all the right people, and they can be beautiful and ambitious. But if they don't have any human *decency,* then I don't care who they are or what they have. They're trash."

Mazzie looks like she might punch Estella. I consider stepping in, pulling them apart. But I don't. "You might be beautiful now, Estella," Mazzie continues, "but it's only because you're eighteen. You might be rich, but it's only because you've got your stepdaddy's money. In a few years, you won't be pretty anymore, and you won't be rich—hell, your mother will probably be on her fourth marriage by then—and you were *never* that smart—and you'll just be the kind of person who goes around talking about how high school was the best time of your life because you ruled the school. And those are the most boring kind of people."

Estella glowers at Mazzie and me for what feels like forever. Finally, forcing the word out with such vile fervor that she almost spits on us, she says, "Dykes."

Drew stands up. "Come on. I'm taking you two home. Linds, you want a ride?"

Lindsey looks hesitant. She glances back and forth between Estella and Drew.

"Don't even think about it. You're staying here," Estella snaps.

Lindsey makes up her mind. "No. I'm going."

The three of us pile into Drew's Land Rover. I sit in the front seat beside him, holding his hand as we drive back to the dorm, squeezing it tightly because I know it might be for the last time. Nobody utters a word the whole way home.

That night in bed, I lie beside Mazzie with my eyes open, unable to stop thinking. A thousand memories, all at once. There are the events of the afternoon, which I'm still reeling from, not quite out of shock, but I'm thinking about Will, too, and the rest of my family. There's a picture that my parents keep on our living room coffee table: me and Will, ages three and eight. We were still poor. Will had helped me to get dressed that morning, in clothes my mother had gotten from the consignment shop, and I'm wearing two mismatched socks, one of the Ghost's undershirts, and a pair of Will's long underwear. Will doesn't look much better. He's holding my hand, and I'm staring up at him, one finger stuck up my nose. It's always been my favorite picture of the two of us.

Once it becomes clear I can't fall asleep, I lie in bed for a long time, rubbing a corner of my sheet between my thumb and index finger on one hand. Other memories—when I was a little girl, I had a habit of rubbing the corner of my blanket between my fingers the same way. I called it "silking the silky."

I'd snuggle up between my parents and beg them to follow my lead. "Here, Mom. Silk the silky."

As I silk the silky now, I look around the room I share with Mazzie, trying to make things out in the semidark. Several tennis rackets are stacked in the corner. Pleated school skirts are tossed over both of our desk chairs. Mazzie's desk is neat; mine is a mess. Bathing suits and swimming caps litter the floor and hang from the corners of all the furniture. The room stinks of chlorine, cigarette smoke (which we blame on the cleaning ladies), and Ben-Gay. Books are arranged in short piles on the bookshelves and the floor—hundreds of books—everything that's been assigned to us over the past three years, everything we've read on our own and dog-eared and shared, making notes in the margins.

The ceiling fan sweeps in a lazy circle on the lowest speed. Its motion creates an easy breeze that moves across the entire room and over my face, fluttering my eyelashes. I don't shut my eyes for fear that this peaceful feeling will stop and never start again, or that I'll wake up and it will all be over. My whole body aches from crying. After he dropped us off, Drew told me he had to think about a few things. I know that, once I get to class on Monday, everyone will know about Will and everyone will treat me like the liar that I am. So for tonight, all I want is to hold on to these moments with Mazzie.

There are so many other things in this room—three years accumulated between the two of us. I don't know how we'll split it all up and move to separate coasts. There are endless boxes of photographs, most of which are snapshots of the four of us girls, and later the five of us with Drew, arranging ourselves in different poses together at various places, only the backdrop and our clothing providing any memory cues, always a different party at so-and-so's house, a different night where someone or another got *sooooo* wasted and did something crazy, like this or that time when . . . well, I know. I know them all. I was there. I was part of it. So I'm in their memories, too—memories that will carry weight someday, not just crumble and disappear over the years.

The best pictures are taped up on the wall, or else in frames on the mantel: Mazzie and me one night after a football game, huddled in the bleachers in our winter coats while the snow falls, smearing against the camera lens and blurring the picture. Drew and me together at the prom last year and the year before. Last year—his senior year—we were prom king and queen, and there's a picture of us, much later that night in Lindsey's pool, where I'm on his shoulders in the water and we're both still wearing our crowns. He's teetering in the water, reaching upward to hold both my hands, and I'm grinning wide like I really mean it—like I'm really happy. You don't forget times like those, ever, I don't think—times when you mean everything. You have to remember them exactly as they happened, because they only last for a moment or an evening. Next year someone else will take my place. Somebody else will be the best swimmer in school. Everything will change.

"Where do you think you'll go to school?" Mazzie murmurs.

"Harvard," I say.

She seems surprised. "With Drew?"

"Well . . . not necessarily with him. We'll be there together, but . . . who knows."

She nods. "That sounds like a good idea. Harvard is better than Yale anyway, Katie."

She falls asleep before me; I barely doze off all night. And in the morning, just as the sun begins to break above the horizon, I kiss Mazzie on the forehead and whisper to myself, *"Ad astra per aspera."* It's the first expression I ever learned in Latin. It means "From the mud to the stars."

chapter 17

The next few weeks of school are rougher than I could have imagined. There are only six weeks to go before graduation, but it's plenty of time for Estella to make my life hell, and I know right from the get-go that she's going to do her best.

She's told everyone about Will. People stop talking when I come into classrooms. Even my teachers—even Solinger—treat me differently. In art class, once again disappointed by my work, Mrs. Averly frowns at my macramé and says, "I thought your mother was an artist, Kitrell?" Then, pretending to think better of it, she says, "Oh, I forgot. You get confused about your family members, don't you?"

The whole class giggles, some more loudly than others. And it's funny—I can't say that I blame them. I know from experience that it's way harder to be the only different one in the room.

But, since I've already gotten into Harvard, I start spending as many art classes as possible under the sink. Most of the time, Mazzie is there, waiting for me, skipping Chem III (her favorite class) so I don't have to be alone.

After a few weeks of silence, I feel certain that Drew doesn't want anything else to do with me. In a way, I feel a sense of relief that things are probably over between us. But one day, when Mazzie and I are walking back from class by ourselves, he's there: parked outside our dorm, waiting for me.

"Let's go for a ride," he says. He opens the car door for me.

Once we're at the highest point of Oglebay Park, Drew puts his car in idle and we roll all the windows down; the wind is blowing hard enough on top of the hill that my hair whips around my face, across my closed mouth. I shut my eyes and enjoy the feeling, trying to soak up the last few seconds of calm in the afternoon.

Drew breaks the silence. "I understand, Katie. You know—everything made so much sense after I found out. It always bothered me that you didn't want me to meet your parents, and that you had Mazzie come home with you for your grandpa's funeral, instead of me." He pauses. "Mazzie always knew, didn't she?"

I nod. "I'm sorry. I didn't mean to tell anybody, but she found out when he called—I mean, besides, we're roommates, and we're best friends, and—"

"Katie. You don't have to explain." He puts his palm over my fist and rubs my knuckles. He has always shown genuine concern for me, no matter how I've treated him. In a way, I think this quality has made it harder for me to like him sometimes. I'm not sure why.

Knowing that he isn't angry with me makes it easier to breathe. If I wanted to, I could leave it at that and we could go on like this, maybe forever. But there's something else he should know.

I close my eyes. "If I tell you something, Drew, can you make me a promise?"

"Anything."

I turn my head and look at him, trying to smile. "Love me?"

"Sure, Katie." His voice crackles a bit with concern. "Hey." He puts his hand over mine. "Tell me."

I figure there's nothing to say but the truth. "The night we were at UVA, when Estella said she walked in on me and Stetson?"

"Yeah . . ." Drew's concern shifts to mild panic.

"Drew."

He shakes his head. "Oh, no. No, you didn't."

I put my head down and start to cry. I can't tell him that it was just after my brother murdered someone, that it was right after my whole family fell apart and I didn't know what I was doing, that I just wanted to be wanted by *someone,* and Stetson had never given me any attention before—because those are all just excuses. They aren't reasons.

For a while we don't speak. And then, after a few moments, I hear Drew feeling around in his pockets for something—his wallet—which he takes out and starts emptying onto his lap.

"What are you doing?" I ask.

"You'll see."

He reaches a hand out and brushes some hair from my face. "Don't cry, Katie. I'm the one who should cry." He adds—and I realize that he *is* crying—"I want to break up with you right now. I want to hate you."

I feel my heart flutter. It doesn't sink—it flutters. "Oh."

"But I'm not going to."

There is silence. Drew passes me a card that he's removed from his wallet. It's a small laminated piece of paper with a passage from First Corinthians: "Love is patient, love is kind," etc.

"What's this for?"

"It's for you."

"Why?"

He shrugs. "Keep it."

"Drew." I put my hand on his arm, leaning into him, and try to wrap my arms around him. For the first time in the three years I've known him, I feel amazed by how lucky I am to have Drew. Not because he's gorgeous or popular or anything like that. Because I've done the worst thing imaginable to him, and he's strong enough to keep loving me, despite what I've done. His faith isn't just something he clings to or hides behind—it's real, and it's amazing. I feel sorry that I've never been able to understand it.

I hold on tight to his body, knowing it's one of the last times we'll be together like this.

But Drew shakes me loose. "Katie, I can't right now. I love you, and it'll be okay—but you need to stop." His whole body is trembling. He punches the steering wheel with his fist. "He's my best friend! You had to choose *him*."

"I'm so sorry—"

"I'm always trying to give people the benefit of the doubt, you know? I thought he was good, deep down inside." He shakes his head. He glares at me. "You were just another notch in his belt. You know that, right?"

I nod.

"He's only interested in getting laid." Drew sighs. "It's kind of like how some girls are the marrying kind and some girls aren't."

I shake my head. "What?"

"You know—some girls you marry, and some girls you mess around with." He fiddles with his keys, still in the ignition. "So I've heard."

I've always known that I am different from my friends

here, and different from Drew. But I want to tell them—don't they know?—I'm not supposed to be different. I might not be going to Yale, but I'm still going to swim my way through Harvard. I'm going to do just as well, if not better than, all the rest of them.

It has never dawned on me that I might just be the type of girl a boy has a good time with, but suddenly I feel like it is impossible for me to be anything else. Is Drew trying to tell me that Estella was right about why I didn't get into Yale?

"What is it?" Drew asks. His tone is still bitter.

"It's nothing." I look at him while I chew at the corner of my bottom lip. "You would marry *me*, right?"

He shrugs. "Sure, Katie. Maybe I'll marry you someday." He stares straight ahead. "If you can stop cheating on me."

I start to cry again. "Oh, shit. I'm one of those girls, aren't I? Have I always been that way? Don't marry me, Drew."

"Look at me," he says.

I look at him.

"I love you, Katie." He takes a deep breath. "Love is about forgiveness. And you're wrong about what kind of girl you are."

"Really?"

"Really."

"Even though I'm from Hillsburg and my brother is in a federal institution for the criminally insane?"

"Yes."

"But what's there to love about me?"

"What's not to love?"

I look down, at the space between us. "Lots of things."

"It doesn't matter." He blinks at me through his tears. He *smiles*. "I mean, you're no Margo Duvall. . . ."

For a brief second, I consider accepting his promise that we can stay together. I could hold on to it, and follow him through Harvard, and if I wanted it badly enough, we probably would get married.

But it isn't what I want. "Drew," I begin, "we aren't getting married."

"Well, not right *now* or anything. But we'll be in school together, and we'll stay together, and then who knows?"

I could stop there. I could let him believe I feel the same way. But Drew has been so good to me—I can't do it.

"I want us to be friends. At Harvard, I mean."

He pauses. "Just friends?"

"Drew, we don't have anything in common besides swimming. I'm not religious like you want me to be. I love you, but not like . . . not like I should. The past three years with you have been the best years of my life. But I think . . . I think we can both have better years. Apart." I put my hand on his arm; he flinches. "I love you," I repeat. "You need to believe me. I've never met anyone like you before."

At first, he doesn't say anything, and for a minute I think he's going to try to talk me out of breaking up with him. But he just nods. "Yeah, I know. I was just hoping . . ."

"So was I." We are both crying.

We put our arms around each other. His hug feels so familiar and warm that I don't want to let it go, but I know I have to. When we pull apart, I say to him, "You'll be the only person I know at Harvard."

He smiles. "You too."

"We'll be friends, then?"

Drew nods. "Sure." He takes a deep breath. "Great."

I think it's the most he can let go, for the moment. As we sit in his car together, staring over the town, my head on his shoulder and both of us still crying without making a sound, I realize this afternoon is the closest I've ever felt to Drew.

The next afternoon, when I come back from freshman intramural practice—which is actually just as awful as Solinger described—Lindsey is in my room, talking to Mazzie. They go silent when I walk in.

"Hi," I say, trying to be casual.

"Hi," Lindsey says. She and I haven't talked since Estella's party. But she hasn't been outright mean to me, either—Lindsey doesn't have it in her.

"I miss you, Linds," I say, after the silence gets so heavy that I can't stand it. "School is almost over, and we won't see each other, and—"

"I didn't think I could forgive you for lying," she says.

I nod. "Oh. Okay."

"But then I put myself in your shoes. And I remembered that, at first, you didn't actually lie. You just misled everyone." Before I can say anything, she adds, "Not that that's any better. And for a while, I didn't want to forgive you. But what Estella did to you that night was so much worse than what you did. What she did was just . . ." Lindsey shakes her head. "It was evil."

I nod. "Yeah. It was."

"I'm still mad at you," Lindsey says. "You should have trusted me. I wouldn't have *cared* about your brother." She thinks she means it, but she doesn't realize the truth. She never could have accepted me the way I was.

"But I want us to be friends again," she continues.

"Okay . . . why?" I'm almost too exhausted for this conversation.

"Because of Estella." Lindsey nods to herself. "She's been awful—my whole life, she's been awful. And no matter how mad I am at you . . . well, you know the expression: 'My enemy's enemy is my friend.'"

After Lindsey leaves, Mazzie and I smirk at each other. "They'll probably be spending the night at each other's houses by the weekend," Mazzie says. She's right, too. It isn't that Lindsey didn't mean what she said; it's just that she's that kind of person. Given the chance, no matter how much she can't stand her, she'll do anything to be close to a girl like Estella.

It's hard for me to hold the fact against her. As Mazzie and I sit alone in our room, as I think about everything that's happened with Drew and how much stronger than me he is, how genuine and kind he's proven to be, it occurs to me that if it weren't for people in my life like Drew and Mazzie, I could have been just like Lindsey. In a lot of ways, that's how I've acted.

It's one week before graduation. The seniors are lined up along the wall of the gymnasium for a rehearsal, shifting back and forth on our feet, fanning our faces with programs for the ceremony. Most of the girls have removed their skirts and tossed them in a pile in a corner, so we stand in button-down shirts, boxer shorts and knee socks rolled down to our ankles. The heat is so intense that I'm dizzy.

Estella rolls her head back and forth against the wall. "This is ridiculous," she mutters. "Like we don't know how to walk single file. This is completely lame. I'm leaving." But she doesn't move. She rolls her eyeballs upward in their sockets, her lashes fluttering.

Behind her, crouching with her elbows on her knees and face flushed to the point where I can see the veins in her neck beating against her white flesh, Lindsey is quiet. Mazzie and I are a few bodies back in line, and it doesn't surprise me that Lindsey is pretending not to ignore us, even though she's actually ignoring us.

"What are you doing after this, Linds?" Estella asks.

"Um . . ." She tries to lower her voice, but we all hear. "Going to Amanda Hopwood's graduation party."

I haven't been invited to many parties lately. I could just show up, and it might not be a big deal—but then again, it might be a bigger deal than I can imagine.

"Good." Estella smiles. "I'll be there. We can ride together."

Lindsey won't look at me or Mazzie. "Okay."

Everybody is quiet again. In front of the crowd, the headmaster and his administrative staff are arranged in a tight circle, his secretary's hairline dark and glossed with sweat.

Classes are over. The upcoming week is finals week, and since seniors don't have to take finals, we are free to do pretty much whatever we please. But it's too hot to do much of anything but stand there, waiting for everything to be over.

In our dorm room, I know, Mazzie's bags are packed, six suitcases and a duffel bag piled in the center of the room. The only thing left is her open backpack, containing loose toiletries and a few changes of clothes. Her bed is stripped down to a fitted sheet.

• • •

The night before graduation, Mazzie and I are awake, the only two students left in the dorm. Mazzie's things are completely packed now, except for the outfit she plans to wear tomorrow and what she's wearing right now. Even her toothbrush has been thrown away; I walk into the bathroom and find her using mine, giving her gums a good scrub.

In our room, the beds are now stripped completely. We'll sleep on my bare mattress tonight. "You should smoke a cigarette in here," she says.

I've been trying to quit for good. "I don't have any. Why should I, anyway?"

"Because you snuck so many with your fat head sticking out the window. You could light up right now in the middle of the room and nothing would happen to you."

"I guess."

". . ."

". . ."

"Mazzie," I begin, but she sees the way I'm looking at her and holds up a quick hand to interrupt. "Shut up, Katie. I know what you're going to say, and I don't want to hear it."

"What do you think I'll say?"

"A bunch of sappy bullshit about how much our friendship means and how important it is that we keep in touch after graduation. That kind of crap."

"Don't you want to keep in touch?"

"No."

"Come on."

She sighs. "Listen, you. Whatever is going to happen is going to happen."

She's right. I lean toward her, as if to give her a hug, but it seems like the most awkward thing I could possibly do right now.

She steps back. "I'm serious, Katie. Don't."

"Won't you miss me?"

"I don't know."

"I'll miss you so much."

I look past her, out our window, at Puff raising his leg against Mrs. Christianson's newly planted tulips.

"I want to tell you something," Mazzie says.

"What's that?"

She licks her lips. I feel the room tilting a little bit as she speaks. "I want to tell you how my mother died."

In three years, I never would have expected this.

"Okay," I say. "So tell me."

She comes close to me, and we both sit on the floor, our legs folded. She closes her eyes—I love the way her eyelashes are long and flutter shut with such grace—leans toward me, and whispers in my ear.

What does she tell me? After so many years of her keeping my secrets, there's no way I'll ever tell a soul. Not ever.

We both stand up. "You ready?" Mazzie asks, staring me straight in the eye.

"For what?"

"For your party, dummy."

As a graduation present, Drew is throwing me a surprise party tonight. Mazzie told me about it weeks ago.

"I guess so. I don't feel like going."

"Why not?"

"Well, for starters, it's going to be you, me, Drew, and his mom at Elbow Room." Elbow Room is a local Italian restaurant. "You know—same stuff, different day. At least, that's how it's been for the past few weeks."

For some reason this is amusing to Mazzie. She cocks her head at me. "But not for long."

"You ready?" I ask.

"Yeah. Do you have everything? Keys? A good surprised expression?"

"Yeah."

"Let's see it."

I flash her my most surprised face.

"Okay, then," she says, "let's go."

"Okay. Let's go."

We don't move.

"I love you," I say. "You're my best friend."

Mazzie's shoulders slump. She's trying not to cry. "Yeah," she says. "I know."

"Don't forget about me."

She nods.

We stand there looking at each other. I remember the first day I ever met her.

"I'll miss you, Madeline Moon," I tell her.

She moves toward the door. "You won't have to. You know where to find me."

I take one last look around the room. With all of our things packed, I barely recognize it. Everything will be different soon. Everything will be new. I don't know what's going to happen. The only thing I know for sure is how to swim.

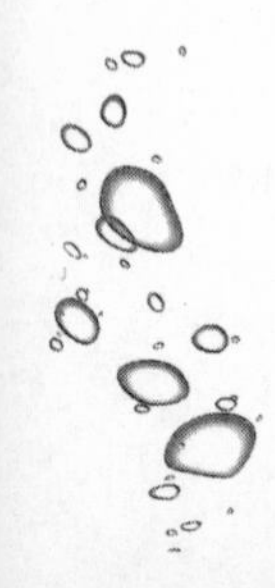

epilogue

ten years later

Once I get through airport security, I easily spot Drew's head of curls above the crowd gathered to meet their loved ones. It's the day before Christmas Eve.

His hugs haven't changed. He squeezes me so tightly that he picks me up off the ground. Once we let go of each other, we stand there grinning.

"Wow," I say. "You never seem to get any older, Drew."

"Neither do you."

"Oh, please."

"I mean it. In fact, wait a second." He pats his coat pockets. "I can prove it to you." He pulls a wrapped package from his inner pocket. "Shelly found this while she was going through our old stuff."

I open the present. "Oh, my God. I can't believe you still have this!" It's a framed photo of me and Drew, taken back in high school. We'd just started dating. We're sitting side by side in our bathing suits, our feet dangling into Lindsey's pool.

"I remember this," I say, clutching the photo to my chest. "I was smiling so hard that my cheeks hurt."

He nods. "What did I tell you? You look exactly the same."

I study the photograph a little closer. I had the same blond hair, the same swimmer's build, but it's obvious from the tension in my shoulders, the lack of confidence in my eyes, that I was just a baby back then. I had no idea what I was getting into—not with Drew, or with anything.

"Shelly's amazing," I say, once we're settled in his car, on our way to my hotel. "If I were married, I don't think I'd ever give my husband's old girlfriend any pictures of them together."

He grins at me. "Come on, Katie. You're the one who *introduced* us. Besides," he adds, "you and I were a terrible match."

"Hey! We weren't that bad."

Drew shrugs. "Oh, whatever you say."

We drive in silence for a few moments. The roads in Pittsburgh are covered with a light dusting of snow, but it's nothing compared to what I'm used to in New York. The afternoon feels calm, a little lonely. I know Pennsylvania will never feel like home again.

"How's Mazzie?" Drew asks.

I shrug. "I haven't talked to her in a while."

He grins. "So you haven't talked to her in, what, a few hours?"

"A few weeks, actually."

"Mmm-hmm."

"Okay, it's been, like, two weeks. She's busy finishing her residency in Santa Monica."

He shakes her head. "I can't believe people trust her with their *kids*. I always thought she'd be a rocket scientist or a brain surgeon."

I smile. I don't say anything. Her choice—she's a pediatrician—doesn't surprise me one bit.

Just before we reach the hotel, Drew says, "Wait—I almost forgot. You have to see this." He reaches across me, into the glove compartment, and pulls out a travel magazine.

"Turn to the back," he says, "to the advertisements."

Sandwiched between two full-page brokerage ads, there's a section for wedding announcements. As I look them over, I gasp. "You've got to be kidding me."

There's a full-page article, along with a glossy color photo of the new bride and groom. It's Estella, looking radiant as ever, standing beside her new husband, whom I don't recognize. I scan the article. Dress handmade from Italian silk . . . reception at the Atlanta Museum of History . . . "Lindsey was the maid of honor?"

Drew nods. "I guess they're still the best of friends. You know, my company buys space in this magazine, and those wedding announcements are technically ads. Can you believe she *paid* just so everyone would know about her wedding?"

I nod. "Sure. Were you invited?"

"Nope." He grins at me. "Thank God for small favors."

Once we're at the hotel, Drew carries my suitcase into the lobby for me.

"Thanks for the ride," I say. "I could have taken a cab." Drew lives just outside the state line, about an hour west of Pittsburgh.

"No problem. I would have insisted you stay with us, but Shelly is in nesting mode. She's going nuts, Katie. Last week I caught her cleaning the floorboards with a toothbrush at three in the morning."

"I hear pregnant women can get like that." I give him a hug.

He pulls away, holding on to my shoulders. "What about you? Any wedding plans yet?"

"Oh . . . I don't know . . ."

"Katie!"

I can't stop myself—I reach out and muss his curls. Just for a moment, I feel a twinge of the same excitement from the first time I touched them. I know it will never go away completely. "I haven't decided yet whether or not I'm the marrying kind of girl."

In general, institutions for the criminally insane are not the most warm and fuzzy places. But Will seems happy enough.

We talk on the phone a lot, but for the past few years, I've seen him only on Christmas. There isn't much we're allowed to give him. This year, I've brought him a game of checkers.

My parents stop by the hotel to pick me up on their way to the prison. We stand in the lobby for a few moments, catching up. I only talk to them every few months, but it feels okay. I think we're as close as we're ever going to get, at least in this lifetime.

My mom smoothes my hair. She has tears in her eyes. "It must be so *cold* in New York. How do you go swimming? Do they have a Y in that little town?"

"Mom," I laugh, "the school lets me use the pool. It's kind of like my office."

My dad gives me a hug. As we're holding each other, I can't stop myself from smelling his hair, his neck, trying to take in every detail.

"You quit smoking," I say, surprised.

He nods. "It's been almost six months."

"Good for you."

My dad looks back and forth, from me to my mother. "Well,"

he says, without a hint of sarcasm to his voice, "let's go celebrate Christmas."

Will loves the checkers. We spend a good two hours playing; each of his moves is slow and calculated and interspersed with frequent commentary and attempts at conversation.

But it's impossible to ignore where we are: there is only one small, depressing Christmas tree in the corner of his common area. None of the other inmates have guests today. My parents and I are the only people not wearing scrubs or robes or worse. And Will still has the scars on his arm; of course, it doesn't matter in here, but every time I look at them I feel a pang and imagine how things might have been different if only we'd found him sooner, or been able to stop him before he got out the front door. But we didn't. And we couldn't. So here we are.

He triple-jumps three of my pieces and lands in my back row. He puts his arms in the air, fists clenched in triumphant victory, and says, "King me!"

So I do. It will be, I know, the highlight of my brother's Christmas. It is the best I can do for him, but for the rest of my life, that is what I will always give to Will: my best. For the rest of my life, no matter what becomes of us, he will always be my big brother. No matter how far I go, I know now that there is no escape—and I know, too, that there was never any point in trying. He will always be with me.

acknowledgments

I'd like to thank my agent, Andrea Somberg, for her seemingly endless support and encouragement, as well as my editor, Stacy Cantor, for her consistent enthusiasm, confidence, and hard work. My gratitude also goes out to my amazing parents and my big brother, whose love, hilarity, and pathology have warped me permanently—I can only hope to return the favor. Thanks to my little daughters, Estella and Esmé, who keep me constantly motivated to show them the endless possibilities that come with being a woman, and to my most enduring and patient friend, Alisa. This book would not exist without all the knowledge and support I received at Seton Hill University, particularly from my wonderful mentors, Pat Picciarelli and Leslie Davis Guccione. My English professors at Indiana University of Pennsylvania—Jean Wilson, Chauna Craig, and Michael T. Williamson—all deserve recognition and thanks. I would especially like to acknowledge Curt Gsell, my amazing trainer, who showed me the peace and meditation that can be found in long-distance running. Thanks to you, I have learned that my most valuable thoughts have room to surface when I am surrounded by the calm of perpetual motion. Finally, I need to recognize the years I spent at the Linsly School, and its fabulous faculty and staff (both former and current) including Matt DiOrio, Robin Follet, Chad Barnett, and Reno DiOrio.